Kick at the Darkness

Also by Keira Andrews

Contemporary

The Spy and the Mobster's Son
Honeymoon for One
Beyond the Sea
Ends of the Earth
Arctic Fire

Holiday
The Christmas Deal
The Christmas Leap
The Christmas Veto
Only One Bed
Merry Cherry Christmas
Santa Daddy
In Case of Emergency
Eight Nights in December
If Only in My Dreams
Where the Lovelight Gleams
Gay Romance Holiday Collection
Lumberjack Under the Tree (free read!)

Sports
Kiss and Cry
Reading the Signs
Cold War
The Next Competitor
Love Match
Synchronicity (free read!)

Gay Amish Romance Series
A Forbidden Rumspringa
A Clean Break
A Way Home
A Very English Christmas

Valor Duology
Valor on the Move

Kick at the Darkness

KEIRA ANDREWS

Kick at the Darkness

Written and published by Keira Andrews
Cover by Dar Albert
Formatting by BB eBooks

Copyright © 2015 by Keira Andrews
Print Edition

Dedication

Many thanks to Amy, Anne-Marie, Becky, Jules, and Rachel for their critiques and friendship. Thanks also to awesome engineers and experts online for providing dissertations on what would happen to our power supplies and other technology in the event of a zombie apocalypse. If it ever happens, I will miss you, internet!

Chapter One

IT ALL STARTED falling apart in *Film Noir from Bogart to Mulholland Drive.*

"*C-minus?*" Parker blinked at the grade, stark and circled in red pen on the front of his paper. His stomach churned. This had to be some kind of mistake. Another student nudged him with her elbow, giving him a look until he backed away from the professor's desk so the others could find their assignments in the pile.

Scrolling through her phone, the middle-aged professor stood by the blackboard, which stretched across the front of the lecture hall. Squaring his shoulders, Parker approached.

"Um, excuse me?"

Professor Grindle glanced up. "Yes? Did you have a question?"

Parker thrust the paper toward her, the red cursive on it a damning indictment. He lowered his voice. "I got a C-minus."

She skimmed over the three pages. "Did you read the comments from the TA? I think there are some excellent points you can keep in mind next time. More analysis and less plot summary, for a start. There's another assignment this month. Don't worry— you'll get the hang of it…" She glanced at the paper. "Parker."

Even though he knew there was no way she could remember all the names of new students, humiliation flashed through him. He'd almost been valedictorian at Westley Prep, but at Stanford, he was no one.

She went on. "I'm sure Adam will be happy to help. Do you have his office hours? They're on the front of the syllabus. He should be there this afternoon."

"Look, I don't…I'm a straight-A student. There must be some kind of mistake."

The rest of the class was gone, and she scooped up the few remaining papers from the desk. "Why don't you talk to Adam, and if you're still unhappy, I'll look it over for you. I'm sorry. I have to get to my next lecture." Her shoes *tap-tap-tapped* as she strode out.

Parker shoved the offending assignment into his messenger bag, wishing he could burn it. Outside, he blinked at the sun and plopped down on the steps of the building, pulling out his phone. He quickly tapped out a message to Jason, his best friend at Westley.

Got a C-minus in a stupid movie class that was supposed to be easy. This is going to screw my GPA! I'm freaking out.

Jiggling his foot, he waited for Jason to reply, watching for the three little dots to appear. And waited.

And waited.

Then he sent the same message to Jessica, who'd lived three doors down from him in Cambridge their whole lives. He waited again. He was tempted to call Eric in London, but his brother would be way too busy to talk to him about a stupid little college paper, and it was probably dinnertime anyway. Although Eric would likely still be at work, trading stocks with the American markets.

Parker stared at his phone as if he could will a text from one of his friends to appear. It was ridiculous. He was being ridiculous. But the wave of loneliness was undeniable, and his breath stuttered. He'd been so excited to come to Stanford and strike out on his own, but it hadn't been at all what he'd expected.

He watched groups of people laughing and talking on the lawn. Other students rushed by him on the steps, and Parker wondered if they'd made friends. He sat there with his C-minus, and felt utterly, pathetically alone.

Jesus Christ. Don't start crying, you loser.

Jason and Jessica were busy at Penn State and NYU. Before college, they'd often spent hours texting each other, and it had rarely taken more than a minute for a response. But in the month since school had started, he'd barely heard from them. Jason was rushing a frat, and Jessica seemed to have a non-stop schedule of classes and partying.

After what felt like an eternity, his phone buzzed, and Parker's heart leapt.

Dude, you need to unclench. You'll be fine. It's not a big deal. School just started.

Parker sighed. Jason had never cared much for academics, much to his parents' chagrin. He would never understand how big a deal it was that Parker had a C-minus. In a *movie* class he'd only taken for the allegedly easy grade.

Jason texted again:

Go get laid. There have got to be plenty of hot guys at Stanford. Later, dude.

There was no word from Jessica, and Parker tapped out a text to Jason:

Yeah, you're right. Thx. Later.

Jason *was* right—he needed to get laid. Parker admittedly hadn't really tried, but he was already overwhelmed with homework. He had no idea how his friends were going out so much when he needed to spend every spare hour studying to keep up. School had always come easily to him, but college felt like being tossed out of the wading pool and into the deep end.

Still, he should make an effort to meet someone. Maybe he needed to check out Grindr or one of those other gay hookup apps and put up his picture. Yes, that would be more productive than feeling sorry for himself. He tapped his camera to face him and ran a hand through his short hair.

It was dirty blond, not the golden color his brother had been blessed with. Parker had bleached it once at Jessica's insistence, but he'd felt incredibly stupid, like he was trying to be in a boy band. It wasn't a good look. He didn't mind his hair, but wished his eyes were something other than ordinary brown. Jess had suggested blue contacts, but he'd put his foot down.

Parker took a selfie, forcing a smile. His wide mouth was decent—his lips could have been a little thicker, but they were nice and red without looking like he wore lipstick. A good cocksucking mouth if he did say so himself. His teeth were white and straight thanks to a small fortune in orthodontics when he was a kid, and his nose was small and inoffensive. He took a few more pics, but hesitated when he went to download Grindr in the app store.

What if no one wants to date me? Or even fuck me?

He thought he was cute enough, but what if no one else did? There were a ton of hot guys at Stanford. What if he put up his picture and there were only crickets in return? It hadn't even happened yet, and already the promise of humiliation churned his stomach. He slipped his phone away. He'd download the app later.

Parker sighed. Ugh, he had to go deal with this bullshit grade. His throat was scratchy, and he guzzled a bottle of water on his way to the building nearby where the TA for the movie class had his office. With every step, the failure seemed to seep into him another inch, and with it mortification and a growing resentment.

It wasn't fair. He had math and statistics pre-reqs for his economics major to worry about—this dumb elective wasn't supposed to be actual work.

I suck. I should have worked harder. What will Dad say if he finds out?

He climbed up to the office level at the top of the four-story building and scanned the nameplates beside each door. His sneakers squeaked on the floor, and it felt preternaturally quiet. At the end of the hall, Parker found the name he was looking for, written on a piece of folded paper and fitted into the nameplate slot.

Adam Hawkins: Film and Media Studies

Parker scoffed to himself. Film and Media Studies. It wasn't like it was a *real* academic discipline. This Adam Hawkins was likely a pretentious douchebag who wore black turtlenecks and horn-rimmed glasses. He probably drank tea and had a minor in existential philosophy. He—

The door opened. "Oh, hello. Can I help you?"

His throat gone completely dry, Parker could only croak. "Uh…"

Adam Hawkins did not wear horn-rimmed glasses.

The jury was still out on whether he had turtlenecks in his wardrobe, but at the moment he was wearing a black leather jacket over a light blue button-up and jeans. He was a few inches taller than Parker's own five-nine, and the leather stretched over broad shoulders. His thick black hair was short and lustrous—it freaking *gleamed*—and his facial hair was artfully scruffy, just the right length to make Parker wonder what it would feel like against his skin.

Adam Hawkins watched Parker with hazel eyes that were strangely golden. "Did you need some help?"

"I'm…" Parker tried to ignore the lust humming in his veins and get it together. "C-minus."

"You're C-minus?"

Cheeks hot, Parker grabbed the paper from his bag and held it up, refocusing on his anger. "That's what you gave me on my assignment, and it's not fair." God, he was whining, and he should leave. Cut his losses. Man up.

Adam Hawkins opened the door wider and stepped aside. He simply said, "Okay." He sat behind his desk and glanced at the round clock on the wall. "My office hours are over, but…" There was a buzzing from his pocket, and he held up a hand to Parker as he answered his cell. "Hi, Tina. Yeah. I'll be there soon. Okay." He smiled, a flash of white teeth and tenderness that had Parker's belly somersaulting. "Yeah. You too." He hung up.

"Look, if you have to go meet your girlfriend or whatever, it's fine," Parker muttered.

"She's running late, so I can stay for a few minutes. You're obviously upset and—"

"I'm not upset!" Parker perched on the guest chair, his foot tapping restlessly. "I just think there's been a mistake. I don't get C-minuses. Ever."

"You're a freshman?" Adam reached for the paper and looked it over.

He nodded. "Economics major, but I'm pre-law."

Adam continued reading through the assignment before handing it back. "A lot of people think film studies will be an easy elective. You're clearly intelligent, but this paper reads as though you wrote it in fifteen minutes the morning it was due and didn't even watch *Laura*."

"I watched it!" Okay, so he watched clips on YouTube and read the Wiki synopsis. That totally counted. He got the gist. Like he was supposed to spend his time watching old movies instead of actually studying? He was already up to his eyeballs in readings. "I'm sure the professor will see that I at least deserve a B."

Adam's eyebrow arched. "Will she? You seem sure of yourself."

"Well, I told you. I don't get C-minuses. I won the state spelling bee when I was nine. I presented for our model UN at prep school and met the Secretary of State! I don't… I'm better than this."

"I'm sure you are. For the next assignment, do the work and put some thought into it, and your grade will reflect that."

Parker knew he was right, but all he could see was the *C-* on the paper, taunting him. Third week of classes, and he was already coming up short. It felt like all his failures were symbolized by this one grade. He could just imagine what his father would say. "*This is what happens when you don't concentrate. Eric never—*"

"I'm not changing it." Adam's declaration jolted Parker from his thoughts.

Pulse racing, Parker tried to keep the desperation from his voice. "My GPA has always been perfect. Except one time. But that can't happen again. I can't get a C-minus. You have to change it."

"Do I?" Adam laughed. He actually *laughed*.

Parker felt hot all over and knew this was all spinning out of control. He needed to cut his losses and leave with a scrap of dignity, but he couldn't stop indignation from slamming through him. "Don't laugh at me! Who do you think you are? This isn't even a real academic subject."

Adam only regarded him with that raised eyebrow. "I think I'm the TA who's not changing your grade, no matter how much entitled crap you throw at him. So suck it up and learn something from it."

Parker wanted to leap up and run away, but he was frozen on his chair, flushed and ashamed in the silence that followed.

Adam sighed, and his tone softened. "I bet you were valedictorian, right? Smartest kid at your school? But Stanford isn't high school. It can be a tough transition."

His cheeks flushed again. No, he wasn't valedictorian. He was salutatorian—a.k.a. second place, a.k.a. *loser*—thanks to Greg Mason's record-breaking perfect fucking score on the calculus final. Like always, Parker came up short, and now he had a C-minus, and he didn't have any friends out here, and he hated himself more than he ever had.

"You're going to have to work hard in every class. Even if you think it's a Mickey Mouse course. I know it can be a real shock when things don't come easily for the first time in your life."

Parker lashed out. "I've always worked hard. I *am* working hard! All I do is study. The important stuff, anyway. I'm going to be a lawyer. What are you going to be?"

Adam's face was impassive. "I'm getting my MFA in documentary filmmaking."

"You'll probably end up working for some crappy reality show," Parker muttered. He was being a dick, but at the moment he didn't care enough to bite his tongue.

Pushing back his chair, Adam stood. "If that's all, I have things to do besides get attitude from a lazy freshman who expects everything handed to him on a silver platter."

Parker jumped to his feet. "You don't know me."

"I know your type. I've met a thousand—" he picked up the paper and scanned the front, "—Parker Osbornes in my life."

Snatching the paper back, Parker tried to think of something to say. He blurted, "I'm dropping this stupid class."

Adam eyed him evenly. "Okay." Then he started scrolling through his phone. After a few moments he glanced up. "Was there something else?"

Teeth gritted, Parker spun on his heel. Mortification warred with anger as he tore the paper in half and stuffed it in a garbage can on his way out of the building. He pulled out his phone to check the time and skipped into a jog with a muttered curse. His stats lecture started in two minutes and he was never going to make it on time. It wasn't even noon, and he was so ready to go to bed and be done with this craptacular day.

HE REALLY SHOULD have gone to bed.

Instead, Parker was in an empty classroom sitting in a circle with a bunch of people who looked as if they should be smoking up and playing hacky sack at the Oval.

He squirmed in his wooden chair, wondering if he could just get up and walk out in the middle of the lesbian's story about her struggle to add vegan items to the cafeteria menu. He had nothing against lesbians or vegans (or lesbian vegans), but he clearly didn't fit in with the LGBT student group. Activism wasn't really his thing.

He'd spotted the flyer for the group meeting after his lecture and had decided it was high time to stop feeling sorry for himself and to try making friends. Or take Jason's advice and maybe pick up a hot guy.

Of course, the only guy he could think about was Adam Hawkins. All day, Parker had replayed their encounter in his mind, devising witty comebacks and scathing putdowns. Not that he'd ever see Adam again, thank God. First thing tomorrow, he was dropping that class. He'd pick up another elective next semester, or in the summer if he had to.

"What do you think, Parker? It's Parker, right?" The blonde girl who'd been speaking smiled encouragingly.

Shit. "Um, I think it's great. Sounds like a plan."

A murmur buzzed around the circle, and a short Asian guy with a pierced eyebrow spoke up. "You think we should stage a sit-in until the school bans all meat and dairy products? Don't you think that's a bit extreme?"

He felt the heat of a dozen pairs of eyes. "Uh…it would get their attention, though. Then maybe they'd compromise?"

The blonde exclaimed, "Exactly!"

As everyone debated the merits of food-based activism, Parker eyed the cute guy sitting next to him. Reddish hair and green eyes, and a tight little body. The guy hadn't said much of anything so far. Maybe he wasn't digging it either? It was hard to tell. But he could be cool. He was definitely hot, at least. *I won't meet anyone if*

I don't try.

Screwing up his courage, Parker leaned over and whispered, "Meat, I get, but no dairy? And no chocolate? Life isn't worth living."

The redhead glanced at him with an unreadable expression. "Chocolate is overrated."

"Uh, yeah, of course." Parker waved his hand. "I was just kidding."

The guy smiled. Hmm. Wait, had he been kidding too? Everyone liked chocolate, right? Heart thumping, Parker whispered, "Want to grab a coffee after this? We could live dangerously and have a latte with real milk."

Please say yes. Please say yes.

The redhead's gaze swept up and down Parker, like a searchlight coming up empty. Parker wanted to puke as the guy pasted on a smile.

"That's so sweet. But I've got a lot of studying to do after the meeting." Then he turned back to the group. "Marjorie? Can we discuss that stunt Kappa Sigma pulled on the weekend at our cruelty-free bake sale? I think we should petition the administration…"

As they discussed something involving an unholy alliance of snickerdoodles and condoms, Parker wished the scuffed tile floor would open up and swallow him whole. Sadly, the floor was apparently vegan, because Parker remained right where he was, his face burning, sure that everyone knew he'd just been shot down.

He cursed himself for thinking it was a good idea to attend this meeting in the first place. Why did he need to officially meet other gay people? Maybe he should just pledge a frat and put his cocksucking skills to good use like he had in prep school. He didn't need a *boyfriend* anyway.

But I want one.

Remembered shame joined the party with the fresh humiliation of being rejected by the redhead beside him. He'd only tried to kiss Greg Mason once. He could still feel the hard tile floor of the shower, cold and wet as he'd landed on his ass, Greg staring down at him with a curled lip. *"Don't be a little faggot."*

The fact that he was eighteen and still had never properly kissed someone was so pathetic he could barely stand it. Sitting there in the circle of LGBTQ students who'd probably all kissed a dozen people, he felt like he had a neon sign blinking over his head.

Loser! Loser! Loser!

But what was the point of finding a boyfriend anyway? It's not like he could ever really bring someone home. His parents tried their best—they really did—but the whole gay thing made them so awkward and uncomfortable. Not to mention he knew their rich pals at the country club would surely not approve. Parker wondered what his father would say if he dated an anti-establishment hippie type. The mere thought made him bark out a laugh.

Heads swiveled. "Is there something you wanted to share?" the blonde asked, her smile a little strained.

Before Parker could answer, a white guy with dreads interrupted, frowning at his smartphone. "Whoa. Did you guys see this? There are some crazy riots or something in New York."

"What are they protesting?"

"Probably not meat and dairy, Abrah."

"Is it Occupy Wall Street? I hope so. I heard they're trying to make a comeback."

"Dunno. Oh wait, it's in DC too. Probably something about police brutality."

As the group talked over each other, checking their phones, Parker slung his messenger bag over his head and made a beeline for the door. He escaped back to the quad and grabbed a sandwich (turkey and Havarti, thank you very much) on the way to his dorm.

The common room was crowded with people watching CNN, but Parker didn't care about whatever protest or riot or whatever-the-fuck was happening. He probably should, but he had way too much reading to do, especially after wasting time at that meeting.

Embarrassment flooded him again as he thought of the dismissive way the redhead had examined him. Then a voice echoed in his head—Adam Hawkins calling him a lazy freshman.

"I work hard at what matters. Ugh, he's such an asshole," Parker muttered as he kicked the door closed behind him.

"Who's an asshole?"

"Jesus!" Parker's heart skipped a beat. "Don't do that."

Grinning, Chris pulled a T-shirt over his shorn head. "Sorry, bro. Just came back to do some laundry." He smelled his armpit. "Febreze is the best invention ever."

"I've barely seen you since NSO." New student orientation had been a week of mandatory activities designed to help frosh settle in and make friends. Parker had learned his way around, but totally failed to meet anyone he connected with. Chris was nice enough, but another pang of missing Jason and Jessica swelled. He cleared his throat. "How's Michelle?"

"Spectacular. Seriously, her tits are just…" Chris raised his fingers to his mouth to kiss them. "Bellissimo. I've found the woman of my dreams." He shrugged. "At least for now. Hey, her roommate's pretty hot too. Wanna come back with me? I got some primo weed. We can hang out and play *Call of Duty*. I bet she'll blow you by the end of the night."

Parker chuckled. He could undoubtedly give Michelle's roommate some pointers. "Nah. I've got a lot of reading to do. Econ test tomorrow already." Maybe he should go hang with them, but he hadn't had a chance to come out to Chris, and he had zero interest in weed. Sometimes he felt like he was eighteen going on forty-five. Partying and getting high had never really been fun for him.

"Cool. If you change your mind give me a buzz." Chris raised his hand as he headed to the door.

Parker slapped Chris's palm and flopped down on his bed. "Later."

In the silence that followed, Parker found himself actually missing the near-constant *thump-thump* of the house music favored by the girl next door. Maybe she was watching the news in the lounge. The news channels always made such a big deal out of everything these days, and Parker didn't see the point in getting worked up.

He stared at Chris's empty bed. Jason had been his roommate all through high school at Westley, so it should have been nice to virtually have his own room at school for a change. It should have been freaking awesome.

But it wasn't.

Parker pulled out his phone. No message from Jessica. He hit her number and waited while it rang, sighing as her voicemail clicked on.

"*This is Jessica. Quick—leave a message before phones become completely obsolete.*"

For a moment, Parker was frozen with indecision. Then he tapped the screen and ended the call. What would he say that didn't sound ninety-nine percent pathetic?

"Okay, enough." His voice was loud in the stillness of the room. "Time to get to work."

After wolfing down his sandwich, he opened his textbooks. The dorm was quieter than usual, and he put his phone on airplane mode and lost himself in free trade theory. By eight o'clock, his eyes drooped. He set his alarm for nine and stretched out for a power nap. He was drifting off when a girl's piercing voice echoed in the hall.

"It's happening in San Francisco!"

With a roll of his eyes, Parker put in his earplugs and curled toward the wall. He'd check the news later when there was actual information to report instead of just fear-mongering speculation. Let them protest corporate America or the police or whatever they were doing. He had his GPA to worry about.

IT WAS TEN-THIRTY by the time Parker dragged himself out of bed. He still wore his jeans and a T-shirt, and he zipped on a dark green hoodie before stuffing his feet into his sneakers. The fifteen-minute walk across campus to the coffee shop would wake him up, and sweet caffeine would keep him going all night. He needed to do better. He needed to ace this test. He *would* ace this test.

He popped in his earbuds and skirted around the people jammed into the dorm's common room.

"Yo, Parker. Are you seeing this shit?" Mike from two rooms down—nice enough guy, but obsessed with sports—called out as Parker hurried by.

"Later, man. Need coffee." Parker gave him a wave and turned on his music. They were probably watching the baseball game since the Oakland A's were one win away from the playoffs, but he couldn't let himself be distracted.

He'd mapped out this shortcut the first week of school after the RA had confiscated his Italian coffee maker. The night air was crisp, and Parker shoved his hands in his hoodie pockets as he navigated the nooks and crannies between buildings.

He caught glimpses of the main quad, where a large number of people milled about. Probably some frat thing; all the better that he avoided it so he could get back to his books ASAP. But he wondered what the riots or whatever had been about, and he thumbed off the airplane mode on his phone so he could Google it.

As the phone reconnected, it vibrated in his palm and the screen filled with notifications. Nothing from Jessica or Jason, and Parker wished he didn't feel the stab of disappointment and hurt. It wasn't their fault they were fitting in and making friends at college. He couldn't expect them to have the time for him that they used to. But it still stung.

He shook it off and focused on the screen. "Seven missed calls from Mom?" he muttered to himself with a smile. "Classic." When she got something in her head, she was a dog with a bone. As he walked, he listened to the voicemail message she'd left.

"*Honey.*" The recording was staticky and garbled, with some kind of background noise. Parker stopped to listen harder. He couldn't make out the next few words. Then, "*Cape house. We love you.*" The message ended.

Huh. That was weird.

Why would she be calling about the Cape house? His parents went to Chatham most weekends in September, but it was Tuesday. Parker deleted the message and started walking again. He'd call her when he got back to the dorm, or maybe wait until morning. It was after midnight on the East Coast.

As he cut behind one of the science buildings, he stopped in his tracks. By a palm tree, there stood Adam Hawkins and his ludicrous cheekbones. Of course—he'd never seen the guy before today, and now he was likely doomed to run into him daily.

Adam had a motorcycle helmet in one hand, and had changed his loafers for black work boots. Wearing earbuds, he peered at the bright screen of his phone with a frown creasing his forehead.

Ugh.

Adam's gaze shot up, his eyes hard as he removed his earbuds. "Excuse me?"

Parker realized he might have said that out loud. He paused his playlist and cleared his throat, trying to remember one of the witty comebacks he'd had a million of that afternoon. "Um, nothing."

Of course he'd think of ten more the minute he left Adam behind. Which couldn't be too soon. In his black leather jacket and stubble, he looked ridiculous. Ridiculously hot, which wasn't really fair since he was a film geek. A documentarian, even! Not to mention a condescending know-it-all. Parker kept walking.

"You didn't have to complain to the dean," Adam called after him.

Parker stopped and faced him. "Huh?"

"Are you seriously going to pretend it wasn't you? I have to meet with Professor Grindle and the head of the department at the end of the week because a student with rich alumni parents put up a stink. She wouldn't say who, but she didn't need to."

"It wasn't me." When Adam snorted and started walking away, Parker couldn't stop himself from following. "Hey! It wasn't me, asshole."

"*I'm* the asshole?" Adam turned, gripping his helmet. His nostrils flared. "Every year I get kids like you taking my courses. Kids who don't care about the arts and just want an easy grade. And now you're messing with my future. This job is everything to me. My degree is everything."

"First off, who says I don't care about the arts? I like the arts just fine, thank you very much. I played viola in my school orchestra, I'll have you know. And like I said, it wasn't me. Whatever, dude. You're not worth it. I have important things to do like study for my econ test."

"Uh-huh."

"What? What does that mean?"

"That eighteen-year-olds think they know it all." Adam shrugged, his flash of passion concealed again behind a flat expression. "If you say it wasn't you, I guess it wasn't."

Jesus, this guy was annoying. "And what are you, twenty-two? So wise."

"Twenty-three, actually."

"Oh, that changes everything. Whatever. I don't have to talk to you."

"Okay." He shrugged again, now completely calm.

"Econ is a hell of a lot more important than dissecting movies."

Adam watched him with an inscrutable gaze. Just like with the cute redhead, it felt as though he was being evaluated and found hopelessly lacking. "Okay."

"Stop saying that! Oh my god, why am I even having this conversation?" Parker brushed by him and pressed play even though now he was going the wrong way for the coffee shop. He'd loop around since he couldn't turn back. "Have a nice life," he called in his wake. If Adam replied, Parker didn't hear it over the music in his ears.

He could not drop that class soon enough. He should have known—

A scream pierced the night, so loud he heard it over the new Macklemore song. Parker ripped out the earbuds and glanced around. He and Adam stared at each other. "Do you hear—"

"Yes," Adam replied, his entire body tensed.

In the distance, the screaming swelled as other voices joined in. Parker's heart thumped. "That's a hell of a hazing ritual."

The din increased, and more shrieks raised the hair on Parker's arms. A girl and a guy raced around the building. "What's going on?" Parker shouted.

"They're killing everyone!" the girl yelled, her eyes wild as she shoved past him.

More students streamed behind the buildings, and Parker watched them as his brain struggled to process what was happening. Then he was being yanked so hard he thought his shoulder might pop free of its socket. Adam propelled him forward, and yes, run. *Run!*

Parker hadn't heard any gunshots, but the screaming filled the night. He had no idea where they were running to, but he followed the crowd—and Adam Hawkins. Ahead, more people flooded the service road behind the library, and in the glow of the safety light by the path, he saw red paint sprayed into the air and over the students who stumbled there. Other people piled on top of them, their eyes unnaturally wide and bugging out.

They swarmed with frantic desperation, and one of them savagely bit the face of a guy wearing a Sigma Nu T-shirt.

Blood. It wasn't paint arcing through the air.

"This way!" Adam shoved him into a narrow alley.

A scream batted its wings in his chest, but Parker sucked in a breath and went on, his feet pounding the asphalt. Adam had pulled twenty feet ahead, and he glanced back.

"Faster!"

Parker's lungs burned, and he pumped his arms. *Faster, faster, faster*. But he couldn't keep up.

Adam looked back a couple more times. "Keep running!" he shouted. Then he streaked off faster than seemed possible and disappeared beyond the end of the alley.

Oh fuck. Oh god.

Parker wanted to scream for Adam to wait, but he was long gone. He still clutched his phone in his hand, the earbuds dangling. He tore them out and illuminated the screen as he slowed. He had to call nine-one-one. He was alone, except—oh Jesus fucking Christ—he wasn't alone, because now the crazy people were coming down the alley, their limbs moving in weird staccato jerks, and—*what the fuck was happening?*

Parker gasped for air as he raced on, the alley endless. He was alone and he was going to fucking die, and he was trapped, and *fuck,* this had to be a dream because this couldn't be real, but they were gaining on him and—

A headlight blinded him. Beyond the bizarre chattering of the people surging closer—like a strange humming and their teeth smashing together—an engine revved. Parker skidded to a stop and raised his arm to shield his eyes as a motorcycle zoomed down the alley. Tires squealed as the driver spun the bike sideways.

"Get on!" Adam shouted, grabbing for him with one hand. He still held his helmet with the other and whipped it at the head of a man who grasped at Parker.

The motorcycle hummed between Parker's legs as he clutched Adam's waist. "Go, go!"

The chattering was louder, and bloody hands clawed at them, one snagging his hood. The material tightened on his throat, choking him for a terrible instant until the motorcycle shot free and careened around the corner.

He hung on precariously, the wind in his face making his eyes water, his fingers digging into Adam's leather jacket. The main roads of campus were clogged with cars, the headlights illuminating packs of jerking people who had become like animals, biting into students while wails echoed across the Oval. Adam deftly maneuvered the bike across campus, weaving around clumps of writhing bodies.

Helicopters circled uselessly in the distance over the pandemonium of Palo Alto. How had he not heard them before? He could only hang on as Adam snaked across lawns and over sidewalks.

"Where are we going?" Parker's voice sounded thin and jagged. God, he was thirsty.

"The preserve," Adam shouted.

This had to be a fucking nightmare. This couldn't be real. It was impossible. His mind spun as they sped around Lake Lagunita, wet and marshy after late summer storms earlier in the week. "Then what?"

Adam steered across the driving range and they plunged into the darkness of the golf course. He didn't answer.

Chapter Two

I N A SWATH of trees, the forest dense around them, Adam brought the bike to a stop and cut the engine. Harsh pants filled Parker's ears, and he jerked around before realizing they were his own. He still clung to Adam's warmth and reluctantly sat back and let his arms drop.

The silence of the preserve was unnerving. Branches swayed in the light wind and leaves rustled. Parker's heart was very possibly going to explode.

"It's okay. There's no one else here."

"How do you know?" Parker craned his neck back and forth. "They could be out here too."

"I can't hear anyone but you."

"What if they're hiding?"

Adam swung his leg over the bike and turned. "Did they seem particularly stealthy?"

"Well, no. Good point. Speaking of those people, *what the actual fuck?* I mean, is this happening? They were like, like..."

Adam pressed his lips together in a grim line. "Zombies?"

"Yes! How the hell?" Gesturing with his hands, Parker jumped off the bike. "This isn't... This *can't*. Zombies aren't real!"

"I don't think those people are actually dead, but they're clearly...infected with something."

"How? And with what?" He paced back and forth. "Earlier tonight I heard someone say it was happening in San Francisco. I should have watched the news like everyone else. I didn't think...

Jesus. Did you hear anything?"

"No." Adam raked a hand through his thick hair. "I was in the AV lab in the basement using the editing equipment. There's no cell service down there." He reached into his jacket pockets. "Shit. I must have dropped my phone back on campus." Suddenly he tensed, his hand raised. Parker froze, listening as hard as he could. After a few seconds, Adam relaxed. "It's just a deer."

Parker squinted into the darkness. "Where?" he whispered.

"You didn't see it? It's gone now."

"Oh. Okay." Parker was quiet for a few moments, the urge to scream still clawing at him as his brain tried to process what was happening. He yanked his phone from his pocket. The light from the screen was harsh, and he blinked at his lock-screen image of the impossibly blue ocean that summer on Cape Cod with white sails bobbing on the horizon.

"My parents. My mom called me a million times." He hit his mother's cell number in the list of recents. "Come on, come on…" He held his breath while he waited for it to ring. Nothing happened. "Come *on*. Ring!"

"The system might be overloaded, Parker."

"Yeah, but I'm still going to try."

"I didn't say not to."

Parker ignored the flash of irritation and tried again, pacing. His throat was getting more and more sore, and his head felt heavy. He needed water. He disconnected and tried again. And again.

As a tinny sound finally echoed down the line, he waved his free hand in the air. "It's ringing!" It rang. And rang.

"Hello. You've reached Pamela Osborne. I'm unavailable, but will return your call as soon as I can. Have a lovely day."

The familiar sound of his mother's voice made Parker want to curl up into her arms and cry. He took a steadying breath. "Mom? It's me. Are you guys okay? It's insane over here. I'm hiding in the woods, but I'm okay. Call me back when you get to the Cape house. Love you."

He tried the Cambridge house phone next, then the Cape house number, his father's cell, and Eric's numbers in London. He left similar messages after each beep. Adam now sat against a tree with his eyes closed and legs crossed. *Is he meditating or some shit?* Parker watched him. "Um, do you want to call your folks?"

"I don't have any family."

Parker blinked. "Oh. But you have a girlfriend, right?" Parker handed him the phone.

Adam took it and tapped in a number. "Tina, it's me. Are you okay? I hope... I hope I see you soon. Love you." He disconnected and handed back the phone. "Thanks."

Pacing again, Parker tried to connect to a news site. "Come on, come on..." The page loaded, and he peered at the wall of red text, his eyes scanning as his brain tried to process it. "National state of emergency. Some kind of virus. Take cover. Washington, New York, Los Angeles, and a bunch of other cities under siege."

"I don't think a virus could spread that fast on its own," Adam said quietly.

Parker bit back a scream when his phone rang and vibrated in his hand, the retro ringtone making it sound like the old phone at the Cape house. His brother's picture appeared on the screen in a shot Parker had taken on the deck of their family's sailboat a few summers ago before Eric moved to London. His blond hair was bleached even lighter, and his face was a little red from the sun and sea.

Parker's heart hammered as he answered. "Eric?"

"Oh, thank fuck. Parkster, are you okay? Are you safe?"

"Yeah. I'm hiding in the woods. What the hell is this? Are you okay over there?"

"No. It's crazy here too. They're saying it's biological terror-ism, but I don't know who the hell would want to spread this. I'm going into a bunker beneath the office. Guess it's a good thing that the president of the firm is a paranoid nut with too much money—apparently he's got some bomb shelter thing."

"Good." He managed a long breath. Eric was okay. "Just stay safe until this blows over. It will, right?" He paused. "Are you still there?"

"Yeah. I'm going to lose you soon, though. Did Mom reach you?"

"She left a message. They're going to the Cape house."

"Right. I told her you'd be okay. Stay out of sight. Are you alone?"

"No. I'm with…a guy from school. We're in the preserve near campus."

"Good. Stay there. Parker, I'm going underground now." His voice got distant. "I'm coming!" Then he was back. "If I don't—if we… I love you, little brother."

Parker's sore throat was unbearably thick, and his eyes stung. "Me too. Eric—"

Then there was silence, and the call disconnected. He gripped his phone, willing it to ring. He tried his parents again, pacing and blinking back his tears. Eric was okay. His parents would be too.

"I'm glad your brother's all right," Adam said.

"Yeah." Parker's voice was hoarse, and he coughed. "Thanks." A half-moon shone through the trees, and Parker met Adam's gaze. "What the hell do we do?"

Adam looked around. "I guess we stay here tonight. Hope that by tomorrow it'll be under control. Whatever *it* is."

"That's the plan?"

"You have a better one?"

"We should… We could…" His shoulders slumped. "Yeah, I have no idea." He stared at Adam sitting against the tree. "Jesus, how can you be so calm? Throw down a red checkered cloth and you could be on a freaking picnic!"

"I'm thinking. This is how I think. I wouldn't call myself calm, but what good will panicking do?"

"No good at all, but *oh my god we just escaped from zombies*. At the risk of repeating myself, what the fuck?" He paced. "Who would do this on purpose?" He tapped on Google and did another search, scanning through the headlines, which all said basically the same thing: take immediate cover. Stay indoors.

"Unless you can find something online, we have no way of knowing, Parker. Not yet, at least."

He clenched his teeth. "I realize that, but it makes me feel better to talk about it instead of sitting there like some, some…Buddha with chiseled abs!"

Adam raised an eyebrow, but said nothing.

Parker tried calling nine-one-one, but he only got an old-fashioned busy signal. "Okay, so Eric said he heard it was bioterrorism, which makes sense if it's happening in England too. I wouldn't put it past the Russians at this point. Maybe that crackpot thinks we're all gay and wants to wipe us out. Or it could be terrorists from anywhere. Or hell, maybe it's just some freak strain of rabies. Maybe we all need to get a bunch of shots and we'll be fine. It'll be fine. It has to be, right?"

"Why don't you sit down? It'll be okay."

Parker tapped each finger against his thumbs in a repeating pattern. "You really think so?"

Adam's gaze skittered away, and there was only the sound of the leaves. Finally, he just said, "We should rest."

The ground was a little damp, but his legs were shaky and it felt good to sit. Parker leaned back against the thick trunk, his shoulder close to Adam's. "The police and the army will take care of it, right?"

"I hope so." Adam seemed to be breathing deeply, inhaling and exhaling evenly.

"They have to. I mean, this is insane. I'm sure I'm going to wake up on my lumpy mattress in my room with annoying house music vibrating through the wall. And this will all be a dream."

Adam only blew out a long breath.

The frantic energy drained away, and Parker suddenly felt utterly exhausted. "I can't believe this is happening. I thought I was going to die. When you left, I just… I thought that was it."

"I knew I could get to the bike. I wasn't going to leave you."

"Were you a track star or something? Because you totally disappeared. And it's not like you owed me anything. So, you know. Thanks. For coming back and saving my life."

"I couldn't exactly abandon you there. I'm not a sociopath."

Irritation flared. "Did I say you were? Geez, whatever. Forget it." He checked his phone again and made sure the ringer was on before resolutely slipping it into his hoodie pocket. He'd drain the battery if he kept turning it on.

Now that the adrenaline had worn off, he started to shiver. It was past midnight, and the temperature had dipped uncomfortably. Clouds rolled in overhead, and he hoped it wouldn't rain. He drew his knees to his chest.

"Here." Adam fidgeted beside him.

Then there was warm leather over his shoulders. "Oh. No, it's fine. Dude, I can't take your jacket." Parker tried to pass it back.

Adam pressed his hand on Parker's shoulder. "Keep it. I'm not cold."

Parker swore he could feel heat from Adam's palm, even through the leather. "You sure?"

He nodded, his hazel eyes that strange golden even in the darkness.

"Um, okay. Thanks. Again."

After a pause, Adam said, "You're welcome."

The jacket was too big for him, and when he pressed his knees to his chest, he could almost wrap it around himself. He was in good enough shape, but he didn't have Adam's bulk. The jacket carried a faint scent of pine and something earthy he couldn't identify. But it smelled nice, and he was grateful for it.

"Go to sleep. I'll keep watch."

He snorted. "There's no way I can sleep. But thanks. If you want to sleep, go for it."

"I don't think so."

Parker checked his dark phone again. He sent texts to his parents, Jason, and Jessica, and then clutched the phone in his hand, willing it to vibrate as the night crawled by. Adam closed his eyes again but wasn't sleeping. Parker wanted to ask him if he actually was meditating but didn't want to interrupt.

In the darkness, they waited.

"SEE ANYONE?"

Adam shook his head.

Parker couldn't decide if the eerie stillness was a good or bad thing. He leaned out from the tree they were crouched behind at the edge of campus. It was misty in the cool, predawn light, but the clouds had rolled out and it would be a sunny day. He tried to focus on breathing steadily, but his lungs and sinuses were increasingly congested. His head was like a brick, and his throat was officially sore. Because he totally needed the flu on top of worldwide catastrophe.

He whispered, "I don't hear that noise they were making either. It sounded like this creepy...chattering or something. You know what I mean?"

"Yeah."

"You think they're gone? Maybe we should go help those people. They might just be unconscious." Bodies dotted the grass in the distance.

"They're dead," Adam said flatly.

"But we can't be sure, can we? Although… It's weird. I expected more. Dead people, I mean. Did they all become zombies? Or infected or whatever those people are?"

"I don't know. Maybe if a person gets injured too badly, they'll still die. We have no idea how it's transmitted or what it is."

"I saw them biting. Eating, really." Parker shuddered. "We need to find someone who knows what's going on. The police must be patrolling. Or the army or someone in charge." He glanced at his phone again, hoping to see a notification from his friends or parents. He still had four bars, but he hadn't been able to get online again. The little circle at the top of the browser just spun endlessly.

"I'm going to check the area. Stay here."

"No way!" Parker grabbed Adam's sleeve. He'd given him back the jacket, and his fingers curled into the leather. "You can't leave me."

Adam shook him off impatiently. "I'm coming back. Don't worry."

"Don't worry? Right, sure, I'll just kick it here and clip my nails or something. No big."

"It's safer for you to stay here."

"And what if you find some rescue squad, and they scoop you up and I'm left out here holding my dick? Uh-uh."

"Parker, I wouldn't leave you." Adam's gaze was direct and his voice steady.

"Why not? We don't even like each other. Why would you come back?"

"I came back last night. I won't leave you. Whether we like each other or not is irrelevant. Right now we have to stick together."

"Right, exactly. Stick together. Which means, you know, *sticking together*." Parker fiddled with the zipper on his hoodie. "I can't just sit here waiting. We waited all night. We need to find the police. We need help. Besides, what if you get hurt? What if you get your face eaten? I'm coming with you."

After a moment, Adam nodded and led the way back to his motorcycle parked between the trees. In the light of day, Parker could see that the bike had dark red trim and was a Harley. And thank God for it, because it had saved their bacon.

Parker climbed on, breathing in Adam's earthy pine scent and wrapping his arms around him even though it felt awkward in the light of day when not fleeing zombies. The guy may not be his favorite person, but the thought of being alone churned his stomach and made his pulse race. He tightened his grip.

"What's wrong?"

"Aside from the zombie apocalypse?"

Adam huffed out a sound that might have been a laugh, and they were off.

The bike's engine seemed unbearably loud as they passed by eviscerated bodies. Parker tried not to look, but they were everywhere—practically in pieces. He saw no signs of life. Or the undead either, or whatever the fuck they were.

The school's buildings appeared deserted. Parker was about to uselessly ask where everyone had gone when he glimpsed a spinning red light beyond the humanities block. "There, there! Did you see it? Go toward the Oval. The police are here." Relief soared through him.

We're going to be okay.

Adam gunned the engine and sped along the sidewalk. Parker's breath caught in his throat as the grassy expanse of the Oval came into view.

The police were there all right.

Lights flashed on squad cars all around the rim of the Oval, stopped haphazardly. And clustered around the police vehicles, dozens deep, were chattering zombie people.

Hundreds of them. Maybe thousands.

He didn't have to tell Adam to turn around. He simply hung on as they raced back the way they'd come. Parker watched over his shoulder, his pulse pounding, but none of the infected followed.

When they reached the dorms, Adam slowed and said, "We need to find a TV."

The doors of one of the dorms stood open, one hanging at an angle and almost ripped off its hinges. Adam drove right up the few steps and into the building before cutting the engine. Silence greeted them, along with several glistening bodies.

Parker looked away from the gore and opened his mouth to say something, but Adam held up his hand. His eyes were shut, and he didn't move. Parker could only see the side of his face, and the sweep of his dark eyelashes against his skin.

Adam opened his eyes. "We're alone."

"How can you be sure?" Parker hissed.

"I can't hear anyone."

"Neither can I, but it's a big building," he whispered.

Adam stood and put down the kickstand. "We'll be careful. Come on, let's find a TV."

Parker didn't really have a choice and followed. Adam seemed to be right—the place was deserted. Chairs were knocked over, and blood sprayed the tiles. At least there weren't that many bodies, and it was utterly terrifying how "only" two dead students splattered across the hallway was somehow already a relief.

He stuck close to Adam as they picked their way down the hall. In the common room, there was more blood.

A lot more.

Blood soaked the couches, but there were no bodies here. The thought that they might have been completely consumed crossed Parker's mind, and he shuddered.

The TV was on, the volume apparently muted. Snow flickered

on the screen. The remote was nowhere to be found, so Parker went to the unit while Adam hung back by the door, checking both ways down the hall every few seconds.

Parker skimmed his fingers over the black plastic casing. "Come on, come on. When I was little they still made TVs with buttons. *Shit*." He hauled the overturned coffee table away from the TV stand. On shelves below the TV sat a DVD player and the cable box. "Can't change the channels on the TV anyway," he mumbled to himself.

He glanced back at where Adam stood, his head turning side to side every few seconds, checking both directions since the common room was in the middle of the building. "We still good?"

"Yes."

"You remind me of the Terminator or something. But it's cool. I'm not complaining."

Adam's lips quirked. "Glad to hear it."

Parker found the channel button on the top of the cable box and pressed it, keeping one eye on the screen above. "Okay, let's see what we have. Snow, snow, snow. Black screen. Black screen. Sn—oh! Here we go." He fumbled with the TV again, finally finding the controls on the side panel. "Volume up..." he muttered to himself.

A high-pitched whine filled the room, and Adam winced. "Volume down."

Parker lowered the sound while he read the message scrolling across the screen over a logo. He forced himself to take deep breaths.

"What does it say?"

Parker read the message aloud. "This is the Emergency Broadcast System. This is not a test. Stay in your home with doors and windows locked. If you are not at home, find a secure location. A state of emergency has been declared in the continental United States. Stay inside and await further instructions. The CDC has—"

He broke off as his palms went clammy.

"What?" Adam asked tightly.

Parker swallowed hard, his throat raw and his nose running. "The CDC has issued a pandemic warning. Avoid contact. This is not a test." He muted the volume completely and watched the message scroll by again.

"Is that all?" Adam asked quietly.

"Yeah. It just repeats." Parker scrolled through the rest of the channels, his chest tightening as he came across nothing but snow or dark screens, and a few other broadcasts of the same message. "Await further instruction. From who? The police are out there dead. But the army will do something, right?"

Adam was silent for too long before answering. "I hope so."

"They have to! I mean, I...I can't..." The pressure tightened on his chest like a vise, and he coughed, his lungs rattling. "I'm supposed to be taking my econ test this morning. I'm not supposed to be... This can't be real. This isn't happening. They have to fix it. They can't just let this happen." Blood rushed in his ears and he trembled.

"Shh. It's okay. Breathe." Adam was there, one hand on Parker's shoulder and the other flat against his chest. "Breathe in."

Lungs stuttering, Parker tried to obey. He gasped and the room spun.

"Now out. Look at me."

Blinking, Parker struggled to focus on Adam's eyes. They were flecked with so much gold they practically shimmered, and he zeroed in on the unusual color as he forced his lungs to expand and contract.

"That's it. In and out. It's okay. You're okay."

The room righted itself, and his pulse slowed. Sweat dampened the short hair at his forehead, and he swiped at his nose. Adam grounded him, his big hands warm and steady and strong. For a foolish moment, Parker wanted nothing more than to throw himself into Adam's arms and be held.

Shit, man. Get it together.

"Are you feeling sick?" Adam peered at him closely.

The CDC has issued a pandemic warning.

Jerking away, Parker shook his head. "I'm cool. Just freaked out. Thanks." He was fine. This was some stupid cold. Or stress. It wasn't anything else. *It wasn't.*

For something to do, he returned to the TV and flipped through more channels. He was about to give up when he passed something new. "Whoa." He backed up.

Adam stood behind him, and they watched. It was one of the TV network newsrooms. The camera was off-kilter, and drops of red dotted the lens. At the top of the screen, the studio lights were almost blinding. Below was the empty news desk, and in the bottom corner, something moved.

"Volume." Adam's voice was hoarse.

Parker unmuted the TV. They both jumped as the chattering filled the room, punctuated by the unmistakable sound of tearing flesh.

Adam spoke quietly. "Let's grab some food and water, and find a safe place. And weapons."

"Yeah. Let's get some of those. How about now?" Parker flicked off the TV and the godawful noise. "I think now is good."

He had a feeling locking doors and windows wasn't going to cut it.

Chapter Three

T HE PROBLEM WITH getting weapons was, well, getting weapons.

"Does Home Depot stock swords?" Parker asked as Adam drove them back through campus, staying far away from the Oval. "People in zombie movies usually have a big sword of some kind. I can't believe I'm talking about this for real. This is crazy. How do we even know what weapons will work on them?"

"Most creatures can't survive decapitation."

"Right. So swords would be good. Where do swords come from? Like, who sells swords in the twenty-first century? It's probably all online. Does Amazon Prime still deliver in the apocalypse? But maybe—" He grabbed Adam tighter. "Over there. Are they…?"

Adam slowed the bike as they neared the library. There was a group of people out front. Parker squinted, lifting his hand to block the rising sun. His heart sank. In the daylight, he could see more clearly what appeared to be the effects of the virus or whatever it was: violently bulging eyes, a jerky motion of the limbs, and hands reaching out with fingers in rictus, curled as if into claws. Blood was smeared on their faces and hands.

But the worst part was the chattering. Their teeth clashed constantly, and over the hum of the motorcycle, Parker could hear a low drone, as if it was coming from deep in their throats. These infected were students, and as the motorcycle neared, they turned in unison, their joints unnaturally stiff.

They swarmed toward the bike, moving faster than should have been possible. Parker's breath came in quick gasps as Adam steered away, seemingly calm as anything. It took Parker a minute to be able to speak again, and when he did, his voice was reedy.

"I think Walmart has guns, right? Too bad we're not in Boston. My dad has a freaking arsenal. Not that he needs it, but you know. From his cold dead hands, second amendment, blah, blah, blah."

At the thought of his father, Parker swallowed down the worry that simmered constantly and resisted the urge to let go of Adam to check his phone. They had to be okay. They *had* to be.

He added, "Or maybe—holy shit."

Around the bend ahead, near one of the campus entrances, an ambulance was toppled on its side, red lights still flashing and engine running. The sun gleamed off the metal, and hundreds of infected crowded around it, their chattering filling the air like cicadas on crack.

"What are they doing? There can't be anyone left in there to eat."

"I don't think they know what they're doing. I don't think they're thinking anymore."

"Doesn't seem like it. That could be us. That probably *will* be us."

"There's a sporting goods store a few blocks from campus. Let's check it out."

"Uh-huh. Sounds good." Parker couldn't look away from the horde of infected, who lunged toward them with bent fingers and arms outstretched as they zoomed by. "How are you on gas?"

"Fine for now. We'll fill up as soon as we can."

The tangle of streets beyond the school came into sight, jammed with abandoned cars. "What do you think it's going to be like off campus?" Parker asked.

"I guess we're about to find out."

To reach the main road, they had to get uncomfortably close to the carnage. There were more bodies—and more infected. Parker caught glimpses of seemingly uninfected people as they weaved through the obstacle course the road had become. There was a flash of blonde hair behind a car; a rifle pointed from a window; two people holding hands and ducking behind a van.

"I think the store's the other way. By the hamburger joint."

Adam didn't slow. "No, it's this way. A couple more blocks."

"Are you sure? I swear it was that way."

"I'm sure."

"Have you been there? How do you know?"

Adam exhaled sharply. "I've lived here for five years, Parker. I'm sure."

"You better be."

"I am."

Parker pointed. "There, there! Sporting goods. Huh. You were right."

"*I know.*"

The parking lot held only a few vehicles, and the store was dark. Adam cut the engine and they sat there for a moment, glancing around. It was unnerving how deserted the streets seemed in less than twenty-four hours. Parker hadn't thought it would be possible.

"What do you think?" he asked Adam quietly.

In the distance, a woman shrieked.

Without another word, they dismounted and hustled to the double set of doors. Parker tried the right one, but it was locked. He yanked on the left. No dice. "I guess we can break a window, huh? Not like someone's going to arrest us. Actually, that would be great if they did. Throw the book at us. Lock us up safe and sound. Okay, how do you break a window?" He looked around for something to throw.

"Wait." Adam was doing that thing where he held up his hand

and listened intently. He sniffed loudly. "There are people inside."

"Huh?" Parker peered through the glass. He could just make out the shapes of aisles, but with the sun bright overhead, he mostly only saw his own reflection. And Jesus he looked like hell—pale with dark splotches under his eyes, and the congestion and sore throat weren't going anywhere.

His kingdom for a venti mocha. "I don't see anyone."

Adam sniffed again, listening with his head cocked. "I'm positive."

What the fuck? "Okay, you apparently have supersonic hearing, but what's with the sniffing? Is there some epic BO going on in there?"

Adam did the strangest thing: he blushed. "Of course not. I think there must be people in there because the doors are locked and I heard voices. You didn't hear them? And I'm sniffing because I have a cold."

"Oh. Okay." It made sense—maybe they were both coming down with it. Then Parker's stomach churned, and he prayed *it* wasn't what had infected the others. Surely if it was, they'd be eating someone's face by now, wouldn't they?

"We should—"

Parker rattled the door. "Hello? Someone in there? Open up. We come in peace. Hello?" He thumped on the glass. "We're going to break it in a minute, so just open the door. Please?"

In the silence that followed, Adam sighed. "I guess that's one way of going about it."

"You have a better idea?" Parker glanced around to make sure his shouting hadn't attracted any infected. Down the block, he could see movement and expected the chattering to reach his ears any moment. "Shit." He turned back to the glass. "Seriously, we need you to open the door. *Now.*"

Silence.

"Time to break it," Parker said, but Adam was somehow already returning from a nearby car with a tire iron. He raised it over his shoulder, and Parker scurried back out of the way.

"Wait!" a female voice cried from the shadows of the store. A moment later three faces appeared faintly in the glass beyond the reflection of the parking lot.

Parker returned to the door. "Hi. We're just looking for weapons. We're not going to hurt you. We're not infected. See?" Parker motioned back and forth between himself and Adam. "We're okay. Can you please open the door?"

The young women looked around Parker's age. They glanced at each other, and then back out at Parker and Adam. One of them leaned her head in and whispered to the others.

"We won't hurt you," Adam said.

Their heads shot up, and they stared mutely.

Parker whispered to Adam, "Okay, that bionic hearing is a little creepy, dude."

Adam didn't reply. Instead, he pressed against him and wrapped his arm around Parker's shoulders. "My boyfriend and I don't mean you any harm. I swear. Please unlock the door."

Boyfriend? Parker opened his mouth, but the question died on his tongue when Adam dug his fingers into Parker's upper arm.

"So they don't think we're going to rape them," he hissed.

Oh, right. Parker cleared his throat and smiled at the girls. He was aware of the unnatural noise of the infected getting louder to the east. "Look, I get that you're scared. We're scared too. I totally would've died last night, but he saved me." His heart tripping, he put his arm around Adam's waist. "Me and my boyfriend here, we really need to get some weapons. Please? We won't hurt you."

Adam looked to the left and tensed. "Open the door. We can help each other."

As the girls exchanged another glance, the chattering swelled. Parker was about to tell Adam to smash the damn glass after all, and Adam was tightening his grip on the tire iron when one of the girls flicked the lock.

With a long exhale, Parker opened the door and held it so Adam could wheel the motorcycle inside. They locked it quickly and backed away from the glass. The front wall of the store was fortunately brick with windows near the roof too high to reach. The double glass doors were the only weak point.

Silently, they watched the infected twitch their way down the street. A few wandered into the parking lot, but were more interested in the cars, reaching for the gleaming metal with bloody fingers. They ignored the store, and after a few excruciating minutes, Parker, Adam, and the young women were alone again.

Parker took in the dark aisles. Sunlight through the doors and high windows and an emergency light at the back of the store cast just enough glow to see. "Did you guys come in here for guns?"

A blonde with a pink stripe in her long hair shook her head. "I'm the night cashier. It wasn't busy, so the manager left me to close up." She indicated her friends, a petite Asian with her hair in two braids, and a tall brunette with the kind of pixie cut Jessica had tried in middle school and regretted instantly.

"Lauren and Daniela came to pick me up. We were going to the Sigma party. Then everything went crazy outside. We turned off the lights and hid. We thought it was some kind of riot. Then we looked online and it seems to be happening all over the place. We saw some videos on YouTube that were…bad. Really bad. San Francisco and Oakland looked like something out of a horror movie. The bridges were blocked with cars, and there were…bodies. And all the news sites said to stay locked inside. They said it was some kind of pandemic or something?"

Parker said, "Yeah. Apparently." Every swallow hurt. But he couldn't have it. He would be eating faces if he did, right? Or he was a cowardly, selfish fuck who couldn't face reality.

In his defense, reality had never looked remotely like this.

Daniela spoke up. "But how is this happening? What kind of

virus or whatever makes people batshit crazy? This is insane, right? They have to do something. Someone will come help us, won't they?"

"I hope so," Parker answered. He wanted to believe it, but with each passing hour, it felt less likely. "Thanks for letting us in. I'm Parker, and this is Adam. My boyfriend." He tried to smile, and likely failed spectacularly.

"I'm Carey," the blonde answered. "As in Mariah, not Underwood."

Lauren's voice wavered and she tugged on one braid. "What the hell happened? We tried calling nine-one-one a million times and it just kept beeping this loud noise, and now it won't connect at all."

Sweat beaded on Parker's forehead. "What about your cells?" He pulled his out and swiped his finger across the screen.

"They have bars, but no one's picking up anywhere."

Parker paced up and down the football aisle and tried all his numbers again. Then he tried his roommate Chris. He barely knew the guy, but would love to hear that he was alive. Straight to voicemail. He left a message just in case.

Chris is probably dead. They're all probably dead. Please don't let them be dead.

We're dead too. It just hasn't happened yet.

He took a deep breath and blew it out. He couldn't panic. That wouldn't help anyone. Eric was in some bomb shelter. He was okay. Their parents would be safe at the Cape house. They had to be. Dad would have been at work, so maybe he'd left early. Maybe Mom had picked him up on her way out of the city.

Maybe, maybe, maybe, maybe.

He rubbed his face and rounded the hunting aisle, calling to Adam. "Want to try Tina again?"

Carey was showing Adam the shotguns while her friends watched. Adam took the phone and tapped in the number. After a minute he silently handed it back, unmistakable resignation pinching his face.

Parker wanted to say something, because it had to really suck to be separated from your girlfriend when this shit was going down, but they were supposed to be boyfriends. Besides, what could he say? It sucked for all of them to be separated from people they cared about.

"Do you have the key for the shells?" Adam asked Carey.

She hesitated. "I do, but…are you sure it's a good idea? Do you guys know what you're doing?"

Parker found himself laughing hoarsely. "Of course we don't. But there are *zombies* out there, for lack of a better word. They're killing everyone, or infecting them, and I think we can skip the background checks." His laughter echoed.

The girls edged away, eyeing him uneasily, and Parker recognized there was a tinge of hysteria to his giggles. Yet he couldn't seem to stop himself. Then Adam was there, standing right against him, his palm cupping Parker's cheek.

"In and out."

His breath was warm on Parker's face, and Parker closed his eyes, leaning into him for a moment. He opened his eyes and looked into Adam's. "Okay. I'm good. Sorry. I won't freak out. How are you so calm?"

Adam smiled for a moment—that flash of teeth and tenderness. "I told you—I'm not. But we can't fall apart right now." He dropped his hand from Parker's face.

"Right." Parker glanced at the girls. Carey and Daniela watched him warily, each with an arm around Lauren, who was crying. "I'm sorry. It's going to be okay. We're all scared. I was being a douche."

Lauren sniffled and wiped her nose. "Are those people really zombies?"

Parker shook his head. "They're…something. We don't

know."

"I can't get in touch with my parents." Lauren hiccupped with fresh sobs. "I can't get in touch with anyone. None of us can."

"Me either," Parker said. "I talked to my brother for a minute, but that's it."

Daniela looked to Adam, who stood awkwardly by the shotguns. "What about you?"

Adam shook his head.

Carey blew out a loud breath and knotted her hair into a bun with lightning-fast fingers, the pink stripe hanging down by her cheek. "Okay. Let's do this. Guns, bullets, knives. What else?"

"Food and water," Daniela suggested.

Parker realized he wasn't hungry, which was a bad sign. He was always hungry. He surreptitiously felt his forehead. Was it warm? He felt tired and shaky all over, but that was to be expected, right? Snot dripped down the back of his throat, and he tried not to sniff too obviously.

Jesus, do I have it? Am I giving it to everyone right now? Did I give it to Adam?

The brave thing would have been to leave and hole up on his own somewhere just in case he was about to get a taste for human flesh.

Parker could admit he wasn't even a little bit brave, because the idea of being alone out there made him want to cry and puke.

Carey started handing out orders. "There's a bunch of granola bars and chips by the cash, and some soda and water. You guys eat, and I'll get the keys for the ammo."

"Oh!" Parker called after her. "You don't have any swords, do you?"

Carey grinned humorlessly. "This is your lucky day."

"THAT'S NOT HOW it goes."

Adam gave him the stink eye. "Yes. It is."

"No. It's *not*," Parker insisted. "I know you're a real tough guy, what with your leather jacket. I mean, as tough as a documentary MFA candidate can get, that is. But that's not the way it goes."

"Fine." Adam handed over the twelve-gauge semi-automatic shotgun and scope he'd been attempting to mount for five minutes. "Please show us all how it's done."

With a flourish, Parker lined up the scope, slid open the joint, and snapped it into place. "Voilà. Please hold your applause until the end of the performance."

Daniela giggled, and to his credit, Adam actually cracked a smile.

"Have you handled a lot of shotguns?" Lauren asked.

"Nope." Parker waved the manual. "I just read the instructions. It's a bold choice, I know." He handed it to Adam with a smirk, and Adam began poring over the pages.

Carey returned from the storeroom with a box of protein bars, which she dumped in the middle of their circle. "There are a few more back there. I guess it just depends on how much we can carry."

They'd barricaded the front and back doors and created a nest of sleeping bags in the rear corner of the store by the emergency light. In the afternoon, they'd heard the distant beating of a helicopter, but hadn't been able to spot it from the parking lot or the service alley behind the store.

As night fell, it was uncannily quiet. They weren't sure where the infected were. Parker hoped that whatever madness had seized them had proved fatal. A stab of guilt followed the thought. He didn't wish anyone harm, but those people...didn't seem like people anymore. He just wanted life to go back to normal.

Would things ever be normal again?

Daniela hefted her knapsack onto her back. "I dunno. If I had to run with this thing I don't think I'd make it far." She pulled it off and began sorting through the contents.

Much of the afternoon and early evening had been devoted to stocking up with supplies. Dried food, water purifying tablets, lightweight shirts, jackets, sleeping bags, and of course, weapons.

Parker had a machete (an actual *machete*) with a back strap ready to go. It wasn't quite a sword, but it was pretty close. He'd tested out handling the blade and hoped to God he would never have to use it on anything living. Or possibly undead or whatever.

Now they were examining the guns. Parker tested the weight of the handguns and went for the lightest. He'd watched his father skeet shooting with rifles over the years, but had never tried it himself since Eric was an amazing shot and Parker hadn't needed to be found lacking in yet another arena.

It was surreal holding a gun. He read the manual and practiced with the safety on before loading it and tucking it away in the side pocket of his pack with boxes of bullets, making sure it was within easy reach.

Seriously, how was this *his life*?

"That's a really cool motorcycle," Daniela said. "Harley, right?"

"Yeah," Adam answered. "Softail."

"Cool. My dad would…" She blinked and tried to smile. "He would totally love it."

In the silence that followed, Parker managed to swallow down a cough. The congestion was getting worse, and his nose was running nonstop. He wiped it surreptitiously with his sleeve. "It's definitely cool. Really classic. Um, everyone have enough bullets? Not that I know what 'enough' is."

"It's not like we're going to have to use any of this stuff." Lauren shredded a granola bar wrapper into long silver slivers. "This isn't like… Someone's going to come for us. This isn't a movie. The army will take over and rescue us. They have to. It's their job."

They all looked at each other around the circle, their faces creased and tired.

"Yeah. I'm sure they'll come tomorrow," Adam replied. "We should hang tight and be prepared. Just in case."

After an awkward silence, Daniela shivered. "It's getting cold in here."

"Sorry," Carey said. "The electricity's out. The emergency light is powered by the backup generator, but there's no heat. It's been a warm September, but you know how the temps dip at night here."

"Why would the power go out?" Lauren asked.

"It wouldn't take much," Adam said. "One pole gets hit by a car, and the line's broken. And if the people in the power plants get infected…"

"But if the lines are okay, the power should still run, right?" Parker asked. He'd never really thought about how electricity worked. Sometimes it went out, but it always came back on before too long.

Adam shrugged. "For a little while, I guess. But those power plants don't operate on their own. I don't know much about them, but I remember visiting one on a class trip when I was a kid. They seemed pretty complex. They gave us a demonstration on how one little thing going wrong could trip the whole system. And the grids are connected. They said it was only as good as the weakest link. That's why blackouts can happen over a wide area." He shook his head. "I don't know why I remember that."

"And I guess the internet won't work without power," Carey said. "I mean, if you had electricity, you could post something, but our ISPs need power for us to read it." She took out her phone and tapped it. "The network's still up, but I can't connect." She smiled wryly. "I guess we get to find out what life's like without smartphones. My mom's always saying I'm addicted." Her smile wobbled, and she took a shuddering breath. "Daniela, let's go get hats."

They disappeared down one of the aisles. Lauren started on another wrapper, and Parker toyed with the laces of his sneakers, untying and retying them.

Carey and Daniela returned with a selection of hats and gloves for everyone. Carey pulled a blue ski hat over her bright hair. "What do you think?"

Lauren frowned. "I don't know. Try the green one."

Daniela rolled her eyes. "Is it warm? Because I don't think the zombies will be judging our fashion sense."

Carey pulled off the hat and patted her hair, tucking stray bits behind her ears. "I guess they won't." Her eyes glistened. "How is this real?"

Lauren's lip trembled, and Parker had to take a deep breath and beat down the rising panic. They were all on the verge of a nervous breakdown, and it wouldn't do anyone any good. He snatched up one of the hats, which had ear flaps and a pink pom-pom on top. He went up to his knees and pulled it over Adam's head. "Yes or no? I think it really brings out his eyes."

Adam scowled but didn't take off the hat. As the girls laughed, he watched Parker intently, and Parker's heart skipped a beat. Crap. Was Adam actually mad?

But then Adam lifted his chin and said, "Only if there's a matching scarf. I have standards."

Parker joined in as the girls laughed harder, and Carey ripped open new bags of tortilla chips and Cheetos and passed them around. The store only carried the small size, so they'd gone through quite a few.

Parker ate a handful, chewing them well and wincing as he swallowed. He found himself shivering and hoped it was because of the temperature and not his worsening symptoms. The chips weren't helping his sore throat, but he'd never been able to resist salty goodness, even when he wasn't particularly hungry.

Just be normal. Everything's fine.

He glanced up and found Adam's gaze on him. Adam had taken off the pink hat, and a bit of his hair stood up at the back. Parker leaned over and smoothed it down, wondering what kind of shampoo he used to get his hair so thick and glossy. When he sat back, he shifted uncomfortably under Adam's stare. "What?" He swiped at his mouth. "Do I have Cheeto dust on my face?"

Blinking, Adam shook his head and looked away.

"Aww. You guys are the cutest," Carey said with a grin.

Although Adam's head was low, Parker could swear he was blushing, and that he'd tensed up. Before things could get weird or awkward, he elbowed him. "Aren't you going to give me your jacket again, Boobear?"

Adam bit back a laugh and nodded to the green nylon coat folded on top of Parker's new knapsack. "You've got your own now."

"True." Parker shrugged it on over his new long-sleeved Dri-fit shirt. "But it's not as warm as leather. Come on."

"Forget it."

"Fine. I'm totally getting a new boyfriend when this is over." Parker crossed his arms with an exaggerated huff.

"You guys will just have to cuddle," Daniela said with a wink.

"You know what? You're right." Parker nudged open Adam's bent legs and jokingly tried to crawl between them. "He's not much of a cuddler," he stage-whispered to the girls, who giggled. It was fun teasing Adam, and they sure as hell could use the distraction.

"That's because you're so ticklish, *darling*." Adam's deft fingers slid up beneath Parker's shirt, rough on his skin but touching him lightly.

Parker made an extremely undignified noise. He really was

ticklish, and he hadn't expected Adam to actually pull him close. He squirmed in Adam's grip, now locked between his powerful thighs. By the time he was able to get Adam's hand away and sit back between his legs, they were all laughing.

He leaned his back against Adam's chest. "There. That's not so bad, is it? Snookums?" He felt the puff of Adam's laugh across the top of his head.

"I suppose not."

Cuddling was actually nice and warm. Parker exhaled and got comfortable, and Adam didn't complain. Parker wondered how he would feel about getting cozy with his fake boyfriend if he knew Parker really was gay.

He thought again of Adam's real girlfriend, and whether or not Tina was still alive. Whether or not Parker's parents were alive. Were Jessica and Jason okay? How long could Eric stay underground? How long—

"Stop thinking for a few minutes," Adam murmured, briefly rubbing Parker's arm.

"How did you two meet?" Daniela asked.

Parker pushed aside his other thoughts since they weren't doing them any good. "He gave me a C-minus on an assignment even though everyone knows it's an underwater basket-weaving course and should be an easy A. He apparently didn't get the memo."

Adam huffed out a breath. "So he complained to the dean and got me in trouble."

Parker sat up and looked over his shoulder. "Dude, I seriously did not narc on you to the dean."

Adam's brow furrowed. "Really?"

"Really. Besides, I'm sure it'll be fine." He and Adam watched each other for a long moment, and then Parker sat back against him.

Would it ever matter again? Had it really only been twenty-four hours ago when that stuff had seemed so incredibly important?

"Wait, he's your TA?" Carey raised her eyebrows. Then she leaned in, her voice lowered. "That's *hot*."

Daniela popped open another bag of chips. "Tell us everything. No detail too small."

Pretending to be Adam's boyfriend, Parker could almost let himself believe this was all just a game. He spun an outlandish tale while Adam just shook his head and actually chuckled occasionally. It felt good to laugh and forget about the shit show going on in the real world. Maybe everything would be okay. Maybe they just had to wait it out together and the cavalry would arrive.

After midnight, Parker's eyes got heavy, and his head felt like mucus was building up by the minute. The girls had curled up together, and when Parker glanced back at Adam, his eyes drooped too. "I guess we should get some rest," Parker whispered. He sat forward to go lie down on his own part of the nest.

But Adam tugged him back between his legs and wrapped his arms over Parker's chest. His breath was warm on Parker's ear. "Sleep."

Despite everything, Parker felt safe. He pulled out his phone. The screen was still blank over the picture of the ocean. No texts. No calls. He checked his battery. Ten percent. It would be dead by morning. He took a shuddering breath and slipped it back into his pocket, trying to keep his mind empty.

Closing his eyes, he wriggled closer. He didn't even *know* Adam, and hadn't liked him at all, and now they were *snuggling*. But he let the exhaustion pull him under...

Parker jerked awake. He didn't know what time it was, but his leg was cramped. He looked back at Adam, who was frozen and alert, his golden eyes practically glowing.

One of the girls whispered, her voice breaking. "What was that?"

Then an unmistakable sound consumed the silence: shattering glass.

Chapter Four

I N THE GLOW of the emergency light, they were frozen—Parker still tucked against Adam, Daniela pushed up on one hand, and the other girls curled on the floor. Then Adam leapt to his feet and somehow ended up halfway down the aisle with the shotgun in his hands.

"Get ready to run," he whispered back to them.

Adrenaline rocketed through Parker as he strapped on the machete and backpack, and the girls gathered their own weapons and supplies. Angry shouts filled the air from the front of the store. Parker and Daniela shared a glance.

Parker licked his lips. "Stay here."

I can do this. I can do this. He crept down the aisle and peeked around the corner to find Adam in a standoff with a group of men in the shattered doorway. A large display of baseball equipment Parker and Carey had shoved in front still blocked their path. One of the men leveled a handgun at Adam, while the others held flashlights.

"Let us in, you son of a bitch!" one of them yelled.

Adam spoke calmly, the aim of his shotgun unwavering. "We have to set a few ground rules first."

"Fuck you!" another intruder spat. "It's every man for himself. We've got just as much right to the guns in here as you do."

There must have been six or seven of them, flashlight beams cutting through the darkness in a zigzag as they jostled for position. Parker couldn't tell how old they were and could only clearly see the middle-aged man with the handgun, who spoke.

"Now I'm sure we can all cooperate and come to an agreement."

"Shoot him! I need guns! Let us in, goddamn it!" a voice cried.

The men began to fight each other desperately, trying to squeeze through the door, the beams of their flashlights spinning wildly. Their leader pleaded for calm amid the shouting and cursing, and then Adam bolted away from the door toward Parker.

"You're letting them in?" Parker shouted.

"Run! Out the back!" Adam grabbed his arm and jolted him into motion before Parker could even process what was happening. In their wake, the shouts of the intruders transformed into screams, and when Parker looked back, he saw blood arc through one of the beams of light. The infected poured into the store, their jerky movements terrifyingly fast.

The girls were waiting by the pile of sleeping bags, their eyes wide and packs on their backs. "Out, out!" Parker called to them. Carey and Daniela bolted, but then skidded to a stop, looking back at Lauren frozen in place.

"Lauren!" Carey yelled. "Come on!"

Daniela turned back to yank at her friend. The back door was through the storeroom at the other end of the rear aisle, and Adam was pushing Parker toward it, the girls on their heels. Adam shoved Parker and the girls through the door and began firing, the shotgun's *booms* reverberating.

But it wasn't enough.

Parker reached back just as Daniela and Lauren were overtaken, their screams piercing as the infected tore into them with hands and teeth. All he could do was grab Carey's wrist and escape into the storeroom while Adam continued shooting, the chattering swelling in the air.

"Adam! Come on!" he shouted.

Then Adam was beside them, and as they raced through the

storeroom, Carey shrieked and stumbled, nearly toppling Parker. One of the infected had hold of her foot. Parker gripped her hand with both of his and heaved as Adam blew off the attacker's head in a spray of gore. They stumbled onward to the rear part of the storeroom, which was separated by a door. Adam kicked it shut, and they plunged into darkness.

"Oh my god!" Carey cried. "We have to go back and get them. They're...oh my god."

Parker couldn't see a thing. Could only hold on to Carey's hand. She squeezed his fingers so hard he thought they might break.

"Adam?" Parker's heart thumped.

"This way."

When Adam's hand found his, Parker had to swallow a scream. They were completely blind, but Adam somehow guided them to the store's back door. Of course they'd barricaded it, but he seemed to shove the storage racks aside in an instant. Holding Carey's hand, Parker tried not to think about Daniela and Lauren. His stomach roiled. They'd been right there, and then...

As they made it outside to the alley, he gulped in the cold night air. Adam circled around, shotgun at the ready. The swell of chattering inside the store was faint, and it seemed like they were alone in the alley.

Adam ducked back into the storeroom for the motorcycle, and Parker thanked whatever deity was in charge of this shit show that they'd put it back there.

Carey trembled beside him, her fingers still gripping his. A sob racked her slight body, and Parker drew her into a hug. "It's okay. We're going to be okay."

"Don't leave me here!"

"We won't. Of course we won't." He rubbed her back.

"Parker."

He looked over Carey's shoulder to where Adam stood a few

feet away with the bike. Adam stared down at Carey's leg.

"Don't leave me!" she cried again.

"She's bitten," Adam said quietly.

Parker jerked away from her. He circled around and stood by Adam.

Her hair had come loose in a tangle, and tears streamed down Carey's face. Below her capri pants, Parker could see the gouge taken from her left calf. Blood spilled over her sneaker.

"Please don't leave me!" She reached for them. "I'm okay. I'm okay!"

Before Parker could formulate a thought, Adam was straddling the bike. "More coming. We have to go." He reached behind and slid the shotgun into the holster strapped to his back.

"We can't leave her! What if she's not infected? We don't know how it's spread."

"Get on." Adam's nostrils flared and he glanced behind. "Both of you. *Now*!"

Parker jumped on, and Carey clambered over his lap so she was facing him, her legs around his hips. They wobbled as the bike sped out of the alley with too much weight on it, but Adam kept control, roaring around the store and onto the sidewalk.

With Carey wrapped around him, Parker couldn't look back, but he prayed to anyone listening that the infected weren't following. They seemed to have gotten faster, but it could just be that there was strength in numbers.

In his arms, Carey sobbed, her face buried against his neck. "It's okay," he repeated, over and over. "It's okay." It took all of Parker's strength to lean forward and clutch Adam's sides so he and Carey didn't go flying off the back of the motorcycle. The handle of the machete dug into the base of his neck, and the backpack strained his shoulders.

He had no idea where they were going, but soon they bounced over grass and there were trees all around. When they finally came to a stop and Adam killed the engine and lights, Parker stumbled off onto the ground, sprawled on his back with Carey on top of him.

A moment later, Carey's weight lifted as Adam hoisted her up and deposited her by a tree some feet away. He backed up, keeping Parker behind him as Carey wailed.

"They're dead! Oh my god, what's happening?" She heaved a great sob. "I want my mom. *I want my mom!*"

On his knees, Parker tugged off his pack and fumbled for the slim flashlight he'd tucked in a side pocket. When he crawled toward her, Adam blocked his way with a strong hand on Parker's head. Leaning around him, Parker shone the light on Carey's gored calf. Her hands were soaked with blood where she tried to stop the bleeding.

"We have to bandage it!" Parker tried to shake off Adam.

"It's too late."

"She might not be—" Parker's words died on his tongue as he watched Carey's eyes bulge. Her limbs trembled spastically, and then began jerking as the chattering sound grew in her throat, her teeth clashing. She tried to speak, but could only scream.

The infection overtook her. Before their eyes, Carey became one of them.

Her wrists swiveled as her fingers curled, the strange rictus setting in. Her eyes stuck out like a cartoon character's, too wide and as if they were pushing out of the sockets.

Parker could still feel the dampness of her tears on his neck. The flashlight was still in his grip, and the light waved back and forth as he scrambled to his feet and gestured with his hands. "What the fuck is this? Jesus, we—"

With a sudden burst of power, Carey lunged toward him, her arms outstretched and fingers grasping.

Adam shoved him out of the way, and Parker hit the ground with a *whoomp*. The flashlight flew from his hand and rolled across the grass as Adam unstrapped the shotgun and fired. He missed, and the bark of the tree splintered as Carey scrabbled across the ground. The chattering swelled as she clutched the flashlight and chomped down on it.

For a heartbeat, they watched.

"I have to kill her." Adam's voice was barely a whisper. "Right?"

"What if there's a cure? What if she'll be okay?" Parker felt hot and shaky all over. They'd known her only hours, but the thought of shooting her was unbearable.

Carey gnawed at the flashlight, her teeth grinding into the metal. A few hours ago, she and her friends had laughed with them, curled up and slept by their sides. Tears pricked Parker's eyes, and the acid in his stomach burned.

He slung on his pack. "Let's go. We'll just... Maybe there's a cure." As long as they didn't kill her, he could keep that tiny beacon of hope alive.

"Yeah. Okay." Adam stared at Carey, transfixed. Then he blinked and backed up to the bike.

When he started the engine and the headlight flashed on, Carey's head jerked up and she vaulted toward them. Parker leapt on behind Adam, his heart in his throat when she caught his ankle through denim, digging her fingers in so hard he thought she might tear off his foot. He kicked wildly, and the motorcycle swayed as Adam hit the gas.

For a terrible moment, Parker felt like he might be torn in two, Carey's unnaturally strong grip not wavering. Then they broke free, the cuff of his jeans tearing as they raced away. Parker turned to watch what used to be Carey chase after them in the red glare of the taillights, her eyes bulging so hard he thought they might explode, a ferociously single-minded expression distorting her face.

Images ricocheted through Parker's mind. The revolving red

police lights on the Oval—the swaying flashlight beams of the intruders—the infected flooding toward the emergency light in the store.

The words scraped his raw throat. "It's the light. They're attracted to the light."

Adam immediately flicked the switch.

Parker blinked. The trees were only shadows, and they might kill themselves navigating the forest before any of the infected could even get to them. "Can you see?" he called. "Maybe we should stop."

"I can see."

Parker didn't argue. He clung to Adam, the shotgun holstered on Adam's back wedged between them. He wasn't sure how much time had elapsed when the bike finally slowed and stopped, and Adam switched it off. The silence felt heavy and unnatural. The engine ticked, and then there was nothing but darkness.

"Where do we go?" Adam asked quietly.

Parker gave the only answer he had. "I don't know."

After a long moment, Adam spoke again—barely a whisper. "I should have heard them. Those men. I shouldn't have fallen asleep."

"It's not your fault."

"They brought the infected to us. The girls…"

Parker realized his arms were still wrapped around Adam's waist even though the bike wasn't moving. He squeezed. "We did our best. We'll do better next time."

After a moment, Adam nodded and turned the key.

They stuck to the woods, making their way as the sky to the east began to brighten. The sound of the engine was welcome, and Parker let himself close his eyes as the steady hum filled his mind, muffling the lingering echoes of the girls' dying screams, and Carey crying for her mother.

PINK AND ORANGE splashed across the sky as they made their way through the winding suburban streets of Palo Alto. The roads were as clogged here as they had been near campus, abandoned vehicles and remains of bodies jammed every which way. Adam steered them along the sidewalk and across lawns. The infected surged toward them from time to time, but for the moment it was relatively easy to evade them.

Parker rested his head against Adam's back, the leather smooth against his cheek. He had never felt so tired. The word felt wholly lacking to describe the weariness that had settled into him. The backpack hung heavily on his shoulders, the machete pressing into his spine. He coughed weakly, totally congested now and his throat burning with each swallow. *It's the flu. If it was what they have, I'd be...turned by now.*

He was filthy with dirt and blood, but at least that was something he could fix. "God, I need a shower," he mumbled. "And something to drink."

Adam heard him, of course. "Let's find a house." He took a turn, driving down a few suburban streets until they came to one that looked normal aside from one car stopped in the middle of the road, what was left of the driver visible through broken glass. Adam glanced around and killed the engine. For a long moment, he just sat there, listening.

Parker let Adam do his thing. If Adam thought he could hear all the way into *houses*, then he could have at it. For the moment, the street was empty, and the only sounds Parker could hear were birds chirping. No chattering, thankfully. He closed his eyes and leaned against Adam. "Any contenders?"

"With the red shutters." Adam jerked his chin toward a house three down and climbed off the bike.

Parker followed on foot as Adam pushed the bike across the

lawn and behind the house. The neighborhood felt oddly peaceful. He could almost believe that coffee makers would be turning on, and the families of Ramblewood Lane would soon be preparing for another day at school, or the office, or maybe the mommy-and-me yoga studio.

Adam parked the bike by the rear door and paused. He turned the handle, but it was locked.

"You sure no one's inside?"

"I'm sure."

Parker eyed the glass window on the upper part of the door. "I guess we can break—"

With a rattle, the door swung inward. The handle hung precariously from its socket.

Adam shrugged. "Shitty workmanship."

Inside, the two-story house was still. The back door opened to the white kitchen, where bananas and oranges sat in a bowl on the island, and pale green tiles gleamed behind the sink. On the white marble counter, fresh coffee did indeed fill a pot, the bitter aroma permeating the air. Parker's nose was clogged, but he sniffed loudly. It was possibly the greatest thing he'd ever smelled.

A finger-painted tree adorned the fridge, along with number and letter magnets. One grouping spelled out:

Ashley is 4 now

"I'll double-check the rest of the house." Armed with the shotgun, Adam disappeared through the dining room.

After a minute of staring at Ashley's tree, Parker made himself useful. He brought the motorcycle in and parked it by the round dining table, resting his pack and machete holster on the polished wood. The house still had power, and he gratefully gulped down a cold bottle of water from the fridge and then blew his nose on a paper towel.

He coughed, and his lungs rattled. Maybe there was some

medicine in the house. The cold water stung his throat, but he guzzled more, then splashed coffee into a mug. He sipped it black, closing his eyes at the soothing familiarity of the flavor.

There were several containers of leftovers in the fridge, and Parker peeled off the lids to find roast pork, mashed potatoes, and some kind of squash dish. It felt weird to eat someone else's food, and he still wasn't really hungry, but he opened each cupboard until he found the dinner plates.

What he wanted more than anything was his mom's chicken soup. He shoved away a pang of longing and worry. They would be fine on the Cape. They would be. Parker pulled out his phone, but it was out of juice.

Floorboards creaked overhead as Adam moved through the house. A pile of local flyers sat on the island, one folded over with a circle drawn around a sale on extra-lean ground beef for three-ninety-nine a pound. Parker peered out the bay window along the back of the kitchen over a cozy breakfast nook. Crumbs dotted the square table. The sun rose over the backyard swing set and nothing stirred.

It could be just another morning.

At the kitchen sink, he washed his hands with peppermint-lavender soap. A pot scrubber rested in a ceramic frog's open mouth, and Parker took it and dug in under his nails. Blood— *Carey's* blood, Jesus Christ—flecked off, sticking to the rim of a mug sitting in the sink. When his hands were raw, he picked up the mug and washed it, reading the words printed on the side:

You're not the boss of me. That's my wife's job!

"Okay?"

Blinking, Parker dropped the mug with a clatter. "Yeah. I was going to… There's food." He grabbed a serving spoon from a jug of utensils and began dishing the leftovers onto the two plates.

"There's a bathroom with a shower down here. Why don't we stay on the main floor? In case we have to leave in a hurry. I brought down towels. You go first—I'll nuke the food." He reached out and gently took the spoon from Parker's hand. "You should rest. You sound really stuffed up."

Parker realized he was shaking. "Yeah. Okay. A shower would be good." He caught sight of a coiled white cord on the counter behind a metal mail holder with bills addressed to a *W. Henderson*. His heart leapt. "Please be the right kind. Please." He pulled out the cord and saw the tiny plug. "Yes!"

The USB end was plugged into a wall adapter in a socket. Parker yanked out his phone and attached the charger. After a long moment, the apple appeared in the middle of the screen.

Minutes passed like hours as Parker watched the red battery indicator creep up. He paced on the pale tiles, drumming his fingers on the marble counter every so often. Adam didn't comment and went about opening and closing cupboards. He pulled out some items, but Parker didn't look to see what. The red bar grew longer.

Finally, there was enough charge to check his messages. Parker opened his phone. There were no red numbers next to his texts or his phone icon. He tapped his recents and tried to dial his mother, but it wouldn't connect. No internet either. He went to settings. "They must have wireless here," he muttered. A secure network appeared, but there were no waves indicated, and he didn't know the password anyway. "Shit."

"Parker."

He felt wired with energy, like he might burst out of his skin. He glanced around the kitchen and realized there was a cordless phone sitting in its cradle on the counter. How had he not noticed that? He pressed the ON button with shaky fingers and thought he might cry when he heard the sweet sound of the dial tone. Parker realized he didn't know anyone's number off by heart and tapped hurriedly at his contacts.

One by one, he tried his family and friends. One by one, the phone rang and either went to voicemail or didn't connect at all. "Fuck!" He barely resisted the urge to smash the cordless phone on the tiles.

"Parker…"

"Shit, did you check the TV? We need to check the TV." He hurried past a rustic pine dining table and chairs to the living room at the front of the house, where a flat screen was mounted over a glass fireplace. Three remotes sat on the coffee table. Parker picked the closest and jabbed the power button. Nothing. He tried the second. Nothing. His pulse raced as he grabbed the third and aimed it at the TV. With a welcoming tri-tone, the screen flared to life.

Snow.

Parker pressed the channel arrow with his thumb, scrolling up past static on station after station.

"Parker, it's no use."

He didn't look at Adam, keeping his eyes glued to the screen. "There has to be something. There has to be." He pressed his thumb rhythmically, up, up, up through the numbers. Finally, a picture appeared. "There!" His breath was shallow as he read the scrolling message.

This is the Emergency Broadcast System. This is not a test. Stay in your home with doors and windows locked…

"It's the same." Parker shook his head. "No, there has to be something else."

Adam was beside him, his touch gentle as he took hold of the remote in Parker's hand. "It's okay."

"No!" Parker jerked away and stabbed the channel arrow. More useless snow and static appeared, or black screens. "They have to tell us *something*!" He pulled his arm back and launched the remote across the room, where it clattered against the fireplace.

"We'll figure it out."

Parker wheeled around to face Adam, who remained infuriatingly calm. "How? What are we supposed to do now?" His throat was raw, but he couldn't stop.

Adam watched him steadily with those strange, beautiful eyes. "I don't know."

"Then what good are you? You don't know anything. We're going to fucking die, and you're just standing there like it doesn't matter. Like you don't even care!"

"Of course I care. Freaking out isn't going to help." He didn't even raise his voice.

It just made the rage rushing through Parker burn hotter. "Well, excuse the fuck out of me for not being as perfect as you. There are motherfucking *zombies* roaming America and England, and the whole world for all we know. *I'm freaking out*! I don't know where my family is. I don't know anything. I can't just be all Zen! What's the matter with you? At least I'm trying to find out what's happening! What are you doing? I might as well be by myself. You're not helping." It wasn't true, and as soon as the hoarse words left his mouth, Parker wanted to haul them back.

Adam watched him for a long moment. Then he turned on his heel, his voice still steady. "I'm taking a shower."

The bathroom door closed down the hall, and Parker was left in the living room, chest heaving and sweat on his brow. His hands were squeezed into fists, and he clenched his jaw so tightly it felt like it might snap. He picked up a tasseled cushion and held it to his face.

He screamed.

Chapter Five

A S THE MINUTES ticked by, he listened to the water run faintly, the pillow still pressed against his face. The anger began to ebb and drain away, and he hurt all over. He wanted to curl up and sleep for days, but fear rattled through him with every ragged breath. What if he woke up and Adam was gone? Parker wouldn't blame him, but the thought made him want to vomit.

His legs weren't steady as he made his way to the bathroom. He leaned his forehead against the door and was about to sink to the carpet to wait.

"Parker?"

He must have made more noise than he'd thought. "I'm sorry," he croaked.

The shower was still running, but a moment later the door opened. Water dripped from Adam's hair, and his skin glistened. He held a towel in front of his waist. "It's okay."

Parker swallowed hard. His throat felt like it had swelled to twice its size. "Please don't leave me."

Wordlessly, Adam took his hand and drew him into the small bathroom. He secured the towel around his hips and lifted up Parker's shirt. "Get in the shower. You'll feel better. The steam will help."

Nodding, Parker unlaced his sneakers and stripped off his clothes. Adam nudged him toward the steamy shower stall and nodded to a folded towel on the toilet seat. "Here you go. I'll heat up that food and make sure it's still clear outside."

"No!" Parker grabbed Adam's arm, clinging to hard muscle and warm, slick skin. The panic swirled in his gut, and he wavered on his feet. "Stay. Please? Besides, there's still conditioner in your hair."

Parker stepped into the shower, and after a few moments, Adam dropped his towel and followed. There wasn't much room to maneuver, but after Adam finished cleaning his hair, he leaned back and let Parker lather and rinse. The hot water and steam really did help, and Parker breathed more easily. His cough still rattled though, and fuck, he was so tired. He wanted to sit at the bottom of the shower stall and let the water pour over him for hours.

As his knees gave out, Adam held him up with strong hands on his upper arms. He shook his head. "You really are getting sick."

Parker could only hack out a cough in response, and his heart rate soared. He was sick, there was no question. It felt like the flu, but what if it wasn't? What if this was how it started? What if—

"You'll be fine, Parker. You need to rest, and we'll get you some medicine." He guided Parker's head under the stream of water and gently rinsed the conditioner from his hair.

Parker closed his eyes, reveling in the touch of Adam's fingers on his scalp. He was used to being around other naked guys—at an all-boys boarding school, there wasn't a lot of modesty—but by all rights, it should have felt awkward as hell to be showering up close and personal with a man who had been a stranger two days ago.

Especially a man who looked like a Greek god come to life, but with chest hair.

Had it only been two days? It seemed like another lifetime. Now it was the only thing keeping him going, having Adam there with him. If he was alone... The thought sent his pulse soaring. He'd lose it.

As if reading his mind, Adam spoke. "I'm not going to leave you."

Parker shook his head. "But why would you stay with me? I'm a loser. I never do things right, and I'll slow you down. You're so fast. How are you so fast?"

"You're not a loser. You're annoying as hell sometimes, but you're brave, and you care about people. I wanted to leave Carey behind. Cut our losses."

"It didn't matter anyway. She's still..." He shuddered as he thought of her bulging eyes and that awful noise coming out of her.

"It matters."

Parker wanted to collapse against Adam's broad chest and weep, but he had to keep it together. "I really didn't mean what I said before. I'm glad you're calm. If we were both freaking out, we'd be in serious trouble. Not that we aren't already in serious trouble."

Adam squeezed Parker's shoulder. "We'll figure it out together." He peered intently. "I don't want to be alone either." Then a ghost of a smile lifted his lips. "We're stuck with each other."

IN THE KITCHEN, Parker rested by the windows, watching drying leaves skitter across the lawn as the microwave whirred quietly. He'd sat on the shower floor until the water had gone cold, and then blown his nose for, like, five minutes.

Now he was changed into some new underwear, jeans, and a pullover hoodie. Adam hadn't been able to grab his pack from the store and had been scavenging through the house for clothes and whatever else might come in handy.

The *ding* when the microwave finished sounded too loud. Parker put in the second plate and brought cutlery, napkins, and cold cans of cola to the breakfast nook.

His phone continued charging on the counter, and he checked it one more time before sitting down. Dark hair dried now, Adam came in wearing a brown Henley and carrying a tote bag of clothing. He joined Parker at the nook and popped the tab on his cola.

After a sip, he sighed. "Damn, that tastes good. We better drink up while we still can."

Parker swallowed a sugary gulp. "Yeah. I guess so." It hurt his throat, but Adam was right that they should enjoy it while they could. The thought that it might be a long time before they had cold soda again led to other thoughts he tried to block out.

They ate in silence, but it wasn't uncomfortable. The hot food tasted better than Parker could have imagined considering he hadn't felt hungry. His stomach gurgled as he shoveled in the first few desperate bites.

Then he slowed down, picking at the leftovers with his fork. He stared out the window at the clouds moving in, obscuring the brilliant blue of the autumn sky. It seemed wrong somehow that nature wasn't reflecting the chaos unfolding.

"Why did you say you were a loser?"

The swings in the yard swayed in the growing breeze. Parker fidgeted, feeling Adam's scrutiny hot on his face. "I screw up a lot." He ate another bite. "These are good mashed potatoes. My mom's were always lumpy. Not bad, but just not this creamy." He had no idea why he was saying this. "What about you?"

Adam chewed and swallowed. "Me?"

"Did your mom—" Parker remembered too late that Adam had said he didn't have any family. "Um, nothing."

But Adam didn't seem upset. "She was a good cook. I've never had red sauce that could come close. She grew her own tomatoes, and she'd let it simmer on the stove for two days. When I first came to the Bay, I tried a bunch of Italian places. Really expensive restaurants. I thought they must have a marinara that was half as good." He scooped up the last bite of butternut squash. "But after a while, I stopped trying."

"Where did you grow up?"

"Minnesota. Middle of nowhere."

Parker wanted to ask about Adam's family, but instead he asked, "How did you end up here?"

"I always wanted to live by the water, and Stanford has a great MFA program." He rubbed a hand over his face and put down his fork, his plate clean.

"So. What are we going to do now?"

"What do you want to do?"

Parker tried to think of a plan, but his mind was blank. "Barricade the doors and windows and sleep."

"Sounds good. You should take some cold medicine. I found cough syrup and stuff upstairs. And before you say it, don't worry. You've got a cold. If you had whatever's causing this chaos, you'd be one of them by now."

Parker nodded. He had to believe that was true, because… Well, if it wasn't, before long it wouldn't matter anyway. So he might as well believe it.

They ended up in the living room with bookcases dragged in front of the picture window and the sheer curtains drawn. Parker curled up on the love seat with a fluffy pillow and blanket, and Adam stretched out on the overstuffed couch. They piled their gear and weapons on the floor between them.

"Where is everyone?" Parker asked quietly. "Why haven't we seen more survivors? Do you think they're hiding like us?"

"Probably. Or they're dead. Or…"

In the dim light, Parker blinked at a framed picture on the side table. A smiling man, woman, and little girl with dark curls sat together in front of a mottled blue background.

As he listened to Adam's deepening breathing, Parker stared at

Ashley Henderson and her parents and wondered if they'd ever come home again.

PARKER BLINKED AS the dark shapes of an unfamiliar room came into focus, barely illuminated by whispers of streetlights through the thin curtains. *Where did*—He bolted up to sitting as he remembered.

"It's okay," Adam said quietly. He squatted by a cabinet beside the fireplace.

"What time is it?"

"Just after two."

"In the morning?" Parker rubbed his eyes. "Why didn't you wake me?"

"We both needed the rest."

Parker nodded blearily and blew his nose. How was it possible to have this much snot in his head? It hurt to swallow, and his mouth was dry. He unwrapped a cherry lozenge from the package Adam had found. "Have you seen anything? Heard anything?"

"Some infected were on the street earlier. I think there are more of them now. You were definitely right about the lights—they're drawn to them. They swarmed a house at the end of the block. I think it has motion sensors, and the lights keep blinking on and off. That really seems to attract them, the flashing. But I think even if they came across you in the dark, they'd still bite. Once you're in their sights, if something else doesn't distract them, they'll keep on you. But I didn't hear... I don't think anyone was home. Didn't seem to be, anyway."

"What's the deal with your hearing? It's freaky."

Still squatting, Adam didn't look at him. "I don't know. It's genetic."

"But like, how?"

"I *don't know.*"

"I was just asking, dude." He blew his nose again. "What are you doing?"

"Looking at their movies."

"Anything good? Maybe we should watch something before the power goes," he joked. "We might never watch a movie again." As he said the words, Parker's stomach twisted. Surely order would be restored. They just had to wait. "But I guess that's a bad idea since they might see the light outside."

Adam reached for a Blu-ray case. "You won't believe what they have."

"How am I supposed to know? Wait—no way they have *Laura.*"

Adam chuckled. "No, but they have *The Asphalt Jungle*. It was next on the syllabus."

"Hey, it'll give me a head start on the assignment. You can tell me what's so great about it."

"I thought you were dropping the class." Adam straightened up and returned to the couch, where he sat with his elbows on his knees.

"Maybe I'll reconsider. I wouldn't want you to have only brown-nosers in your class." He stretched his neck one way and then the other. He'd slept, but he'd had strange dreams that he remembered now in snatches of imagery.

It was surreal, waking up in someone else's living room in the middle of the night. The world seemed utterly still. "I feel like I'm sleeping. Like this is all some horrible dream. I was studying, and went for coffee, and then…this."

"I was on my way home to clear a couple episodes of *The Amazing Race* off the TiVo."

"I guess we're doing our own race now. Except if we lose a leg, we might actually lose a leg."

Adam laughed, then peered at Parker quietly.

"What?"

"Nothing. You're just…"

"An idiot? I know, believe me."

"Funny. I was going to say you're funny."

"Oh. Um, thanks."

"You make me laugh. I don't… Not many people do."

"What about Tina?" The question was out of his mouth before he could stop it. "I'm sorry. I didn't mean…"

Adam smiled softly. "It's all right. And no, she's not really funny. She's kind, and generous, and she loves to laugh. But she's not funny. Unless knock-knock jokes are your type of humor."

The tender expression on Adam's face sent a surge of sticky jealousy through Parker. *Jesus, get a grip. He's not even gay, and she's probably dead. I'm such an asshole.* He coughed and reached for another lozenge. "How did you meet?"

"In undergrad. I took a women's studies class, and I was the only guy. It was intimidating, but she sat right beside me and talked to me. I thought it was because she felt sorry for me, but later she said it was because she thought I was hot." He smiled faintly.

She wasn't wrong. "Um, is your place around here? Do you think she would be there?"

"No."

"But maybe?"

With a sigh, Adam closed his eyes. "She went into San Francisco that night for a concert. I'd texted her earlier to say enjoy the show, and I saw her reply right before I ran into you. It was from an hour earlier, and there was nothing after it. She said there was something weird happening in the crowd, and she was going to go find out what the holdup was."

"Oh." Parker didn't know what to say, so he started babbling. "It must have been pretty bad downtown. So many people, and it all happened so fast. And if she was in a crowd inside a building, and the infection spread…"

Stop talking immediately.

"Yeah." Adam's sorrow was palpable as a faint smile flickered over his mouth. "That was Tina. She'd march right in with her hands on her hips and demand answers." He opened his eyes, blinking away a hint of tears. "That *is* her. I can still hope, I guess."

"I'm sorry," Parker whispered. It wasn't enough, but it was all he had. "And you don't have any other friends or family?"

He shook his head. "No close friends here. And my family died when I was nine. My parents and two sisters."

Jesus. Parker couldn't even imagine. Although now *he* might be the sole survivor. He pushed the thought from his mind. He didn't know that. Eric was in a bunker, and the Cape house might be safe. And there was always the boat, if they'd been able to get to the marina. "That must have been terrible." He wondered how it had happened, but didn't want to pry.

"Yeah." Adam sat back against the floral couch cushions. "I guess I learned that's the way the world works. Nothing's forever. We think it will be. It never is." He peered around the dark room. "I wish I could film this place."

"Did you always make movies and stuff?"

Adam's gaze was unfocused, like he was far away. "After the accident, my shrink gave me a camera. Told me to record anything that interested me."

"And what interested you?" Parker curled up again, tucking his feet under him. He dabbed at his nose. His head was so heavy.

"People. I'd record them when they weren't watching. But sometimes when they were, and they'd talk."

"There's a camera on my phone. You could use it and—" He sprang to his feet, wobbling and grabbing the side of the love seat. "My phone. I need to check." He shuffled to the kitchen, feeling his way down the hall in the darkness.

The phone was where he left it on the counter, plugged into the charger. He tugged out the cord and went into the bathroom just in case the light from the screen could be seen from outside. There were no messages on his lock screen, and the bars at the top had disappeared. He tapped in his code and tried to dial his mom's number. No connection. Parker closed his eyes and breathed deeply. It was okay. It would be okay.

Adam was leaning against the wall in the hallway when he came out. "Anything?"

"Uh-uh. No network. I guess we're lucky there's still power here. Probably won't last for long."

"Probably not."

As if on cue, a scream tore through the stillness.

Without a word, they raced back to the living room and strapped on their gear and weapons. Parker's head spun and coughs racked him.

More shrieks rang out. They inched the bookcase away from the front window, and Parker squinted into the night. The picture window jutted out from the house, and he knelt on the ledge so he could look left and right. The streetlights were still on, and groups of infected circled them. But two doors down, a light shone from inside, and infected streamed into the house, shattering windows and shoving in their desperation.

Parker and Adam shared a glance. Parker knew the options: hide, run, or help. "We could try going around the back. See if they're still…"

Adam nodded. "But if not, we get out fast."

He wheeled the bike out the back door and they peeked over the fence. Next door, all was quiet and dark, but the invaded house two down seemed to pulsate with the buzz of the chattering. It had to be too late, but as Parker opened his mouth to say that, a child's wail pierced the terrible racket.

Before he could think twice, Parker scaled the fence. But when he reached the top, Adam was somehow ahead of him, already on the ground. He shouted as he ran.

"Get the bike and bring it around back!"

Parker flipped onto his belly and dropped back down to the Hendersons' lawn. The backpack overbalanced him for a moment, and he swung his arms to stay on his feet. Past the swing set, he hopped on the motorcycle and looked for an exit.

He couldn't go the way they'd come, around the front of the house. Too many infected on the street. Fortunately, there was a gate at the back of the yard, where the ground sloped down to a small ravine. Now he just had to figure out how to start the bike.

He twisted knobs desperately, trying anything that might work. "Key, key, key. There has to be a key, right? Fuck it." He jumped off and tried to push it. "Jesus!" It felt like it weighed five hundred pounds. With a grunt, he dug in with his sneakers and wheeled the bike to the dry ravine, his muscles straining and his breath rattling as he panted. He couldn't see any keys or a place to put them. Maybe Adam still had the keys and didn't realize it?

There was a new, terrible sound from the house under siege— a growl that roared through the night.

Parker left the bike and squeezed through the gate into the dark yard of the house next door.

Adam, Adam, Adam.

Parker was almost to the top of the fence when a floodlight blinded him. He scrabbled for the wooden slats but lost his grip and tumbled back onto the lawn. The air *whooshed* from his burning lungs. The machete handle dug into his neck, and his back arched where he sprawled like a turtle over his pack.

The floodlight snapped off, but a shadow jerked into view at the top of the fence. The light came back on, illuminating the bulging eyes and grasping bloody fingers of an infected man. Parker scrambled back, but it was too late. More contorted faces appeared, and then the infected were tumbling over the fence. On his feet again, Parker's Jell-O legs somehow moved and he raced around to the front of the dark house.

Too late he realized his route back to the motorcycle was cut off—not that he could even work the damn thing. There was nothing to do but keep going.

Parker yanked the machete out of its sheath on his back, praying he could outrun them. On the street, the infected milled around the streetlights, and he angled toward another house, seeking the darkness. Through backyards and over fences he raced, with the infected gaining on him. At least a dozen chased him, their twitching limbs too quick.

Thoughts crashed through his mind, images and memories and fragments pushed out by the frenzy of panic and the need to survive.

Faster, faster, faster.

Gasping, he stumbled over a lawn chair and slammed to the grass, the machete still in his grip. The ground vibrated with the approach of the infected, and he forced his feet under him and ran on. When he glanced back over his shoulder, they were only ten feet away, and panic choked him.

No, no, no!

Then the ground disappeared.

Chapter Six

A S HE PLUNGED into water, the breath *whooshed* from Parker's lungs. He seized up in the unexpected cold. He plummeted beneath the surface in a heartbeat, flapping his arms and kicking his legs, the backpack a leaden weight dragging him down.

Dying, dying, dying!

His lungs burned, and he saw stars. Parker kicked desperately, and when his head broke the surface, he sucked in as much air as he could, coughs racking him. For a moment, all he could do was tread water and try to breathe. As the spots of light behind his eyes faded, he focused again. He was in the middle of the deep end of a backyard pool, and fuck, where were the infected?

He blinked up at them streaming around the concrete deck, none of them even glancing his way. They seemed to bypass the water with some kind of instinct, giving a wide berth around the pool and leaving Parker behind.

He treaded water as quietly as he could, careful not to splash. Perhaps they couldn't see him in the dark pool? It seemed not. He kept only his face above the surface, trying to disappear as much as he could beneath the depths as he breathed through his mouth.

After a minute, he was alone.

Still taking care not to splash, he kicked his way to the side of the pool and grabbed the ledge. He realized he'd dropped his machete when he fell. In the dead of night, the water was utterly black.

Cursing himself, he eased off the backpack and set it on the deck. The infected droned from the way he'd come, but he needed to go back. He needed to find Adam.

The panic swelled once more, and he fought it down. It had only been minutes since he and Adam had stood side by side, and now he felt a million miles away.

Adam could be dead.

The thought was a punch to his gut, and he took in a shaky breath. No. Adam had to be okay. He just needed to find him.

There were a hundred infected in that house.

He shook his head as if he could physically banish the idea that Adam didn't make it.

He made it.

Shivering, Parker tried to get himself together. His head was so full of snot that he could barely breathe, and as a coughing fit overtook him, he tried to muffle the sound in the soaking crook of his arm.

Finally, it passed, and he drank a mouthful of the pool water to soothe his throat even though the chlorine burned. He needed a weapon. Peering down, he couldn't see a damn thing, but the machete had to be there.

It's just like snorkeling off the boat in summer. Eric's here, and we're playing a game like we used to.

Somehow the lie gave him the confidence he needed, and he dove down blindly, his arms outstretched. His fingers grazed the concrete bottom of the pool, and he swept his hands from side to side, praying he'd find the machete and nothing—no one—else. His eardrums felt like they were going to burst as the pressure built.

Lungs burning, he returned to the surface empty-handed. It took four more tries before his fingers closed over the steel of the machete's blade at the bottom of the pool. He hefted it onto the deck and hung on to the side as he gasped and coughed. Normally he'd push himself out of the water easily, but he trembled all over and had to haul himself up on the ladder.

It was quiet now, the chattering receded into the night. He slung on the sodden backpack and hurried back the way he'd come, the machete in hand. He muffled his coughs again in the crook of his elbow, helpless to stop them. As the minutes passed and he skulked by dark houses, he realized he had no idea how to find the Hendersons' home again.

He'd zigzagged through countless yards, and as he hurried back into the shadows, all the houses and streets looked the same. He wanted to scream Adam's name but kept silent. What if it wasn't just light that attracted the infected? What if he called them right to him?

He dragged himself onward, wondering if other survivors were watching from dark windows, unwilling to give refuge to a machete-wielding stranger. He actually reached for his phone to look up Ramblewood Lane on the map. He laughed, a high-pitched squawk that sounded far away.

When he tripped over the eviscerated remains of what looked to be a dog, its gnawed collar abandoned a few feet away, his stomach heaved. He vomited up what little was left in him.

The sky was lightening when he reached the edge of what might have been the preserve, but could have been a park for all he knew. He'd searched so many streets and was hopelessly lost. He'd been in Palo Alto a month and only knew which way was east from the rising of the sun. He walked on, machete in hand, his eyes flicking back and forth across the trees and bushes. The preserve and foothills were in the south, he thought.

The reality that he might never see Adam again was a lead ball in his gut, growing heavier with each step. They should have discussed a plan in case they got separated, but it was too fucking late now. For some reason, Parker thought Adam would go back to the preserve. He seemed more at home there amid the trees than on the Hendersons' floral couch.

Parker's eyes burned, and he shivered uncontrollably. He was really alone. He'd be grateful to see any other uninfected human, but he longed for Adam and his scruff that was turning into a beard, his wry smile and infuriating calm.

It had taken only a blink of an eye and they'd been separated. Adam could be one of them now. Parker closed his eyes against the awful image of Adam transformed. He choked down a sob. "Fuck, fuck, fuck."

Pain flared in his knees, and he realized his legs had given out and he was on the ground. Fingers digging into the dirt, he fought the wave of nausea. There was a thick bush nearby, and he crawled toward it, the machete awkward in his right hand. He squeezed in amongst the brambles, finding a small hollow in the center of the bush where he could curl into a ball.

Behind the cover of the shrubbery, he trembled and coughed, his nose running.

I need to get it together. I need to survive.

Yet when he tried to move, his body didn't seem to want to cooperate. Wet and freezing but hot all over, he remained hidden in the bushes, his cheek pressing against the earth. He needed a plan if he was going to make it. He had to make it.

Why?

He tried to ignore the other voice in his head, but it persisted.

They're all dead. Mom, Dad, Eric. Everyone. Adam. The world is fucked. It's hopeless. Might as well give in now. There's no point.

"No." His voice sounded hoarse and foreign. "No," he repeated. He couldn't give up. He wouldn't. He needed to figure out what to do next. He wasn't sure what time it was. He instinctively reached into his pocket again for his phone, but it was in his pack and soaked now.

Grief returned, and he squeezed his eyes shut against it. His last connection to the world was gone. Intellectually, he knew it had been gone before tripping into the pool, but the finality of it gutted him. He should have listened to his mother's message again while he'd had the chance. His last piece of her. But wait, had he deleted it? Did the recording even exist anymore in the cloud or some shit?

"How is this real?"

Now he was talking to himself, although his voice sounded hoarse and foreign. He wondered how he would have done on his econ test had the world not gone insane. By now he would have gone ahead and dropped the film course. He probably would never have seen Adam again. It was a big campus, and their paths might never have crossed.

Tears pricked his eyes, and he curled tighter into himself. Had he really only known Adam a few days? It was unfathomable.

"Stop, stop, stop," he muttered. His mind was a jumble of thoughts and scenarios, and the images of Adam were unbearable. Parker had to leave everything behind. He was on his own now. He willed himself to uncurl and get moving, but he shivered and stayed put.

Just a few more minutes. Then he'd go…

The gray day was brighter when Parker realized the growing drone in his consciousness was real. Gripping the machete, he jolted his head up and got tangled in the bush. It didn't sound like the calling of the infected, but his ears might have been playing tricks on him. He closed his eyes as the low noise grew louder.

It sounded like…a motorcycle.

His pulse raced. It couldn't be Adam. It was impossible. Even if Adam had somehow survived, how would he find Parker? But maybe… *No.* He couldn't get caught up in wishful thinking. Whoever was out there, odds were they were human, unless the infected had learned to ride motorcycles.

Jesus, let's hope not.

The bike neared. In a few moments it would be gone. He had to act now. Now! His soaked backpack caught on the bush branches as he clawed his way out, opening his mouth to shout for the driver's attention. The words died on his tongue as the motorcycle screeched to a halt several feet away.

Blood stained Adam's hands and flaked on his face. For a moment they could only stare at each other. Parker's heart leapt, and he'd never been so happy to see another person in his entire life.

He made a noise that was half laugh, half sob. "Adam."

Adam was off the bike, closing the distance between them in a few seconds. He hauled Parker to his feet and took his face in his hands. "Parker." His voice was gravelly. Then he was examining Parker's limbs, his eyes scanning and hands surprisingly gentle. "You're not hurt? God, you're freezing." He put his hand to Parker's forehead. "But hot. Shit."

Parker couldn't stop shaking, but he tried to smile. He wasn't sure he'd be able to stand without Adam holding him up. "I'm better now. How? Are you real? Am I going crazy?"

A small smile lifted Adam's lips. "I'm real." He exhaled heavily, his breath warm on Parker's face. "I wasn't sure I could find you."

Parker wavered on his feet, and Adam gripped his upper arms. "I thought you were dead. It all happened so fast. I didn't mean to leave you. Did you…was there anyone still…? That kid?"

Adam's gaze dropped, and he shook his head.

"At least you tried."

He stared intently at Parker. "Next time we have to stay together. If we can help someone we will, but we have to make sure we have a plan. I don't want to lose you again." He brushed back Parker's matted hair. "Did you get wet? I lost your trail for a bit. I thought…I thought you'd been infected."

"My trail?" Parker's head swam.

Adam grabbed the machete from the ground and slid it onto Parker's back before leading him to the bike. "Come on. We need gas. And you need to rest."

Parker climbed on behind him, eager to wrap himself around Adam's warmth. "How did you find me? It's impossible. You drove right up to me."

Adam turned the key, and the engine hummed to life. He was silent for a long moment. "My parents taught me to track. You left an obvious trail."

"I did? Oh. Were they hunters?"

"Kind of. Yeah." He gunned the engine and they were off.

When they reached a main road, it was jammed with abandoned cars—and the dead—like most of the other streets they'd seen. Adam stayed on the sidewalk, and Parker glanced left and right warily. As they passed a strip mall with a blinking neon sign, he saw a pack of infected, their clothes tattered and bloody as they surged into the store.

Farther up the road by an IHOP, Parker was blinking at a tangle of mauled corpses when Adam tensed.

"People."

Parker squinted over Adam's shoulder. Down the road, an SUV bounced over the sidewalk across the street. "Should we talk to them?"

"I guess so. Carefully."

Adam steered onto the road, weaving between cars to get to the other side, and the SUV rolled to a stop ten feet away. Parker could see a man and a woman through the windshield, and they all watched each other uneasily. The man unrolled his window and leaned out. He wore an Oakland baseball cap and looked middle-aged. "Any news?" he asked.

Adam answered, "Not from the authorities. You?"

The man chewed a piece of gum. "Nope. But the word is that it's happening up in Canada too, and down in Mexico. Don't know about overseas."

Parker spoke up. "It was happening in London. I don't know

about anywhere else."

The man sighed. "Well, shit. That isn't good." He rubbed his face. "Heard from a guy that the army's organizing at the base near Big Sur. We're going to head that way and see what we can see."

"Good to know," Adam replied. "Anything from Moffett airfield?"

"Overrun with creepers."

Creepers. Sounded about right. "Do you know what the hell this is?" Parker asked, his voice scratchy and weak.

The brunette woman leaned out her window. "Wish we knew, kid. Never thought I'd see the day those stupid zombie movies Dave loves became real life."

The man—Dave, presumably—barked out a laugh. "And aren't you glad now I paid attention? We're still alive, which is more than I can say for most. Population seems to have been decimated practically overnight. Whatever this thing is, it's goddamn effective. You guys keeping the lights off?"

Adam nodded. "Attracts them."

"I don't think they like water either," Parker added. "They were right on my tail, but when I fell into the pool, they kept going and forgot about me."

"Handy to know," Dave replied. He tipped the brim of his cap. "Good luck to you."

"And you." Adam nodded.

They went their separate ways, and Parker's mind whirled. "You think it's true about the army?"

"Maybe." Adam pointed. "Gas station."

"Think we should follow them?" Parker coughed violently, shivering.

Adam pulled into the gas station, which was jam-packed with abandoned vehicles. He skirted around the edge of the lot and pulled up as close to the pumps as he could. "I don't know. You need to rest, and we don't know if we can trust them."

Fat, cold drops of rain began to fall. "Do you think the rain will affect them? The infected, I mean."

"Maybe?" Adam answered. "Let's not wait around to find out. We should get some more supplies while we're here."

Parker stumbled off the bike, and Adam put the nozzle in the tank. He pressed a few buttons, but nothing happened. Then he barked out a laugh and took out his wallet. He swiped a credit card, and the gas began to flow. "Guess we still have to pay for gas."

Parker smiled, but it faded quickly. "What happens when there's no more power? Will gas pumps still work?"

Adam frowned. "I don't think so. Let's check the garage for a hose. We'll have to siphon once the power goes everywhere."

"Because it will. It's only a matter of time, isn't it?" The world they'd always known was vanishing. Was already gone.

Adam didn't reply. They both knew the answer.

UP ON A craggy mound in the foothills that night, they found a little cave with enough overhanging rock to keep off the rain. Adam parked the motorcycle while Parker huddled on the ground.

"I'll be fine soon." His throat felt like he'd swallowed razor blades. "Should we go to Big Sur?"

"We'll see." Adam eased the pack from Parker's shoulders and soon covered him with a weatherproof heat blanket they'd grabbed at the sporting goods store. He pressed the back of his hand to Parker's forehead and then eased up his head. "More cough syrup. I think antibiotics would do you more good, but this is all we have." He filled the plastic measuring cup and tilted it to Parker's lips.

Parker winced at the sickening cherry syrup but swallowed it all before flopping back. "In a few hours, I'll be fine," he mumbled. His tongue was thick, and his head pounded.

Adam folded a sweatshirt under Parker's head and tucked the blanket around him. "Okay. Just sleep now."

"Uh-huh." Parker wanted to say more, but he was so cold, and he drew himself into a ball. He'd tell Adam later.

IT WAS COLD, and wet, but so hot. Parker kicked at his blankets. Why was his hip so sore? He struggled onto his other side. The mattress was hard, and he couldn't stop shivering. Everything hurt. *Mom.* Why wasn't she there? Was he at school? Jason would call her. She'd come.

SOMEONE WAS PULLING at him, and he wanted them to stop. A low voice told him to hold still, but he thrashed his arms and legs. His feet were cold, but the rest of him was too hot. Where was he? He tried to open his eyes and saw a flash of gold before he went under again.

OH GOD, THEY were after him. He was trying to run, but his legs kept folding beneath him. He got up again, staggering, and he sprawled out. They swarmed over him, all teeth and eyes and sharp fingernails, and they tore him open.

Then he was one of them, and he was choking on blood and someone's guts.

HE WAS IN the pool again, and he was drowning. The infected were toppling in over him, and he thrashed, struggling for the surface, a cry stuck in his throat. Why did it hurt so much? He could barely swallow.

Then he was on the Cape, and it was summer, and the sun beamed overhead, and everything was good. Everything was *perfect*. He and Eric were diving off the boat, the last week of vacation before Eric went to college and Parker started Westley.

"Think there's any buried treasure down there?" Parker sat on the side of the sailboat, his feet dangling over the edge.

"Sure, squirt. Didn't you ever hear about the Damned Manta?" Eric plopped down beside him and shook his hair, water flying off the golden strands.

Droplets sprayed Parker's bare, sun-warmed chest. His trunks were still wet since he never spent long enough out of the water for them to fully dry. "Uh-uh. Tell me!"

Eric gazed at him thoughtfully and lowered his voice. "I guess you're old enough to hear it."

"Of course I am!" Eric was four years older and thought he knew everything. Parker wasn't a stupid baby anymore.

"All right, I'll tell you. But you have to swear to keep it secret."

"I swear, I swear!"

"Two hundred years ago, the Damned Manta was the fiercest pirate ship that sailed the Atlantic. Every vessel with the misfortune to cross its path was savagely plundered. The captain and crew showed no mercy. Navies tried to hunt the Manta down, traveling the waves month after month, year after year, without ever so much as spotting its mast on the horizon. It might as well have been a ghost."

"Did they ever catch it?"

Eric leaned in closer. "In the end, it wasn't a flotilla of warships that put an end to the Damned Manta's reign of terror on the sea. It was a woman."

"A woman?" Parker's eyes widened. "How did she do it?"

"Well, this was no ordinary woman." He paused. "It was Mother Nature."

"Oh." Parker deflated a bit. "So it was a storm?"

"Not any ordinary storm. No, it took more than that to sink the Manta to the ocean's floor. For ten days and nights, the wind howled and the seas swirled. The Manta's hold brimmed with gold and jewels, a lifetime of spoils the pirates had won through bloodshed. The waves grew stories high, crashing over them. No matter which direction they sailed in, the storm followed mercilessly until finally, it was as if the seas simply opened up and swallowed the Damned Manta whole."

"It sank? Where?"

Eric whispered, "Rumor has it the Manta went down right around here. Close enough to the Cape that the pirates could have abandoned ship and saved themselves, but not a one would leave his treasure behind."

Although Parker knew this story was probably bullshit, he grinned anyway. "No one's ever found it?"

"Nope. Not so much as a single bullion." His gaze darted over to where their parents reclined on the deck, their mother tanning with a sedate smile and their father reading The Wall Street Journal *with his customary frown. Eric lowered his voice. "Wanna look for it? Legend says that only the most bold and fearless have a hope of finding it."*

Parker grabbed his mask and snorkel. He knew they couldn't go very far without proper diving equipment and oxygen, but in the shallows of the reef they could go deep enough for it to be an adventure. Eric slapped his on and stood beside him on the deck. "Ready, Parkster?"

Parker nodded, bouncing on his toes.

"Into the great unknown!"

They leapt in unison, cannonballing beneath the surface.

HE COULDN'T STOP shivering.

Parker flickered in and out of consciousness, but he wasn't sure what was real. He flailed out, his fingers scrabbling over rock. Then there was warmth, and the faint scent of pine and leather, which meant everything would be okay. He exhaled, coughing.

Someone moaned, and Parker realized it was him. He was on fire, but he was so cold. A bottle pressed against his lips, and he opened up, swallowing as much water as he could.

"That's it. Drink. Go back to sleep. Everything's okay."

Everything's okay.

A voice in his mind screamed that it was a lie. Everything was wrong, and it could never be right again. But Adam was there, and his arms were around Parker, blocking out the rest of the world.

Parker burrowed closer and believed.

Chapter Seven

H E WAS DROOLING.
Parker licked his dry lips and opened and closed his mouth, swiping at it with his hand. It was nighttime, and he was...outside? He could hear rain falling but could only see dark shapes as his eyes focused. The memories came rolling back, slotting into place one by one with sickening clarity. Eric and their parents...no, he couldn't think about them.

Focus. His head was pillowed on something warm, and there was denim...

Parker seized up. He was drooling on Adam's thigh. Because his head seemed to be in Adam's lap. Which was surprisingly comfortable given the dude had thighs of steel.

"It's all right," Adam said softly. "You're safe."

Inch by inch, he relaxed, breathing again. His throat was raw, but his head felt clearer. Groaning, he shifted onto his back, his head still on Adam's outstretched legs. Adam was leaning against the stone wall of the cave with his hands in the pockets of his leather jacket. In the dark, Parker could make out Adam's golden eyes watching him.

Adam opened a bottle of water and lifted Parker's head so he could sip. Then he unwrapped a lozenge, his fingertips grazing Parker's lips as he fed it to him. Parker sucked, the lemon honey soothing his throat. He hacked out a few coughs and then settled. "Thanks."

"Sure."

It really should have been weird, being so close to Adam, but Parker liked it. The foil blanket was tucked around him, and Adam was nice and warm. Parker felt remarkably dry. Adam pressed the back of his hand to Parker's forehead, and he had to stop himself from leaning into the touch.

"I think your fever's breaking."

"What time is it?" Parker croaked.

"A little after ten or so."

"Is that all? It felt like longer."

"It's been two days, Parker."

"What?" He jerked up, and this of course caused another coughing fit. His lungs rattled, and he horked up a huge wad of phlegm into a sodden tissue Adam gave him. Parker wiped his mouth and settled back down. "Ugh. Sorry."

"It's okay. It means it's clearing out. It's a good thing. You should have more medicine in a minute."

"Two days? Jesus." Horror gripped him. "Did I piss myself?" It didn't feel like it, but...

Adam chuckled, a warm sound Parker could have listened to for hours. "You don't remember? You barely went since you're dehydrated. I helped you."

Parker groaned. "That is way above your pay grade. Thanks." He squinted out at the dark shapes of trees in the distance. "I guess you don't have any news."

"No."

"Thank you for staying with me. Most people would have ditched me."

"Would they?"

"I don't know. Some would have, I bet." He blew his nose noisily.

"You wouldn't have left me."

"No. But we've lost so much time."

Adam shrugged. "You couldn't ride a motorcycle. You were

totally out of it. Besides, maybe things will be better out there now."

Parker peered up at Adam. Part of the moon gleamed through the clouds, and he could make out Adam's features. Especially his amazing eyes. He resisted the urge to reach up and run his fingers over the darkening scruff on Adam's cheeks and chin. "I had the weirdest dreams. I didn't try to eat your face, did I?"

Adam looked at him for a moment, then burst out laughing, his teeth gleaming. "You really are funny."

A warm rush of pride filled Parker. "Am I?"

"You are. Hasn't anyone ever told you that?"

"I don't know. Jason was always the funny one at school. And Eric at home—my brother."

"Well, you're funny. And I'm glad. It helps." He brushed back Parker's hair from his forehead, and a shiver zinged down Parker's spine.

Careful.

Adam was being super cool and nice to him, but it didn't mean anything more. Parker turned his head and looked out from their perch over the darkness of the foothills and the preserve beyond. When a flicker of light caught his eye, he froze. "Do you see that?"

"Yeah. It's a campfire. Must be other survivors. I think I've seen a few little groups out here."

"How long until the…" He thought of the word the man in the SUV had used. Had that been real? He wasn't sure. "The creepers make their way into the forest?"

"Not long enough." Adam unwrapped a protein bar. "Think you can eat?"

Normally the answer would always be a resounding *hell yes*, but Parker's eyes were heavy again. "I don't know."

"Try a few bites." He slid his arm under Parker's shoulders and lifted him up enough to chew. Parker dutifully ate as much as he could. It was some kind of chocolate-based flavor, and it tasted remarkably good, like his taste buds had been dying for stimulation.

"That's it. Now some more medicine. You should be able to sleep okay now."

The cherry syrup tasted like crap on the heels of chocolate, but Parker got it down. As he settled his head back on Adam's lap, he realized he was wearing different clothes. The pants were cargos, and the sweater was dark cotton. "Did you…um, thanks. For getting me out of the wet clothes." He realized they were spread over the other side of the little cave, along with some of Adam's. "I think I dreamed about that. I might have kicked you."

Adam snorted. "You definitely kicked me. But you wouldn't get better in damp clothes, so it had to be done."

Parker's cheeks flushed. "Sorry." Okay, so Adam had seen him naked again. And helped him piss. It wasn't a big deal. They'd already showered together. It wasn't sexual, and the guy wasn't even gay. He sternly repeated this to himself a few times until the embarrassment faded. Jesus, it was the end times, and he was being *bashful*.

His eyes were getting too heavy now, and he closed them. "I don't want to drool on you again," he mumbled. "It's such bad manners. My mother would be shocked and appalled. She'd be shappalled."

As he faded away, he heard the soft rumble of Adam's laughter.

PARKER GINGERLY PUSHED himself up and swiped a hand across his mouth. He gazed at Adam blearily. "Hey."

"Hey." Adam reached out to touch Parker's forehead. His palm felt cool, and he held it there for a moment before dropping his hand with a little nod. He passed Parker a bottle, and Parker noticed there were a few of them outside the lip of the cave, full of rainwater. "Drink up."

Parker did, his throat finally feeling more normal. He'd apparently spent the night with his head pillowed on Adam's lap again. "You didn't have to... You could have shoved me off and rested too. Jesus, I must stink."

Adam hitched a shoulder. "I stink too. I slept pretty well, actually. All things considered."

"Good. I hope I don't give you this bug. You were sniffing before."

"Nah. I feel fine. I'm not worried."

Parker blinked out beyond their little cave. The dawn was gray, with rain still drizzling down. The expanse of trees below them was blanketed by fog. His hip was numb where he'd curled on it, and he coughed up some more lovely mucus, which was hopefully the last of it. He definitely felt rested for the first time since the world went to hell.

"Another day in paradise, huh?"

Adam's lips twitched. "Indeed."

Parker scooted over and leaned against the rock beside Adam, wincing at the stiffness in his back. Adam had taken off Parker's sneakers and put thick wool socks on his feet. He rubbed his feet together, enjoying the friction. "Okay. Still living in a zombie apocalypse, it seems. I guess it's time we get our shit together and make a plan."

Adam raised an eyebrow. "Any suggestions?"

"I know that, aside from this whole flu thing, I've been kind of freaking out a little. And by 'a little' I mean a lot, and I appreciate that you didn't just leave my whiny ass behind days ago."

Adam huffed softly. "I'm freaking out too. Don't be so hard on yourself."

"Yeah, well, your version of freaking out is a lot more...stoic.

But anyway, we need a plan."

"You're right." He gazed out at the foggy dawn. "We could try Big Sur?"

Parker mulled over going south. "I don't know about having the ocean on one side. It would make it easy to get trapped. Unless we had a boat." A memory of salt on his tongue and summer wind in his hair swelled in him, next to his parents as they watched a pod of whales splashing. He was filled with a resolution he felt down to his bones.

"Parker?"

He swallowed hard. "I think... Adam, I need to know if my family made it. My mom said they were going to the Cape house. They could be okay there. If the people were able to block off Cape Cod, the infection might not have spread. They might be safe. They might be waiting for me. They would wait."

Adam was silent for a moment. "It's possible."

"And completely unlikely. I know. I realize what the odds are. But if there's even a tiny chance they survived, I have to try to find them. I *have* to. I can't give up without trying."

"Okay."

"Okay, what? Okay, you understand? Or okay, you'll come with me?"

"I'll come with you."

Warmth bloomed in Parker's chest. "Really? You will?"

He nodded. "I can't just sit around hoping to not get eaten. At least we'll have a goal. A destination. Without something to work for, I think I'll go crazy. And it makes sense to stay together. Right?"

"Right. Definitely." Parker exhaled, some of his tension draining away. This was something, at least. A plan. "So, we go east?"

"We go east. Well, we should go a bit south first. There are preserves and parkland below the eighty-five. I think we're safer in the forest. We can bypass San Jose."

Parker nodded. "Stay away from populated areas." He tried to picture the US map in his mind. "If we keep in the parkland, we'll hit Yosemite, right? Then up to Tahoe and into Nevada?"

"Yeah. We should try to find a map."

"They had some at that gas station. Sorry. I should have grabbed one."

"We'll find one. We should fill up again before we leave the area."

"Will the bike be okay off-road?"

Adam smiled with something that looked like pure affection. "She'll be good."

"Does she have a name? This love of yours?" Parker teased.

"Mariah."

"*Mariah*? As in, Carey?" As soon as the name left his lips, he blanched. Memories flickered through his mind—grasping hands and eyes sticking out too far—that awful noise starting in her throat, and her teeth smashing together.

He shuddered. "God, I can't believe that was...what? A few days ago? She was so scared. I told her everything would be okay. And the other girls..." He could hear their screams and see their blood spurting as the creepers tore into them.

"I know." Adam leaned closer, pressing their shoulders together. "I know," he quietly repeated.

"It's weird, isn't it?" Parker ran a hand through his greasy hair. "I mean, of course it's weird. What day is it?"

"Sunday, I think." Adam shook his head. "I was worried about my thesis proposal. This weekend I had so much work to do on top of grading."

"More C-minuses to give out?"

His lips twitched. "Mmm-hmm. A ton. I was holding one in reserve for you, though."

"I totally would have gotten an A on my next assignment if I kept that class."

"I bet you would have. When you set your mind to something, I bet you can do anything."

Parker shifted and looked away, not sure what to make of the praise. "Um, thanks."

"Let's do this. Let's get you to Cape Cod."

"IT'S THAT WAY." Parker pointed to a range of hills to their right.

"No. Would you look at the map? It's *that* way." Adam nodded in front of them.

"I did look at the map!" He coughed up another wad of phlegm, spitting it onto the ground. Ugh.

Adam held it out. "Look again."

Snatching the folded paper, Parker huffed. "Oh my god, fine. I bet you five hundred bucks I'm right."

"You're on. Not that five hundred dollars will do me any good."

Parker examined the map and zeroed in on the swath of preserves south of the Bay area. "See? We're right here." He jabbed his finger on one of the green zones.

"No. We're *here*." Adam pointed to a spot three inches away. "There's the Stanford golf course. There are the foothills. This is us."

"Oh. Okay. Yeah, that makes sense. Uh, do you take AMEX?"

With a laugh, Adam folded the map and handed it back. "I'll bill you. You're sure the pack isn't too heavy?"

Parker zipped the map into the front pocket, which was lined to keep contents dry. "Nah. It's fine."

"I wish I could go home and get my saddlebags."

"Saddlebags? Like for horses?"

"Yeah, but plastic and designed for the Harley. But we can't risk it. There were too many creepers near the gas station today, and that was on the outskirts."

"I'm fine with the pack." He swung it on over the machete and approached the bike. "Okay, show me one more time."

Adam handed him the keys. "Flip the ignition switch. Put in the key and turn it."

"They really had to *hide* that?" Parker grumbled under his breath. "Okay, got it."

"Make sure it's in neutral and the run/stop switch is on run. Push the start button."

The engine came to life, rumbling under Parker. He pointed to the hand controls. "And I twist the throttle, and that's the brake."

"Right."

"Let's hope I never have to drive."

Adam clapped him on the shoulder. "Let's hope. Well, I guess we're off."

"How far can it go before we have to refuel?"

"She gets about two hundred miles. Maybe a little less if we're going over rugged terrain."

"Oh yes, *she*." He leaned down. "My apologies, Mariah."

"All right, all right. Scoot back."

It felt good to finally have a plan, even if it was only to find their way east without being eaten. They made their way through the hilly preserve and onto the dirt roads that cut through the Santa Cruz mountain area.

Parker felt more at home than ever on the back of the motorcycle, his arms securely around Adam, the shotgun on Adam's back digging into Parker's chest. He kept watch for any signs of life—or death. He thought of Dave and his companion in the SUV and wondered what they'd found down the coast. He hoped they made it.

Unlike the streets of Palo Alto, the back roads were unnervingly empty. No tangle of cars, no bodies, and—so far—no creepers.

They stopped by a small river and coasted down to the grassy bank. The gray sky was still heavy with the threat of rain, and the air was thick. But for the moment, they remained dry.

Parker knelt by the water and refilled their bottle while Adam sat on a large, low rock and spread out a little picnic of chips and trail mix. They perched together on the rock and ate silently for a minute. Parker blew his nose, glad they'd found more tissues at the last gas station.

"My kingdom for a Big Mac," he said. He still wasn't super hungry, and his throat was tender, but he craved the taste of hot food.

"With extra-large fries. Chocolate milkshake."

"Oh my god. I might never have another Shamrock Shake. Think this whole thing will be cleared up by March?"

"Probably," Adam deadpanned.

They rode on, but before long Parker's eyes were heavy, and he started listing to the side, having to jerk himself back awake as Adam applied the brakes. Parker rubbed his face. "Shit. Sorry, I'm really tired. I felt so much better this morning."

"Not surprising. That bug really drained you. Let's find a place to camp."

"No, no. I'll be fine. I want to keep going. We've only made it to the state park. We should be in Yosemite by now."

Adam shook his head. "You need to rest and get your full strength back."

"But I already cost us two days." Two days further away from seeing his parents again. "I can keep going."

"It won't do you any good if you fall off a moving motorcycle. Don't be an idiot."

Tensing, Parker was immediately on the defensive. "I'm not an idiot."

Adam pressed his lips together. "Not yet, but you will be if you insist on not stopping when you need more sleep. Your body's still recovering."

He wanted to argue, but Adam was right. "Fine," he grumbled. "I just... I feel so...ugh."

"Can you be more specific?"

"Useless. I shouldn't have gotten sick. And now I'm slowing us down even more."

Adam lifted his eyebrows and regarded him skeptically. "Yes, Parker. You shouldn't have gotten sick. Because you totally *chose* to get the flu at the same time we had to run for our lives. Yep. Completely your fault. You really need to think about your life choices."

Parker huffed out a laugh. "Point taken. Fine. I'll rest. Let's find a place."

Fortunately, they stumbled on a ranger station before long. Adam followed the arrow off the main road and pulled the bike up outside a squat, small building. He cut the engine and seemed to be listening intently. After a few moments, he nodded and led the way inside.

Parker was too tired to comment and let him do his thing. He seemed to have a good sense of when people were around, so Parker was going with it.

Inside, the station was one room with a kitchenette on one wall, two twin beds with wooden frames against the other, and behind a door, a bathroom with a bathtub and shower. Parker went to use the toilet, which felt like absolute luxury. He wanted to cry when it flushed. He turned the taps and there was running water. He wondered how long water still flowed in a situation like this and vowed to enjoy it while he could.

He sat on one of the beds, managing to take off his shoes before flopping back. It was Adam's turn in the bathroom, so Parker would just close his eyes for a few minutes before he had a shower...

IT WAS DARK when Parker bolted up on the thin mattress. *Where? What?* He caught his breath as he remembered. Ranger station. Right. He rubbed his face. He'd slept for hours, apparently. There was a little kerosene lamp burning in the kitchen, and the dark curtains had been drawn and duct-taped against the window frames. The blankets on the other bed were mussed, and he could hear the shower running.

A shower.

The need to get clean again was suddenly all-consuming. Parker felt like his whole body was itchy with grime. With a burst of energy, he knocked on the bathroom door. "Hurry up. I need a shower too."

"I'll be out soon," Adam called back.

Okay. Cool. Totally fair. But Parker paced in front of the bathroom door. He was so *dirty*, and not in an ironic, Christina Aguilera way.

He froze for a moment, struck by a memory of being a little kid and singing along to that song on the radio at the top of his lungs while Eric laughed his ass off and their mother looked scandalized in the kitchen doorway, one hand to her glossy lips and the other on her waist. She'd told him sternly not to let his father hear that song but had smiled soon after when she let him lick a wooden spoon, cake batter dripping from it.

His throat tightened. *Mom.*

"Stop it," he muttered. "She's okay." Ugh, he was going to cry, and he needed to stop thinking. He knocked again. "Seriously, hurry up. Stop bogarting the hot water."

Adam's muffled, laconic response came a moment later. "You know that the more you bug me, the longer I'm going to take."

"Dude! Don't make me come in there."

"Go ahead. I dare you."

"Oh yeah?" Adam had already seen him naked, so what did he care? He opened the door, already stripping off his clothes. "Dare accepted."

Through the clear shower curtain, Adam whirled around and stared. Then he laughed, his head tipped back, and Parker decided he wanted to hear more of that sound. He pulled back the curtain and stepped in. "Come on, shove over."

The hot water was like heaven coursing over him. Parker closed his eyes and moaned softly, tipping his head back under the stream as Adam shifted to give him room. When he opened his eyes, Adam's smile had vanished, and his throat worked as he handed Parker a little bottle of shampoo. His voice was tight. "There's even conditioner."

"This is perfect." Parker lathered up his hair and then scrubbed his body with a bar of soap. "Jesus, I never thought soap would be so amazing. I guess I'm going to find out all the things I've been taking for granted my entire life."

Adam's voice cracked. "Yeah." He cleared his throat. "Yeah," he repeated.

"I feel so much better after sleeping in a bed. You were right." Parker rubbed his scalp with another round of shampoo.

"Can I get that in writing?" Adam asked playfully.

"Well, you were right this time. Doesn't mean you will be next time. No guarantees in life, Adam."

Adam's smile faded, his lips pulling down and his eyes hooding with clear sadness. "I guess not," he murmured.

They looked at each other through the steam, and before he could think better of it, Parker hugged him tightly, pressing their bodies together. "Thank you for everything you've done for me." Adam was warm and breathing and *alive*, and Parker soaked it in with a kind of need he'd never felt. After a few heartbeats, Adam hugged him back.

For a minute, they simply held each other close, the water

beating down. They were safe in their little cocoon, the rest of the world fading away. It probably should have been weird, but their lives had become such a nonstop parade of crazy that he supposed they were getting used to it. It felt so damn good to be held, and Parker closed his eyes.

They were safe in here.

He skimmed his fingertips over the muscles of Adam's back, needing to touch. His face was pressed into the side of Adam's neck, and without thinking, he kissed the soft skin there. Adam's breath caught, and Parker sucked lightly as he continued caressing him.

Wait, what am I doing? He's going to punch me out.

But it was so good to be in Adam's arms and feel his body, and Adam hadn't shoved him away. In fact, Adam's cock came to life, thickening against Parker's belly.

Adam went rigid all over. "Sorry. I should—"

But Parker was already sinking to his knees. "Can I? Please? I need... Oh fuck, I really need it." He circled the base of Adam's dick with his hand, eager to taste. "Please?" He glanced up. Adam might have been straight, but in Parker's experience, all men would take a blow job where they could get it. "I'm really good at it."

Adam was frozen in place, his voice strangled. "You like men?"

Parker's stomach flip-flopped, and he forced a light tone. "Yeah. I'm a total homo." *Shit. Oh shit, shit, shit.* Had he messed everything up? "Is that a problem for you?"

"No," Adam choked out. "I just didn't know."

He was still holding Adam's shaft, and with a deep breath, he stroked lightly. "Will it be too weird for you if I—"

"No." Adam shook his head sharply. "Do it."

Parker didn't need to be told twice and swiped his tongue along the shaft as he worked it in tandem with his hand. Adam wasn't cut, which sent desire shooting through Parker's veins. It had always turned him on; maybe because he was cut himself, and it was different. Holding Adam's hip with his free hand, he worked the foreskin down and sucked the head while his own cock came to life.

Adam stroked Parker's hair, and when he looked up, Adam was watching him with parted lips and eyes that somehow seemed to shine more golden instead of darkening. Sucking deeper, Parker's nostrils flared, glad for the steam that loosened his lingering congestion. He stretched his lips over the thickness of Adam's big cock.

He'd always loved the sensation of being filled—of the taste and musky smell of cock consuming him, of a dick almost choking him while he pushed it toward the edge of release. With Adam in his mouth and the little breathy moans and pants coming from above, Parker was alive and in control.

As he worked Adam's cock, his gaze flickered over Adam's body, drinking it in. Dark hair peppered Adam's chest, and a trail led down below his belly button. His arms and legs were dusted with hair as well. He was very much a *man*, when Parker had only ever been with boys his own age in school.

It made his cock throb and swell, and he reached down to give himself a few strokes. He moaned around Adam's shaft before forcing his hand back to Adam's hip. Adam had to come first—he needed to give him that.

With the guys at school, Parker hadn't usually thought much about them beyond wanting to get off. But with Adam, he could swallow him whole and climb into his skin.

He sucked harder and faster before sliding off with a loud *pop*. Adam's fingers tightened in Parker's hair, and he made a sound in the back of his throat that might have been a whine. It made Parker's blood sing in a way he'd never felt, and he cupped Adam's balls in one hand to lick and suckle them, lapping fiercely.

Adam moaned so loudly. "Parker," he muttered.

The sound of his name on Adam's lips, said with so much *need*, made him feel better than he could remember feeling in so long. It didn't matter what was happening out there—all that mattered was here and now. Making Adam feel good.

Adam's cock was red and straining, drops of pre-cum at the tip. Parker licked them up, savoring the salty tang. When he swallowed the shaft again, spit dripping from his mouth, Adam gasped.

"I'm going to…"

But Parker ignored Adam's warning and kept sucking desperately, desire vibrating through him as Adam came in his mouth. After swallowing every drop he could, he pulled off and inhaled deeply, the steam doing wonders. He was already reaching down for his own dick to stroke.

"Here." Adam almost wavered on his feet, his voice breathy. "Let me." Adam tugged on Parker's arm.

Parker shook him off. "It's okay." It was nice of Adam to offer, but he had plenty of experience jerking himself off, and he was so close. He rested his head against Adam's thigh and worked his dick. He stroked his tingling balls with his other hand and tightened his grip on his cock as he jerked it.

Adam's hand closed over his head, caressing him lightly, and Parker leaned into the touch. Closing his eyes, he came with a strangled moan, milking himself until it was too much and he had to stop. Still on his knees, he leaned heavily against Adam as the haze of pleasure wore off.

Adam's hand still rested on Parker's head, but Parker knew from his days at Westley that straight guys didn't like to bask long in the afterglow. Besides, the water had begun to run lukewarm. He pushed to his feet and switched it off. Now it was time for the awkwardness, but it couldn't be helped.

He pulled back the shower curtain and reached for a scratchy towel. He held it out to Adam, who stared blankly at it before taking it. Parker dried off with another towel, keeping his gaze averted. "Thanks. I needed that."

After a few moments, Adam answered. "You're welcome?"

Parker rubbed his hair. "We're still cool, right?"

"Uh…yeah."

"Great. I'll make us something to eat." Parker escaped the bathroom, picking up his clothes as he went. So it would be a little awkward. They were both adults. It would be just fine.

Chapter Eight

SPOILER ALERT: IT wasn't fine.

Parker found a can of alphabet noodles and one of baked beans, heating them on a little gas Coleman stove. Adam periodically went outside to check the perimeter or something. Parker left him and his Spidey senses to it.

They avoided looking at each other whenever possible.

There was a little table with two chairs, and Parker dished out the canned delights on chipped plates while Adam was outside. When he returned, Parker nodded to the other chair. "Um, dinner, I guess." He winced. *How eloquent.*

"Thanks." Adam sat and picked up his fork.

They ate in silence, the only sounds their swallowing and forks scraping the cheap plates.

Parker felt completely full when he was half done. "You want the rest of mine? I can't."

"Sure. Thanks." Adam held out his near-empty plate, and Parker scraped the rest of his food onto it.

While Adam finished eating, Parker got up to put the pot soaking in the sink. The air felt thick with... He didn't know what. Tension, but why? Was Adam freaking out that a guy had sucked his dick? Was it because it was *Parker*, and Adam had regret for getting that desperate? Was this elephant in the room going to be riding the motorcycle with them tomorrow?

I screw everything up.

He took another capful of cough syrup, the cherry tasting

particularly gross after cheap tomato sauce and baked beans. While Adam still sat at the table, playing with a few last beans, Parker escaped into the bathroom. He opened the cupboard under the sink and could have wept with joy when he saw the little collection of new toothbrushes wrapped in plastic and stuffed into a cup. There was toothpaste too, praise the Lord.

It wasn't late when he finished, but he shucked off his cargo pants and curled up on his bed anyway, burrowing under the musty blankets in his sweater and boxers. "I left out a toothbrush for you in the bathroom. I'm tired again, and we'd better get an early start tomorrow. Night." He faced the wall, closing his eyes.

"Night." Adam's voice sounded…neutral? Tense? Parker couldn't quite tell.

Why the fuck did I do that? We were friends. What if he leaves me now? What if he'd rather be alone than with me?

His mind whirled, and the canned dinner gurgled in his stomach. But soon enough the sedative in the cough syrup kicked in, and he drifted off.

"NO! *NO!*" PARKER flailed about, desperate.

There were strong hands on him, trying to catch him, and a calm, steady voice filled the air. "Parker. Wake up."

Wake up? He forced his eyes open. It was pitch black, and he whimpered.

"You're okay. It was just a dream."

"Adam?" He squinted in the darkness. Where was he? He was on a hard floor, but it was so dark.

The hands left him, and a moment later, moonlight flooded the station as Adam opened one of the curtains on the wall by the beds. "We're here at the ranger station. Remember?" He came back and crouched in front of Parker. "Everything's okay."

"Right." Parker rubbed his eyes. "Ugh. I was dreaming about..." He shuddered. "Scary shit."

"You want to talk about it?" Adam was only wearing a white T-shirt and briefs he'd taken from the Hendersons' house, and it was rather distracting.

"Uh, no. But thanks." Parker straightened his bunched-up sweater and winced as he tried to stand. He poked at his knee. "I think I need a Band-Aid. I scraped the shit out of it on the side of the bed frame."

Adam eased him up to sit on the side of the mattress. "I'll get one." He closed the curtains again, briefly plunging the cabin into complete darkness.

Parker could hear him bustling about. "You must have a really good memory. How do you—" A match was struck, flaring to life as Adam lit the lantern. "Remember where everything is?"

"Like you said: good memory." He disappeared into the bathroom with the lantern and returned before long.

Kneeling at Parker's sock-clad feet, he put the lantern on the floor between the beds and dabbed at Parker's scrape with antiseptic that burned. Parker felt ridiculously like a little kid, but it was nice to be looked after. The blood had slowed, and Adam wiped it away before unpeeling a Band-Aid and carefully smoothing it over the middle of Parker's knee.

"There." He sat back on his heels.

"Aren't you going to kiss it better?" The stupid, stupid words were out of his mouth before he could stop them. "I—I... I didn't mean..."

But Adam only smiled, leaned down, and gently pressed his lips to the Band-Aid.

A pleased laugh bubbled out of Parker's chest, and warmth buzzed through him. "Thanks." Maybe things would be okay after all. Maybe everything would get back to normal after their detour to blow jobs and awkwardville. Maybe—

Watching him intently, Adam's smile faded as he went up on his knees and took Parker's face between his hands. He leaned in, and their lips met softly. His heart thumping, Parker stopped breathing.

Adam was kissing him.

With so much tenderness, Adam pressed their lips together. Parker's pulse kicked into high gear as his brain tried to catch up and make sense of it. He tilted his head and tentatively kissed back, Adam's hands still cupping his face.

Adam was *kissing him*. And *he was kissing Adam*.

It wasn't all tongues and wild passion like he'd always imagined his first kiss to be. But it was somehow so much better as Adam's lips teased his, and his scruff rubbed Parker's skin. They breathed each other in, and Parker was sure he would have floated away if not for Adam's big hands so gentle on his cheeks.

Their lips were parted just a bit now, and it was wetter. Adam sucked Parker's lower lip before pulling back and searching his face. Parker leaned after him, his breath coming faster. "Why did you do that?" Parker whispered.

Adam dropped his hands instantly and sat back on his heels. "I'm sorry. I thought... I wanted to kiss you so badly. I shouldn't have."

"You...wanted to kiss me?" He waited, dumbfounded, as Adam nodded. "But why?"

Adam's brow furrowed. "What do you mean?"

"No one's ever wanted to kiss me before." Parker touched his lips with his fingertips. Was he dreaming again? In the golden lantern light, Adam watched him, waiting. "No one ever *has* kissed me before. And I thought you were straight?"

"No. And wait, surely you've..." He glanced toward the bathroom. "That wasn't your first time."

"No, I've done that a bunch of times. It's not the same. I never...wait, you're gay? I didn't think...you're not...you have a girlfriend." He couldn't bear to say *had*.

Adam frowned. "No, I don't."

"You do too. Tina."

"Tina? She's my best friend."

"You said she was your girlfriend."

"No, I didn't."

"Yes, you did!" Parker waved his hands. "Remember? When I came to your office, you said you were meeting your girlfriend? And then later after everything happened, when you left her a message you told her you loved her."

"She's my best friend. Of course I love her."

"But you said she was *your girlfriend*."

Adam shook his head firmly. "I never said that. You might have heard that, but I didn't say it." His brows drew together and he was quiet a moment. "I think you said girlfriend, and it didn't seem important at the time to correct you."

"So you've been gay or bi this whole time?"

A smile tugged at Adam's mouth. "Yes. Gay, for the record."

Parker found himself smiling back. "And you wanted to kiss me."

"I did." Adam leaned closer, but he still kept his hands at his sides.

"Since when?"

"Since about the time you put that ridiculous hat on me in the store to make the girls laugh."

Parker could swear he actually felt his heart swell, which was so corny and dumb, but he *felt it*. He wanted to throw Adam down and climb on top of him and kiss him until tomorrow. He played back what had happened in the bathroom earlier like a movie in his mind. "In the shower…"

"I wanted to touch you. You said no."

Duh. I'm an idiot.

"I thought you were just being nice. Returning the favor and all that, even though most straight guys don't. Should have been my first clue, I guess. Wow, my gaydar needs a tune-up."

Adam smiled softly. "Guess so. I thought maybe you were, but I wasn't sure. Everything's been so upside down."

"Do you still want to touch me?" Parker blurted. *In for a penny.* "Because I really want to touch you."

He could have sworn Adam's eyes flashed pure gold just for a moment before he hauled Parker off the bed and onto his lap to straddle his thighs. Adam licked his lips, and Parker lunged for them. Mouths open now, they kissed and licked and sucked, tongues tangling. Parker's whole body flared to life, *want* burning through him.

This was *real* kissing, and he couldn't get enough. It was wet and messy, and smacking sounds filled the air. He rolled his hips, rutting while Adam gripped his ass and urged him on. Parker wanted to take off his sweater, but he couldn't bear to stop touching Adam. Their moans and grunts echoed off the cheap wooden walls of the station, and he was sure he was going to come in his boxers.

Leaning back, he broke the kiss. Adam made a low sound that was almost a growl, and Parker grinned. "Don't worry. I'm not going far." Lifting up just enough, he freed his straining cock from his boxers. Then he fiddled with Adam's stretched briefs, and Adam batted his hands away, quickly yanking out his hard dick.

They groaned in unison as Parker settled back down and took them both in his hand, rubbing their shafts together. Adam latched onto Parker's neck, nipping and sucking the tender skin there. He rolled his hips up in time with Parker's rhythm, his hands roaming under Parker's sweater.

Every time Parker thought about pulling away and moving to a bed, Adam kissed him again, or tweaked his nipple, or ran his fingers up and down Parker's spine. Yeah, right here on the floor was good. It was *great*.

It was hard to believe that only days before, Parker had been so annoyed by Adam. Now he wanted to devour him. "God, I wanna be naked with you," he muttered.

Adam's fingernails almost felt like claws digging into Parker's ass through the cotton of his boxers. He kissed Parker again deeply, and Parker increased his pace, stroking them faster, his other hand dipping down to roll their balls together.

That was all it took, and Parker cried out as he came over his hand, the pleasure sweeping through him like a tidal wave. He kept jerking their cocks, milking his and driving Adam to the edge.

Releasing himself, he concentrated on Adam. "I love your dick. I love that you're uncut," Parker murmured. He couldn't seem to activate the filter on his mouth, and it all poured out. "I wanna feel that inside me."

Face buried in Parker's neck, Adam moaned as he came, splashing hot between them and dripping over Parker's fingers. He shuddered as Parker coaxed another few drops from him. They panted softly, and Adam raised his head. He ran his thumb over Parker's lips.

Parker lifted his hand and sucked his fingers clean one by one as Adam watched avidly with lips parted. When he was finished, they kissed slowly this time, their tongues sliding together. He was still straddling Adam's lap, and they were sticky.

He waited for it to get awkward, but Adam simply wrapped his arms around Parker and drew him closer. He rested his head on Adam's shoulder, listening to his steady breathing, the world a million miles away.

Chapter Nine

PARKER WASN'T SURE what time it was when he woke again, but weak light was coming in the open curtains. He was alone in the narrow bed, but when he blinked the room into focus, Adam was looking over his shoulder where he fiddled with the Coleman stove in the kitchenette. He was naked, and *damn*. It was quite a view. Adam's ass was round and firm, and just...wow.

"I could get used to this. Do I get breakfast in bed?"

Adam's tone was playful. "If you play your cards right."

Parker yawned widely and stretched his arms, pushing the blanket down to his waist. After cleaning up, they'd slept tangled naked together on his bed, and even though there hadn't been enough room, Parker had slept deeply. His throat wasn't sore, and he didn't feel like there was a pound of mucus clogging his head and airways. He felt so good he could almost forget everything else.

Almost.

But there was plenty of time to worry about the world later. "So, are you still gay this morning? And into me? I didn't dream that, right?"

The smell of coffee brewing filled the air, and Adam chuckled. "Right."

"Cool." Like, *epically* cool. He watched as Adam crossed the room, swallowing thickly at the sight of his big cock and balls. He'd seen him naked before, but somehow there was something more intimate about Adam's casual nudity now.

Adam sat on the side of the bed. "How are you feeling this morning?"

"Better. And like I totally want to kiss you again, but I have morning breath, and—"

Adam's lips were soft and seeking, his hand coming to rest on Parker's bare chest. Parker opened his mouth and met Adam's tongue. He sucked in a breath as they parted. "Okay, so you don't mind about morning breath. Good to know."

"Mmm-hmm."

Parker leaned up and kissed him lightly. It was nice, this kissing business. "You feeling good this morning?"

"Mmm-hmm." Adam pressed Parker back onto the mattress.

As Adam's weight covered him and they kissed again, Parker mused that the kissing/sex combo was pretty awesome too. "This is a great wake-up call." He thrust up his hips, wanting the blanket out of the way.

"Mmm-hmm." Adam sucked on Parker's neck, sending a shiver down his spine as his tongue teased.

"Is that all you can say?"

He raised his head. "Is talking really how you want me to use my mouth right now?"

The coiled desire in Parker's belly whipped through his body, and he moaned. "Uh-uh. Carry on."

The wet heat of Adam's mouth on Parker's nipples had him panting and arching his back, and his morning wood was now rock hard. But Adam ignored Parker's lower half and nipped his tender flesh before doing some kind of swirl with his tongue that was probably illegal in some states. Parker wouldn't have been surprised if sparks were actually flying from his nipples.

He threaded his fingers through Adam's thick hair. "Oh my god. Is this real life?"

Adam's shoulders shook, and he puffed warm air over Parker's skin. He moved down, his scruff rasping wonderfully. The combination of his soft lips and rough hair was somehow the most perfect thing ever.

He dipped his tongue into Parker's bellybutton while he teased the trail of hair leading down with his fingertips. He was so close to the tip of Parker's dick, which Parker could feel was leaking. Adam was heavy on top of him, the blanket still trapped between them. Parker was completely pinned down and confined, and it only made him harder. He pushed at Adam's head.

With a wicked grin, Adam glanced up. "Was there something you wanted?"

Groaning, Parker tried to arch his hips again. "Please."

"Please what?"

"Please *suck my cock before I explode.*"

Adam shimmied down and pulled the blanket away, tossing it onto the floor. Parker's dick strained against his belly, but Adam moved lower, mouthing at Parker's inner thighs until they were trembling.

By the time Adam licked up Parker's shaft, Parker was moaning so loudly his face flushed. He could hear Greg Mason's voice in his head. "*You sound like a slutty fag.*" He pressed his lips together, his nostrils flaring as he muzzled his cries.

Adam looked up after a few more licks, his hazel eyes doing that gold glowy thing that was so breathtakingly beautiful. "Why did you stop?"

"You don't mind? If I'm…loud?"

With their eyes locked, Adam took Parker's leaking cock in his hand and caught a drop of pre-cum with a feathery flick of his tongue. "I like it."

Groaning, Parker threw his head back. He wriggled, his limbs electric as Adam sucked down the length of his shaft. Parker moaned freely, and the more noise he made, the more it seemed to spur on Adam.

Adam gripped his hips, holding him down as he worked Parker's dick, the slurping sounds mixing with Parker's cries and filling the ranger station.

Greg had only sucked him once, and that had been nothing compared to this. Adam took him in so deeply, and the hot pressure on his cock made blood rush in his ears. His legs twitched, and he thought that if he had to die, at least he had an honest-to-god amazing blow job before he went.

"So good, Adam," he muttered, gripping Adam's head.

Adam hummed around him, and Parker's whole body tingled. The delicious torment continued, and Adam brought him close to the edge more than once before backing off. Parker whimpered— he actually *whimpered*—and tried to spread his legs more. Adam mouthed at his balls.

"Please. I need it. Can I..."

Adam's breath was hot against his sac. "Tell me."

He tried to block out the memory of a furious Greg, spitting repeatedly on the shower room tiles. "*Don't be so uncouth.*" Because Greg was the kind of pretentious twat that used words like *uncouth*. But what if Adam thought it was gross too? Parker throbbed with need, and he took a deep breath. "Can I come in your mouth?"

With a groan, Adam swallowed his cock again, sucking fiercely. Parker could only cry out, his head back and mouth open as the orgasm tore through him. He felt as if he was levitating off the thin mattress, shuddering as he spurted. He managed to open his eyes and watch as Adam swallowed it all, his lips stretched wide.

Parker realized he was gripping Adam's hair too tight, and he relaxed his hands. "Thank you," he whispered. He couldn't remember ever feeling so warm and peaceful.

Catching stray drops, Adam licked him clean and pressed tender kisses to Parker's inner thighs and hip bones. He sat back on his heels and jerked himself off. Parker wanted to offer his services, but all he could do was lie there, utterly sated, listening to

Adam's grunts and watching him work his cock.

"You can come on me, Adam," he murmured.

And Adam did, leaning forward onto one hand and splattering Parker's belly and groin as he shuddered and milked himself. Breathing hard, he dropped his head and licked Parker clean, which was possibly the most surprisingly hot thing Parker had ever seen in his life, and he'd watched a lot of porn. The wet drag of Adam's tongue on his skin sent shivers over him, and he ran his fingers through Adam's thick hair.

When Adam moved back up Parker's body to cover him again, they kissed lazily, and Parker loved tasting the remnants of their spunk. He wondered briefly and belatedly about safety, but dismissed the thought since his odds of surviving long enough to contract an STI were slim to none. He was going to enjoy this, goddamn it.

Adam rested his face in the crook of Parker's neck, and Parker rubbed his back, sliding his fingers up and down Adam's spine. "You're really good at that."

Adam smiled against Parker's skin. "Am I?"

"Why do you sound so surprised?"

"It's been a while."

"Really?"

"Why do you sound so surprised?" Adam asked back.

"Um, have you seen you? The cheekbones, for starters. The eyes. The lips. Jesus, that mouth. And this is all above the neck. It's not bad to the south either. Shoulders. Chest. I'm pretty sure there's a six-pack down there, and you could crack walnuts with your thighs. We haven't even talked about your ass or your junk yet. Do I need to go on?"

With a chuckle, Adam shook his head. He propped himself up on one arm and traced a finger down Parker's chest. "You're not so bad yourself."

"Me?" Parker laughed sharply. "Come on. I'm all right, but—"

"You're a lot more than all right." Adam kissed him again soundly.

The way Adam said it, and the way he looked at him—no one had ever made Parker feel like that. He couldn't help but ask, "Really?"

Adam's brow furrowed. "Of course. Your eyes are so expressive, and the lashes are so long. So pretty." He leaned down and ever so gently licked the shell of Parker's ear. "Just the right size ears."

Parker shivered. "Ticklish."

Smiling, Adam ran his hand over Parker's chest and belly. "I love that you're lean and strong." He teased the hair scattered over Parker's chest. "Just the right amount. Smooth, but not too smooth." His hand drifted down over Parker's thigh. "Narrow hips, and those long legs. Your ass is amazing. Even that first day, in my office? When you stormed out, I was thinking about what an amazing ass you have."

Parker knew he was blushing, and he bit his lip. "Really?"

"Mmm-hmm. It was pretty damn inappropriate given I was your TA."

"It was. You're a total perv." He grinned. "Good thing I am too."

Adam lowered his voice and confessed, "I wondered what you'd look like in a Speedo."

"You did not!"

"I did." Adam chuckled. "In high school, I had the biggest crush on the entire swim team." He ran his finger over Parker's lips. "And your mouth is perfect."

"But don't you think my lips could be more—"

"Nope. Perfect."

For once, Parker couldn't find any words, so he kissed Adam instead. Their mouths opened, and their tongues stroked lazily. He ran his hand through Adam's hair, and down over his shoulder and arm, enjoying the sensation of just touching. He'd never actually done anything in a bed. At school, it had usually been in the bathroom, or against a dorm room door, since they didn't lock.

As Adam nuzzled his neck, Parker mumbled, "I can't believe you were gay the whole time. I might have died without experiencing that blow job."

When Adam laughed, his whole face brightened and his eyes twinkled. "Glad to be of service."

"So, how long is a while?"

"Huh?"

"You said it had been a while. Since you'd…" Parker shrugged. "Just curious. Not to mention nosy as hell."

Adam's gaze skittered away. "More than a year, I guess."

"Seriously? Wow." Although he knew circumstance had played a huge role, Parker couldn't help but be flattered.

"Why is that so surprising?"

"Again, have you *seen you*? Cheekbones, abs, etc. Ass that won't quit. Not that it's *big*, but it's just…damn." He swore Adam was blushing. "And that meaty cock I want to make a meal of daily. Eat your hearts out, vegans. Because I have some prime beef in my bed."

Adam burst out laughing. "Vegans?"

"It's a long story. Probably won't make much sense outside of my head."

"I'll take your word for it. And thank you." Adam leaned in almost shyly and kissed Parker. When he sat back, he exhaled slowly. "I've hooked up with guys over the years. Just sex, pretty much. There was never anyone special. I'm not…I dunno. Sometimes I felt like I was looking for something different than everyone else."

"What were you looking for?"

He ran his finger over Parker's lips. "I'm not really sure."

Parker wanted so badly to say something unbearably cheesy, like, *Maybe you finally found it with me.* For once he managed to bite his tongue. He kissed Adam instead, and for a minute they just nuzzled each other. Parker knew they had to get moving again, but… Just a little while longer.

Adam rolled onto his hip and propped his head on his hand. He ran his foot over Parker's shin. "What you said about straight guys…why have you been with them? I assume you have, at least."

Parker shrugged. "Boarding school. I was the resident queer. I wanted to suck cock, and guys knew I would do it no questions asked. Oh, but don't worry. I got tested recently, and it all came back negative."

"I'm not worried. Me too. For the record." Adam frowned. "There were no other gay kids there?"

"A few, but they weren't keen on admitting it. It wasn't a big school. There were two guys who were into each other. They were roommates and happy as clams. There was no one else that would admit it, except for one guy who'll probably end up marrying some lucky girl and making her miserable while he cruises the public bathrooms." Parker's smile faded as he thought about where Greg might be right now. His stomach clenched.

Adam flattened his palm against Parker's chest. "What is it?"

"Just wondering if Greg's still alive. Or if he's infected." He shuddered. "It's weird to think about."

"I'm sure he's okay." Adam rubbed soothing circles with his hand.

"Yeah. It's not… I mean, the guy was a douche. Super closeted, but somehow I couldn't stay away from him. We'd fool around, but he wouldn't kiss me. Not ever. He always thought I did things wrong. Then he beat me for valedictorian for the final humiliation. I don't know why I put up with his shit. I never even liked him." He blew out a long breath. "But I still hope he's okay. I'm pathetic, huh?"

"What's pathetic about caring for people? Even when they're jerks? That's not pathetic in my book."

"I guess when you put it like that. Thanks." Parker was smiling, and he kissed Adam briefly. Being able to just kiss him when he wanted made him stupidly happy. He did it again, a press of lips, and Adam caressed his chest before pulling back with a sigh.

"We should get moving, I guess." Adam ran a hand over his face. "There's shaving gear in there, so I'm going to clean up."

"Okay. I'll get our stuff ready." Parker had never been able to grow much of a beard, which he supposed would come in handy now that he wouldn't be able to shave regularly.

Reluctantly, they went about dressing and cleaning and packing up their gear. As the minutes ticked by, the tranquil haze evaporated, and Parker was on edge again as he zipped up his green rain jacket and shouldered the backpack over his machete holster. Adam strapped the shotgun to his back.

They mounted the motorcycle, and Parker gave the ranger station one last look as they drove away. He knew he had to try and find his parents, but part of him wanted to tell Adam to turn around so they could hide away for another day.

They still had the back roads to themselves as they made their way across the scrubby grasslands and flat expanses of the interior. It took longer, but they carefully picked a route that kept them away from major areas or roads, although they had to venture close to a town for gas. They saw only bodies—or what little was left of them—as the hours passed.

Parker's thighs and butt were sore from a day on the bike by the time they stopped to eat a dinner of cold canned pasta. But the day got a lot better when they kissed for longer than they should have, sitting by a fast-flowing river while the sky darkened.

Even when they got back on the road and cold rain began to fall, Parker couldn't stop smiling. *Adam likes kissing me.* He knew it was silly, and probably awful to care about it when so many people were dead, but he needed to focus on something positive.

Although they'd both shaved that morning, Adam's five o'clock shadow had left Parker's skin a little raw. Parker touched his face, reveling in it. Being with Adam was like a little oasis in a desert of terrifying awfulness.

As night fell, they were almost at the Sierra National Forest. The back road was twisty, and according to a sign, there was a town not far ahead. Parker squinted. "You sure you can see without the headlight? It really clouded over. The moon is barely out."

"I'm sure," Adam called back. "But we'll find a place to stop soon."

"However will we pass the time tonight?" Parker unzipped Adam's leather jacket and snuck his hand inside.

Adam laughed. "Don't distract me."

"Oh, is this distracting?" With his other hand, Parker squeezed Adam's crotch through his jeans. "How about this?"

Groaning, Adam shook his head. "Unless you want me to throw you over the bike and fuck you right here, you'd better stop."

The thought sent all of Parker's blood rushing to his groin. "Uh, I'm not seeing the downside." He rubbed Adam, who groaned again.

"We should bypass this town unless—" He eased up on the throttle, suddenly tense.

"What?" But as they came around a bend, Parker saw what.

Creepers.

Dozens of them milled around, and Adam swore as he dodged two who reached out at the last moment. Parker unsheathed his machete, adrenaline zipping through him. While they weren't drawn to the noise of the engine the way they were lights, it did get their attention, and they zeroed in on the new stimulus, coming at Parker and Adam in a strange shuffling unison. Adam twisted the throttle, and Parker slashed at an outstretched hand.

Ahead, the ranks closed in, and blood rushed in Parker's ears. *Fuck, fuck, fuck!*

Adam had to slow to twist the Harley to the right, and in an instant, a tug on his backpack threw Parker off balance as he lashed out with the machete. The tires screeched, and Parker was flying back, the impact on the ground shoving the air from his lungs. He desperately raised the machete and hacked into the head of one of the creepers as it leaned over him, bulging eyes wild and its mouth open.

I'm going to die! Help! No! Fuck!

Parker hacked again, panic and adrenaline taking over.

An inhuman sound reverberated through the air, a roar that set all the hair on Parker's arms on end. The creeper that he'd cut into suddenly disappeared, tossed into the night like a rag doll. Parker's mouth opened and closed, and he tried to breathe as his mind screamed.

A hairy animal with golden eyes and sharp fangs tore the head clean off another creeper using wickedly sharp claws. Parker jerked his head left and right, searching for Adam. But Adam wasn't there, and Parker choked down a scream. In a horrible instant, his brain caught up with what his eyes were seeing.

Sprawled on the blacktop with his machete still in hand and heart in his throat, Parker could only watch as the leather-clad thing that used to be Adam massacred the infected one by one.

Chapter Ten

*N*EED. AIR. FUCK.

His heart was about to explode, and Parker gripped the machete handle too tightly as the creature—*Adam?*—slashed a creeper's throat so deeply that the head lolled off, bug eyes rolling until the head was torn free and tossed into the trees. Creeper corpses littered the dirt road. The motorcycle engine still hummed, and the beast turned to Parker, blood and gore dripping from its claws.

Claws.

Scrambling back, Parker choked on a scream. His heels slipped in something that was probably entrails, and fuck, fuck, *fuck*, he was going to die. "No!" His voice was barely a croak.

The thing moved closer and extended its hairy hand. "It's okay. It's me."

"*What?*" It was *talking*. It still sounded like Adam, except growlier. But it couldn't be. "You're infected. Jesus, something's wrong with you!" Parker was finally able to make his legs work, and he staggered to his feet. He held out the machete with a trembling arm. "Stay back."

"I'm not infected." Somehow, Adam's calm, rational voice was coming out of the mouth of this thing. A mouth dripping with blood.

How was it—*he?*—talking? "You have to be! Look at you!"

Before Parker's eyes, the animal in front of him transformed. The claws and fangs retracted, the hair that had covered much of

Adam's face and hands seemed to fade away, and his eyes lost their glow. In only seconds, it was Adam again.

Parker shook his head frantically. "I must be dreaming. You can't...what is this?" Adam took another step, and Parker jumped back, nearly tripping over the body of a headless creeper. "What just happened?" he shouted.

Adam's shoulders were hunched in his jacket, and his gaze was on the ground. "I can explain," he said quietly. "Please give me a chance." Then his head shot up, and he stared to the right. "We have to go. There are more coming this way. That town must be infected. We have to get into the woods and away from the road. Now."

The road curved ahead, and Parker could barely make it out. But over the bike's still-running engine, he thought he heard the din of that awful chattering. He couldn't stay out here on his own, and Adam...*what the fuck?* Had Parker hit his head? He couldn't even form a sentence.

"We have to go." Adam strode to the motorcycle and straddled it. "I'll explain it all once we're safe. Come on, Parker."

For a long moment, Parker could only stand there. Then as another creeper twitched into his peripheral vision up the road, he took a step toward the bike.

Adam stared back at him. "Please. I promise I can explain."

With a deep breath, he sheathed his machete and climbed on behind Adam, the pack heavy on his shoulders. If he didn't want to fall off the back again, he needed to wrap his arms around Adam and hang on, the shotgun between them. He did, breathing in the whiff of leather and faded hint of pine that probably came from some cologne Adam had used before...well, before.

Did monsters wear cologne?

Pressed against him, Adam felt the same as he had earlier, and looked to be completely normal again. Parker wanted to ask a million questions. He wanted to run. He wanted to open his eyes and be back in his dorm room, with only his econ test and that C-minus on his mind.

All he could do was hold on as they bounced along a hiking trail, deeper and deeper into the forest.

He wasn't sure what time it was when Adam slowed Mariah. Parker squinted at their surroundings. "Is there something here?"

"A cabin. To the left."

The path was barely big enough for the motorcycle, and Parker had no idea how Adam had spotted it. *Probably something to do with the fact that he's some kind of shapeshifting demon spawn. Likely has x-ray vision.* As soon as the bike stopped, Parker leapt off and backed away. Adam killed the engine, and the silence was startling.

Parker ran a hand through his hair. "Seriously, what the fuck. What the hell just happened? What's wrong with you?"

Adam didn't look at him as he stood. "I'll explain everything. Let's just go inside. Get cleaned up."

"No. I'm not going anywhere until you tell me what the fuck is going on."

Adam slipped out of the shotgun holster. After a few moments, he met Parker's gaze and shrugged. "I'm a werewolf."

Parker's bark of laughter was like a gunshot in the stillness. "A *werewolf?*" he sputtered. "Wh—what the fuck? Is that supposed to be funny?"

Adam sighed. "Nope. It's what I am. I'm a werewolf."

"I… What? *What?* That's ridiculous."

Adam's jaw tightened. "I'm telling you the truth. Why would I lie?"

"I don't know, but 'I'm a werewolf' can be filed under insane-comma-batshit."

"You saw me back there!" Adam tightened his fists, his nostrils flaring. "I know it's a shock, but what more proof do you need?"

"I don't know! But what if it's the virus?"

His voice rose sharply. "I'm not infected! I've always been this way."

Parker battled the urge to back up as his heart thumped. "Okay, fine. Sure. Let's say I believe you. You're a werewolf." Parker waved his hand. "Tell me more, by all means. Tell me all about it."

Adam seemed to deflate, the anger seeping away. He closed his eyes and inhaled deeply, steadily breathing in and out a few times. When he spoke, his voice was low, and he stared at the ground.

"I was born this way. My family were all werewolves—my parents and my sisters. Our parents taught us how to hide it. How to control it. But they died before I could learn everything I needed to. Everything I wanted to. There's so much I don't know. I don't know why I'm like this. I don't know how many of us there are. My parents didn't have any other family. Hardly any friends. They drilled into us that we had to keep the secret at all costs."

"You can't expect me to believe this." But how else could it be explained? Parker had seen it with his own eyes.

Adam raised his head. "All I can give you is the truth. This is the truth, Parker. This is who I am."

"I feel like I'm dreaming. This can't be real. First this virus turns people into monsters, and now you're a werewolf? I mean, that's crazy." Like a movie in his head, Parker saw it all again— Adam transformed into a hairy creature, killing the infected with a strength that couldn't possibly be normal. Or even human.

The next thing Parker knew, he was on the ground, his legs folded under him. Adam took a step toward him, his face pinched in concern.

"I'm fine." Parker waved a hand. "I guess I needed to sit down. This is the kind of news where people say, 'You should sit down.' So I am. And now I'm babbling, aren't I? Yeah. That's what I do. I babble."

Adam only watched him warily, hovering a few feet away with his arms stiffly at his sides.

It was as though someone had dumped a jigsaw puzzle into his head, and Parker was slowly piecing it together.

After a minute, he tried the words out loud. "You're a were-wolf." Somehow, it was seeming less crazy as he considered the strange little things about Adam that now made sense—the supersonic hearing and the sniffing for starters. "You're a were-wolf," he repeated.

"Yeah." Adam's voice was low and hoarse.

"Have you ever? Back on the road, that was…"

Adam held up his bloody hands, staring at them as if he'd never seen them before. "I've never killed anything. I never had to." He trembled all over. "It was like I was watching someone else do it. I let the instinct take over. I couldn't… They were going to kill you. I couldn't let them."

Guilt flared in Parker's gut. "I know I don't seem it, but I am grateful. Thank you."

"You don't have to be. I know you can't… I know I'm a freak." He closed his eyes, curling his fingers into fists. "I understand. I hated myself for so long," he whispered.

The urge to comfort drew Parker to his feet, and he stepped closer, a tentative hand reaching out but not touching. "I don't hate you. You're not a freak." He wanted to smooth out the creases in Adam's face where his eyes were squeezed shut and his mouth a taut line. "Adam, you're not." The wind whipped through the trees, rustling the leaves. "Let's go inside and talk."

"You can take the bike. You'll need it if you're on your own."

Parker thought he might be sick. He was still holding out his hand, and he drew it back. "You want me to go?"

Adam opened his eyes and finally met his gaze again. "No. I'd never want that. But I understand if you do."

Now that the shock had worn off—as much as it could considering he'd just discovered *werewolves were freaking real*—and Adam was himself again, the thought of leaving him was pretty much the worst thing Parker could think of.

"I want to stay together." He reached out again, and this time he snagged one of Adam's hands, not caring about the blood. He squeezed tightly. "Can we go inside now?"

Adam looked at him with wide eyes. "Okay."

Tugging Adam along, Parker approached the worn, unadorned cabin and tried the door, which creaked open. "Do you think I can use a flashlight?"

"Huh? Oh, uh…" After a moment, Adam continued. "Yeah. I can't hear anything nearby. Just some animals in the forest."

The slim flashlight's beam found one room with two bunk beds in the left corner, one against each wall. No fridge, and there didn't seem to be any electricity. A battered wooden table and four chairs sat in the middle of the room, a kerosene lantern resting on top. There was no bathroom, so there was likely an outhouse somewhere nearby.

"Hunters, probably," Parker noted. "Doesn't look as if there's been anyone here in quite a while." A layer of dust coated everything in the Spartan space.

Adam gripped Parker's hand, his gaze a little dazed. Parker led him to one of the chairs and gently pushed on his shoulder. "Sit down."

"I'm fine," Adam murmured, but it was clearly an automatic response.

"I know. Just sit." Parker hurried to tightly close the musty curtains on the one window. Using the flashlight, he uncovered boxes of supplies stashed under the beds. "Jackpot," he muttered.

Once he'd filled the lantern and lit it, he unscrewed a jug of water. He held it up to Adam, who obediently drank. Then Parker took a few gulps himself, marveling at how damn good tepid water could taste. Next, he filled a plastic wash basin and unwrapped a bar of soap.

Adam didn't argue as Parker eased him out of his boots, jacket, Henley, and jeans. In his briefs, he sat on the chair and let Parker scrub his hands clean. There was blood on his face and neck and splattered in his hair, and Parker tried not to think about what he'd looked like with fangs. *Fangs.*

It's okay. He's a werewolf. And that's okay. He's not a creeper. He's not going to eat my face. He's still Adam.

Parker rinsed off the blood, gently working his soapy fingers into Adam's hair, Adam pliant beneath him, his eyes open but unfocused. Parker wanted to ask a million questions, but he kept silent.

When Adam was clean, Parker peeled off his own shirt and knelt on the floor, scrubbing his face and hands in the low glow of the lantern. He sat back on his heels. "I guess we should get some rest?" There was so much more to say, but he wasn't sure Adam was in the right frame of mind. He likely wasn't either.

Adam nodded, and Parker took off his sneakers and jeans before shaking out the blankets folded at the end of one of the bottom bunks. He settled in, squeezing over on the mattress in his boxers and T-shirt.

But when Adam doused the lantern and walked over to the bunks, the floor creaking with his steps, he went to the other bed. Parker swallowed the surge of hurt that threatened to bring tears to his eyes and curled up under the scratchy blanket.

Even though Adam was only a few feet away, Parker felt utterly alone.

THE DARKNESS WAS absolute.

It had been at least an hour, and although Parker had screwed his eyes shut and willed himself to sleep, his brain had refused to shut off. He couldn't make out his hand in front of his face, and he wondered if it was worth the risk of keeping the lantern on low. He thought about the creepers, and their horribly wrong eyes and industrious teeth, and sighed. Not worth it. He pulled the scratchy, musty wool blanket up to his chin.

"You okay?"

Adam spoke quietly from the other bottom bunk a few feet away, but it seemed loud. Parker cleared his throat. "Yeah. It's just dark. But it's okay. You'll hear anything coming, right?"

"Yes." After a few beats of silence, he added, "I should have known those creepers were there on the road. I'm sorry."

"I'm the one who distracted you." Touching Adam had felt so natural, and now here they were in separate beds. Did Adam not want him now? Parker didn't know what to think, or how to feel. But in the dark, it somehow felt easier to talk, and Adam sounded more like himself again after kind of zoning out there for a bit. "So, you can hear things from pretty far away, huh?"

His question hung in the dank air so long that he thought Adam had fallen asleep or spaced again.

"I spent years trying to suppress it—my hearing and sense of smell. The vision I couldn't change, but I tried my best not to pay attention to my other senses. Tried to make them as…normal as possible."

"With your eyesight, is it like, you know, night vision goggles? I mean, what you see, is it like that?" He tried to keep his tone neutral.

This is totally normal. Just talking about special werewolf abilities. NBD. Ain't no thang.

"Something like that. I see movement much more sharply."

"But you've tried not to use your senses? Didn't they come in handy even before all this?"

After another prolonged silence, Adam answered. "I didn't want to be different. I had to hide who I really am. I couldn't take any chances."

"You never told *anyone*? What about Tina?"

"Yes. She's the only one I told who's still in my life." There was a brief silence. "Who was in my life."

Parker wanted to soothe him and say that he'd see Tina again, but couldn't push the pretty lie past his tongue. He cleared his throat. "Who else did you tell?"

There was another silence. And then he said, "My foster parents. After the accident, I bounced around a few homes. I was nine, and it's not easy to place older kids. Then I got lucky. The Taylors were really great. They already had four kids under the age of twelve. All fosters they'd adopted, or were adopting. They took me in, and it was good. For a while, at least. Before I messed it up."

"What happened?" Parker asked softly. In the darkness, a confessional mood had settled over them, and Parker was almost afraid to speak in case he broke it. He had a feeling Adam hadn't told anyone this. Adam was silent again, and Parker added, "I've messed up plenty of things, trust me. It's not just you."

"I told them the truth."

"Oh."

Adam exhaled a long breath. "At first, they thought I was acting out, or that I was coming unglued or something. PTSD. They said they'd take me to a therapist and we'd get to the bottom of it. That everything would be okay. They didn't believe me, which I understood. So I had to show them. I'd worked so hard since the accident to suppress it. The wolf."

Parker swallowed hard. "Is it like…a beast you can't control? Are you going to howl at the full moon and go feral?"

Holy shit, when is the next full moon?

There was a hint of amusement in Adam's voice. "Don't worry—it's only like that in movies. The moon doesn't affect me any more than it affects you. It's a myth."

"Oh. Really? Well, that's good to know. Okay, so going back to your foster parents. You had to show them. Did you, like, get all fangy and stuff?"

"A little. The fangs and the claws and the hair were already a lot for anyone to deal with, but when I transformed again after the first time in so long, I roared so loudly it shattered all the windows in the house. And a few next door."

"Whoa."

"The Taylors were terrified. I tried to explain, but I could see that they were afraid I'd hurt them, or the other kids. They didn't know what to do. They told me to never do anything like that again, and that everything would be fine. For a couple days, we pretended like it was, and that some freak storm had blown out the windows."

Forcing himself not to start babbling in the silence, Parker waited.

"But I knew I'd ruined it," Adam finally whispered. "They couldn't even look at me, and their hearts would pound when I came in the room. I could hear them. They'd seen the real me. They were scared. So I ran. I never saw them again. I ended up on the other side of the state in a group home."

"God. I'm sorry." Again, he wanted to reach out, but Adam had chosen to take the other bed. Parker was usually too pushy, and he didn't want to mess up. "What happened after that?"

"I bounced around group homes. Started getting into fights. Shoplifted and vandalized. I was angry and scared."

"And hurt."

Adam's voice was small. "Yeah."

"I'm sorry if I made you feel bad tonight." The guilt was acid in Parker's stomach. "I didn't mean to. I really didn't."

"It's not your fault. I'm a freak, Parker. I can't expect anyone to accept me once they know the truth."

"But I want to. I… It was scary. I'm not gonna lie. Seeing you sprout claws and fangs and a whole bunch of hair was really unexpected." He laughed with a healthy dose of hysteria. "Understatement of the year."

When Adam didn't speak, Parker kept talking, because of course he did. "I thought you were infected. In a split second, I thought that was it. That I was going to be on my own. I was going to lose you and probably die too. But I'm really glad I didn't lose you or die, and I'm just trying to process all this." He was silent for a moment as his brain whirred. "How many werewolves are there out there in the world? Are there vampires? Sasquatches? Loch Ness Monsters?"

"Not that I know of."

Parker wished he could see Adam in the darkness to see if he was smiling. He thought from his tone he might have been.

"As for werewolves, I'm not sure. Growing up, it was just my parents and sisters. They taught us to hide our true natures so we could go to school and be normal. I was too young to really wonder why we didn't know any other werewolves. They said there used to be packs of us, but that in-fighting decimated the population. Scattered us all around. They wanted to keep us separate. Safe. They told us if we ever thought there was another wolf there, we should leave and tell them right away. That it was vital for us to live normal lives and keep our secret."

"So you don't know, like, where you come from? How you exist?"

"Not really. I wish I'd asked more questions. I know Maddie and Christine did. They'd get in these fights with our parents sometimes, and I'd come home from Scouts or soccer and everything would be crazy tense. But they'd never tell me why. I guess I was still at the age when I wanted to please my parents more than I wanted to satisfy my curiosity." He was quiet for a moment. "Every once in a while over the years, I've felt like I could sense another wolf. Could smell something distinct that made my hair stand up and my nerves go raw."

"What did you do? Did you talk to them?"

Adam exhaled sharply. "No. I ran. Every time. I was too afraid. I'd managed to turn my life around, and I didn't want to mess it up with…werewolf stuff. I got a scholarship to Stanford. Spent all my spare time filming. God, I miss my camera."

"Where did you go to film?"

"Have you been to the Palace of Fine Arts?"

"No. It was on my sightseeing list, but I was too busy already with school." It was likely he'd never see it now, and regret waved through him.

"It's beautiful there. Gardens and paths weave through these grand stone outdoor structures. There's a huge rotunda and archways. A big pond. On pretty much every weekend in the summer, you can see couples getting their wedding pictures done there. There's often someone playing the harp. It's just…magical. Peaceful. I think something about that place made people open up. Made them happy to be alive. Happy to share little pieces of themselves with me. It was like…this little connection, and I had it on film forever."

"That sounds really nice." *Nice* didn't seem adequate, but Parker couldn't think of another word.

"I hate thinking of it overrun now. But I'm sure it is."

"Yeah. It sucks." There was another understatement. In the heavy silence, Parker thought back to what Adam had said about other werewolves. "So, I get that you'd gotten your life on track. But weren't you curious to meet people like you?"

"Of course."

"You didn't want to at least talk to any of them?"

"It wasn't as though I bumped into them often. It was rare. And I wasn't even sure exactly who they were. I got the sense when they were near, but they didn't have a neon sign flashing over their heads."

"But you could have figured it out if you tried?"

"Yes. Probably. If I actually talked to someone and shook their hand, I think I'd know right away. But..." He was quiet for a few moments, and then his voice was small. "But what if I found other werewolves, and they didn't like me? What if they didn't want anything to do with me?"

"That would have been awful," Parker answered quietly. "Yeah. I get it."

"And I had no way of knowing if they were friendly or not. They could have hurt me—ganged up on me if they wanted. So I kept to myself. Me and my camera."

He pondered it. "It was like, you could go and talk to people and connect with them, but stay separate. Protected. They shared with you, but you didn't have to give anything back." It sounded so damn lonely, but Parker would probably have felt the same way.

"Were you taking Psych one-oh-one too?" Adam asked dryly.

Parker smirked. "Dr. Freud, eat your heart out. I've got your number, Adam." His mind raced with questions. "So, that sense of smell—that's how you found me after we got separated?"

"Yeah. Took me longer than it should have, but the chlorine from the pool made it harder. And like I said, I'm rusty."

"Can you smell the creepers?"

"I'm starting to, now that I'm concentrating."

"What do they smell like?"

"Like people, but...wrong. They're still alive. I can hear their hearts beat, and their blood pump. But it's like the infection has rotted them from the inside out. It smells rancid. It's getting stronger, but I'm not sure if that's them or just that my senses are coming back."

"It's weird. Don't you feel like there should be more of them around? I know we saw lots of bodies of people who got killed, but maybe there are more survivors than we think. Maybe they got out somehow."

"Or the creepers are congregating somehow, and we haven't run into a really big group yet since we left campus."

Parker shuddered. "Let's hope my theory is the right one."

"Let's hope."

"What else can you do? I've seen the claws and super strength in action. Can you run really fast? Do you ever turn into an actual wolf?"

"You really want to hear all this?"

"Uh, *yeah*. Look, we're already dealing with sort-of zombies. We need to capitalize on all your mad werewolf skillz, yo."

"Did we travel in time back to two thousand and eight, homie?"

Parker's burst of laughter filled the stillness of the cabin. "I admit my street language is a little dated."

"I'll try not to throw any shade your way."

"Thank you. Okay, seriously. Spill."

"I guess along with the strength, claws, and fangs—and the heightened senses—I can heal quickly."

"Like, how fast?"

"It depends on the injury."

"What about a cut or a bruise?"

"About ten seconds," Adam answered.

"Totally healed?"

"Yep."

"Like it never happened?"

"Uh-huh."

"Wow." Parker upped the ante. "What if you got stabbed? Or shot?"

"I'm not sure. Maybe half an hour. It would depend."

"What would happen to the bullet?"

"My body would push it out."

"Seriously? That's kind of awesome."

Adam chuckled. "I guess."

It was so good to hear him laughing again. "No, it is. Time to embrace your abilities. It's awesome."

"If you say so."

"Can you turn into a wolf? Like, a full-on animal?"

Adam was quiet in a tense way. Finally, he said, "I never have. We can only do it when we're fully grown, so I couldn't try when my family was still alive. But it takes skill to manage it. Control it. Skills I don't have."

"Wait. You've never even tried? How is that possible? It would be so cool!"

Another silence. "If I didn't control it properly, it would be bad. I might hurt someone. *Kill* someone. I can't risk it." He blew out a breath. "And I'm afraid, okay? I'm afraid to try."

"Oh. Well, that makes sense. I'm sorry if I was a dick. It's just an exciting possibility." A thought occurred to Parker, and he changed the subject. "The night on campus when everything went down—how far away was your motorcycle?"

"Not that far. I can run fast, but I'm not the Flash or anything."

"Oh." Parker couldn't help but be disappointed. "But you're faster than a normal human? What about Usain Bolt? Dude, maybe he's a werewolf too."

"I suppose it's possible."

"Okay, what else? Tell me! Hey, wait—if you heal so easily, how did your family die in that accident?" He blurted it out before he could think better. "Shit, I'm sorry. I don't... You don't have to talk about it."

"It's okay."

Then it was silent, and still pitch black, and Parker wasn't sure if Adam was going to tell him or not. He was opening his mouth to apologize again when Adam started talking softly.

"We were coming home from my sister's hockey tournament.

We lived in Minnesota, and we were all hockey crazy. But Madison, she was really good. She played goalie for the boys' team because there was no older girls' league. Most girls her age were worried about whether someone would ask them to the homecoming dance, and who was dating who." He paused. "I guess I shouldn't say *most*. But Maddie never cared about all that stuff. She was a tomboy. Of course, she did have a huge crush on one of the boys on the team, but she'd never admit it to anyone. Not that it wasn't insanely obvious."

The affection in Adam's voice was palpable. Parker said, "I bet you were an annoying little brother and teased her mercilessly. It's our job as little brothers, after all."

"Yeah. I was ruthless. But we didn't fight much, me and Maddie and Christine. Sometimes, of course. The girls bickered with each other more than with me. But I think because of our family secret, it made us all closer. That night..." He swallowed audibly. "We were on our way home, and it was snowing. The roads were icy. Christine was bitching about wasting the weekend in another ice rink. She was in the middle in the back of the sedan between me and Maddie. I was getting bigger, and they were already tall. She kept elbowing me as she gestured. So I started elbowing her back."

"Sounds like me and Eric in the back seat." Parker pushed aside the ache.

"It all happened so fast." Adam's voice was barely a whisper. "My parents were telling us to knock it off, and Christine took my little video game thing and tossed it by Maddie's feet. I was so pissed. I took off my seat belt and squeezed onto the floor to reach the game. Then my mom slammed on the brakes, but it was too late."

Parker held his breath.

"It was so loud. Metal screeching above me and glass shattering. I was lying there on my sisters' feet, and my ears were ringing.

Maddie and Christine weren't moving, and it was dark. I tried to move, but I was jammed between their legs and the front seats. Outside, there was a man on the phone, and he kept repeating, 'Oh my god, oh my god' over and over. Then there were sirens in the distance. Other than that, it was so quiet. Too quiet…"

He trailed off and breathed harshly. "I realized I could only hear my own heartbeat, and I could smell so much blood. Could feel it wet on me. It was like I could taste it. I tried to scream, or shout, but I couldn't breathe. I was trapped until the fire truck got there to cut me out."

His heart breaking for Adam, Parker waited, blinking back tears.

"There was a tractor trailer stuck in the right-hand lane. I heard later that it had broken down, and the driver had just gotten out to put up the flares when we crashed into the back. My sisters and I distracted her with our arguing, and my mom didn't see it until it was too late. We drove right under it, and the top of the car was sheared almost clean off."

Stomach clenching, Parker murmured, "Jesus." Although it was pitch black, he screwed his eyes shut as if he could erase the mental picture of the accident.

They were probably decapitated.

"Your family, they… The injuries were too bad even for healing?"

"They died instantly."

There was nothing Parker could say, since everything that popped into his head sounded unbearably trite. He climbed out of bed, feeling his way over to the other bunk with his arms outstretched.

"Are you sure?" Adam whispered.

Parker felt for the wooden frame and squeezed onto the thin mattress as Adam shifted over and their arms went around each other. Parker rested his head on Adam's chest, and Adam pulled the blanket over him.

"I'm sorry," he whispered into the cotton of Adam's T-shirt. Adam's grip around him was almost painful, but Parker didn't mind at all. He burrowed into Adam's heat, hoping he was giving some of his own.

"Thank you." Adam's fingers skimmed over Parker's ear.

"We're stuck with each other, remember?"

He felt the press of Adam's lips on the top of his head, and they held tight as the night wore on.

Parker was almost asleep when a question tumbled out. "If it's always your choice, then tonight, you chose to...transform."

"I couldn't let them hurt you."

That Adam had exposed his deepest, darkest secret to save Parker made his heart skip a beat, and he fumbled for Adam's hand, twining their fingers together as sleep finally came.

Chapter Eleven

PARKER WOKE SLOWLY, aware of an all-over ache and a cramp in his right leg. He realized the former was from falling off the back of a motorcycle, and the latter was from sleeping curled on his side on the thin mattress. But he couldn't really move because Adam was spooning him, their T-shirts bunched up between them.

The events of the previous night rushed back, and his stomach flip-flopped. He was being spooned by a *werewolf.*

More than that, he had morning wood in his boxers, and he could feel Adam was hard too. In this brave new post-werewolf world, some things had definitely stayed the same. Maybe he and Adam could…

Am I crazy? Should I be having sex with a werewolf? What if there's some freaky stuff I still don't know about?

Sure, Adam had seemed normal when they got off before, but now Parker's mind was filled with visions of fangs and claws and hair.

Or had it been fur?

Weirdly enough, his erection swelled.

He blinked in the murky light at a knot of wood in the cabin wall. He couldn't tell if Adam was awake or not. Adam wouldn't hurt him. Of that, Parker was certain. And he still wanted to be with Adam. Of that, Parker was also certain. Before he could fully organize his sleepy thoughts, Adam yawned.

"Hi."

With difficulty, Parker maneuvered onto his other side, nearly taking out Adam's eye with his elbow. "Hi."

Adam watched him carefully. "Are we…good?"

In reply, Parker leaned in and kissed him soundly. Adam drew him closer, his arms around Parker's back. "I really do like this kissing thing," Parker murmured.

A tentative smile played on Adam's lips. "In the station—was that really your first kiss?"

"Aside from when Amber Hardy laid one on me during a particularly competitive game of spin the bottle in seventh grade. She slipped me the tongue, and I almost choked on it."

The gust of Adam's laughter tickled Parker's nose. "Smooth."

"Yup. But I think I'm getting the hang of it now." He kissed Adam again, then moved lower, shimmying down to pull Adam's hardening cock out of his tight briefs.

"You still want to?" Adam blurted. His cheeks reddened. "Even though you know?"

"Adam, you could be a lesbian vampire succubus who moonlights as a golem and I would still want to suck your cock twenty-four-seven."

A laugh burst out of Adam, and he looked achingly young. Tenderly, he brushed back Parker's hair. "You really do have a way with words, you kn—"

The rest of the sentence was lost on a moan as Parker swallowed him almost to the root. He spread Adam's legs and got him on his back, kneeling between them as he tasted the musky heat of Adam's cock. Mindful of the upper bunk above them, Parker stayed hunched over, kneading Adam's muscular thighs as he sucked him.

There was nothing outwardly different about Adam. He still gripped the mattress and moaned softly as Parker teased the ridge on the underside of his shaft before licking his balls. Even though Parker had seen what he could become, he was still just Adam, and Parker wanted more than anything to make him feel good.

He nuzzled at Adam's sac. "You like my mouth?"

Panting, Adam murmured a yes.

"You want to fuck it?"

With a low groan that was almost a growl, Adam took hold of Parker's head. Parker planted his hands on the mattress. "Yeah. Like that. Do it." When Adam paused, he met his gaze. "I trust you."

Digging in his heels, Adam lifted his hips with a moan. He clutched Parker's head, keeping him in place as he thrust into his mouth. Parker concentrated on breathing through his nose and keeping relaxed, letting Adam in as deeply as he could. Adam was pulling his hair, and Parker's eyes were watering, saliva dripping from the corners of his mouth.

And he loved it. He was painfully hard in his boxers, and he shoved them down to free his dick and tug it.

Adam was almost whining now, his eyes locked on where his shaft disappeared over and over into Parker's mouth. When he came, his rhythm stuttered, and he splashed over Parker's face. With a small cry, Adam painted Parker's cheeks and mouth. It dripped down to his chin, and Parker swiped at it with his tongue.

Then Adam was kissing him like his life depended on it, messily licking up his own spunk and shoving it into Parker's mouth with his tongue. It was salty and bitter, and Parker swallowed every bit he could. He'd always loved swallowing, and with Adam it was even better somehow. Everything was better.

Adam flopped back and urged Parker up to straddle his face, opening his mouth wide. Parker was only too pleased to oblige and fucked Adam's mouth in return, clutching one of the slats on the top bunk as he worked his hips. It didn't even take thirty seconds before he shot down Adam's throat, shuddering as his toes curled.

They kissed again, and Parker could taste them both now.

Adam ran his hands up Parker's sides, and then he shoved his face into Parker's hairy armpit and inhaled deeply.

Parker couldn't bite back a giggle. "Ticklish, dude."

Of course, then Adam was tickling him in earnest, his fingers under Parker's T-shirt and feather-light over his ribs. Parker smacked his head on the upper bunk trying to get away, but Adam kissed it better, so in the end it was a win.

THEY WERE DRESSING when Parker blurted out a question that popped into his mind. "Do you bite people and turn them into werewolves too? I mean, can you? Not that you *do*. I'm sure you don't run around biting people."

Adam smiled stiffly. "No, I don't bite people, and even if I did, I can't turn them into werewolves. My parents told us all that stuff in movies isn't true. It's genetic. We're just like everyone else. You were born a human. Bears are bears. Dogs are dogs. Werewolves are werewolves. We can't bite people and change them."

"Oh, okay. That makes sense. I was just curious. I wasn't trying to say you'd bite me or anything. I know you wouldn't."

Sighing, Adam ran a hand through his hair. "I'm being defensive. Sorry. I'm not used to talking about this."

"It's cool. I get it. Well, I might have to ask more questions in pursuit of getting it, but getting it is my ultimate goal."

"I know." Adam zipped up his jeans and kissed Parker softly. "Most people would have run for their lives by now," he murmured.

"I guess I'm not most people."

"Lucky for me."

Parker couldn't help but preen.

I am a pretty awesome boyfriend, it's true. Whoa. Boyfriend?

Adam frowned. "What's going on in that head of yours?"

"The usual overthinking." He waved his hand dismissively. "Standard issue. You'll get used to it. Okay, we'd better get on the road. There's a gas can in that storage box out back. Hunters probably bring ATVs up here. We can fill up, at least."

As they left the cabin, the sun was peeking over the horizon through the trees. Adam tossed Parker the keys. "You should practice driving for real." He strapped on the backpack.

"Hey, what about the shotgun?" Parker stood in the cabin door and glanced back. The gun and box of shells rested on the old table.

"Leave it for someone else. Once it's out of shells, it's useless, and... I don't need it. It was really just for show."

"Right. Okay." Claws and super strength did seem quite effective against the creepers.

"Unless you want it?"

"Nah. I'll stick to my machete." Parker pulled the door shut and tossed the motorcycle keys from hand to hand. "I've still got the pistol just in case. It's a lot lighter than the shotgun."

Adam motioned to the bike. "It's all yours."

With a deep breath, Parker straddled the red metal and chrome. He put in the key and went through the steps Adam had taught him to turn on the bike. He patted its console. "Okay, Mariah. Sing me a sweet song. Do you have any favorites, Adam? I assume you must. Let me try and guess."

Adam rolled his eyes. "Whatever. She's got a great voice."

"I'm not denying that! My mom loves her, and I may or may not know all the words to the *Daydream* album. I was too young to know any better. I was brainwashed, really. But Mariah's got pipes. That I will admit."

Adam's tone was wistful. "My mom liked her too."

He climbed on and wrapped his arms around Parker's waist, his thighs powerful against Parker's hips. It felt good to have Adam pressed up against him, and it sent heat through Parker's veins even though they'd just gotten off.

Hmm. Maybe they could fool around a bit more, since it wasn't like they had a strict schedule to follow, aside from penciling in: *Don't get eaten by creepers.*

Then he thought of his mom humming "Always Be My Baby" as she cut his toast into soldiers he could dip into his eggs. He had to get home.

Parker took a deep breath and revved the engine. "Hold on to your butts," he shouted as they shot forward, since quoting Samuel L. Jackson was always, *always* the right thing to do.

BY LATE AFTERNOON, they were skirting Yosemite, looking for a way into the park that wasn't clogged with creepers. They'd beaten a hasty retreat from the one entrance they'd tried and now headed north on a paved road. The odd time, Adam picked up the sound of another vehicle or people in the area, but they had only seen bodies. It was frightening how normal that was becoming.

Parker had never been to Yosemite, and the sheer rock faces and sparkling lakes were breathtaking. As they drove around a corner and a new vista unfurled—a waterfall cliff that jutted out over a swath of green, the water thundering, Parker's breath caught. The sun shone, reflected in the water, and a rainbow arced through the sky.

For a moment, he could only stare, soaking it in as he let up on the throttle. The absurd thought that they should take a picture flitted through his mind, and the magic evaporated. How could he be admiring the view when so many people were dead or infected? When his parents, brother, and friends could be?

Behind him, Adam asked, "Okay?" He squeezed Parker's thigh. "That rainbow is amazing, huh?"

"Yeah." He concentrated on a light tone. "I keep waiting for a cop to pull us over for not wearing helmets." He'd gotten the hang of driving the bike, and he honestly felt like a bit of a badass.

Adam snorted. He spoke loudly so Parker could hear, even though Parker could talk in a normal voice and Adam heard every word just fine. "I wish they would. Wouldn't mind seeing a cop or twenty out here. Either they're hiding, they're dead, they're infected, or they're planning some amazing creeper takedown."

"Oh, like the SWAT team, maybe? Any second now, they'll swoop in and take out all the creepers, and we'll never have to hear that godawful sound they make again."

"Yep. Any second now. Or Thor and Iron Man are going to arrive and save the day."

Grinning, Parker nodded. "With the Hulk. And Hawkeye, although I dunno how much help he is with just those arrows."

"He's hot. That's help enough."

Parker laughed. "True, true. But fuck, man. Looks like we might never see that next *Avengers* movie."

"I guess not."

It made his stomach churn to really think about how completely different the world was going to be if this pandemic was everywhere. Eric had said it was in London, so it could well be in the rest of Europe. And if it was in Europe, it could spread to Asia even if Asia hadn't been targeted.

Considering how quickly it had spread in the US, bioterrorism seemed to make the most sense. But to accomplish *what*? For all they knew it was on every continent. If it wasn't, it didn't seem like any of their allies were in a rush to come help.

"What's wrong?" Adam rubbed a hand over Parker's thigh.

He realized he'd tensed up and tried to relax as he slowed to take a curve on the tree-lined road. "Just thinking." Their lives had already been hugely turned upside down, but there would be all the little changes too. The shit they took for granted, like superhero movies.

If he pondered it too much, he wanted to cry. He forced a light tone. "What do you think happened in Hollywood? Like, are Clooney and Pitt twitching their way through the hills with bug eyes, trying to eat the Botoxed face of every starlet they come across?"

"It would be only fair, really."

"Maybe Hollywood was contained, and they can keep making movies and TV shows. I was really looking forward to that next sequel."

"And we'll never get to see—" Adam broke off and gripped Parker's waist harder, digging in his fingers. "Slow down. People ahead."

Parker let up on the throttle. As they went around the next corner, he saw the people. More importantly, he saw the two pickup trucks parked across the road, nose to nose. "Fuck. This gives me a bad feeling." He slowed even more.

"Stay on the bike." Adam still sounded calm. "Get ready to go without me." Then he was fiddling with the pocket of Parker's jacket, pushing something heavy inside. "The safety's on. It's loaded."

"I'm not going without you! What the fuck?" Parker's heart thumped.

"In case this goes bad. I'll catch up. I'm fast, remember?"

"But—"

"Just be ready."

Parker wanted to crawl out of his skin as they approached the trucks. To the right was a small clearing with a few more vehicles. He counted four men and one woman. One of the men walked onto the road, a shotgun leaning casually on his shoulder.

He had dark hair and was about thirty, wearing jeans and a plaid shirt. Parker stopped twenty feet away. He didn't like the man on sight.

"Hi there, boys," the man said. He smiled and spat onto the

blacktop. "How goes it?"

"Fine," Parker replied warily. "You know, there's this whole sort-of zombie attack thing happening. But other than that, we're great. How are you folks doing?"

The man's teeth gleamed. "Making the best of it. We've claimed this land. Have a whole community sprouting up over yonder." He nodded to indicate the forest.

Adam was a wall of tension behind Parker, and Parker struggled to keep his voice light. "That's great. We're just passing through, so. Good luck to you all. Be careful. There were a lot of creepers at the park entrance. They're attracted to light, so keep them off at night."

"Is that right?" He spat again. "Thanks for the tip. Where you headed?"

"East Coast. I have family there." Although he didn't trust this guy as far as he could throw him, he couldn't resist asking, "Have you heard anything about what's going on out there?"

"Nothing concrete. But we've got a ham radio and antenna, and word is this shit's all over the damn place. Had to be coordinated. Guy down in Mexico said they're just as fucked as we seem to be."

"Anyone know why?" Parker asked. "I mean, what's there to gain?"

His smile was sharp. "I guess the strong will survive. Maybe the good Lord's got a plan for us like he did for Noah."

Parker tried to laugh, although he was afraid the man was serious. "Maybe. Well, we'll get going now. Take care."

"Sure, sure." The man pulled keys from his pocket. "We'll back up here and let you through."

The shoulders were narrow, and the huge trucks blocked the entire road. There was a ditch on each side, and Parker wasn't confident about taking the bike into one of them. He smiled. "Great. Thanks." Maybe it would be okay and they could just go on their way.

The guy pivoted by the truck. "Say, that's a fine ride you boys have there."

Shit. "Um, thanks. We really should keep moving." Adam was vibrating behind him, and Parker thought he could hear a low growl.

"Must come in handy having a bike, huh?" The man appeared only mildly interested, but Parker could feel the weight of other eyes on them as well.

The others came closer, too casually, and Parker's gut clenched. "So, uh, like I said—"

"Get out of our way." Adam's guttural command hung in the air. "Now."

All eyes turned to him as he stepped off the bike. He appeared still and calm, yet there was a menace pulsating in him that made the hair on Parker's neck stand up. The others could clearly sense it too.

One of the men cleared his throat and spoke to the man in the road. "Joe, maybe we should let these fellas be on their way."

Joe, the obvious leader, gritted his teeth, his gaze locked with Adam's. "Sure. Just get off that bike and you're free to go."

Adam moved so quickly Parker barely knew what was happening as Joe was hurled into a tree, his shotgun flying in the other direction. There was a moment of stunned silence before the rest of the group cried out, the men disarmed and scattered with a roar.

Adam's fangs and claws were out, his eyes bright gold as the hair spread over his cheeks. He was still wearing the backpack with their gear, and Parker hoped he wouldn't bust the straps.

The young woman had a gun in her raised hand, and it trembled violently. Parker aimed his pistol at her. "We just want to leave."

Mouth agape, she stared at Adam and his extended claws.

"Sweet Jesus."

"Put the gun down," Parker ordered.

Blinking, she lowered her arm as if she hadn't realized the weapon was in her hand. She stared back and forth between Adam and Parker. "Sweet Jesus," she repeated.

Parker gunned the engine. "Come on."

Still wolfed out, Adam took the front of one of the trucks and gave it a mighty shove into the ditch. Then he climbed back onto the motorcycle behind Parker, pressing against him.

"Wait!" the woman cried. "Was that true what you said? About the light?"

"Yes," Parker answered, his gun still trained on her just in case. "And don't we have enough problems with the creepers without this bullshit?"

She nodded. "I'm sorry."

He shoved the gun in his pocket and tore off down the road with Adam's hot breath on his neck. Blood rushed in his ears, and the throbbing of the engine between his thighs went straight to his dick.

He'd actually *held a gun* on someone, and he'd been so fucking afraid, but they'd made it. Those assholes didn't know who they were dealing with. Parker realized he was *smiling*.

He put ten miles behind them before veering off on a dirt road. It was darker here, the trees growing close overhead, and they bounced along until the road ended at a lookout high above a lake. The sun was almost at the horizon, glowing orange and reflecting on the water below.

There were a hundred things Parker wanted to say as he jumped off Mariah and turned to Adam, whose fangs, claws, and extra hair had receded. But there was still something different about him as he came down from his transformation—a dark, dangerous rumble to him that made Parker want to hump his leg even more than usual.

"That was... You were..." Parker's blood sang. There was so much adrenaline pumping through him that he thought he might burst.

Adam kept his gaze on his hands as he dismounted. "I know. I'm so ugly like that, but those people were—"

Parker launched himself at Adam, kissing him hard. "More like so fucking hot," he muttered, hitching up one leg so he could *actually hump him.*

He swallowed Adam's surprised yelp, and then Adam yanked him closer, shoving his thigh between Parker's and gripping his ass. They were all tongues and teeth as they kissed messily, hands all over each other. Lust burned through Parker, and he gasped for air. Denim rubbed together as they got hard.

"I want you so much," Parker mumbled. He unzipped his jacket, mindful of the gun in the pocket as he dropped the jacket to the ground. His gray tee was sweaty, and Adam lifted Parker's arm so he could stick his face in his armpit. Maybe it should have been weird, but it made Parker feel good. With a groan, Adam gripped Parker's hips.

"You want me?" he whispered in Adam's ear, one hand tight in his hair. "You want to fuck me?" He'd never dirty-talked like this before. With Greg he'd kept his mouth shut, afraid he'd say the wrong thing and make Greg mad.

But with Adam, he felt free. So powerful. So *alive.* "Want to shove that big cock in me?"

Adam full-on growled, a low snarl of need and possession that made Parker leak in his boxers. With considerable effort, Parker pulled back an inch to speak. "Nothing around for miles, right? No people or creepers?"

Closing his eyes, Adam turned his head to both sides and inhaled deeply before blowing it out. "Nothing."

"So, we could keep going. Or you could bend me over that picnic table."

In a blink, Adam hoisted Parker right off his feet. He wrapped his legs around Adam's waist and kissed him desperately as Adam strode to the table and deposited him on top. Adam tugged off the backpack, and they both moaned as they kissed again, rubbing together.

Parker was so hard he thought he might come in his pants just from rutting. He gulped in a breath. "You need to fuck me now." He shoved at Adam's chest so he could stand at the side of the table and turn around.

He yanked at the zipper and button on his jeans and shoved them down with his boxers before pulling off his T-shirt and leaning over the wooden table. It hadn't been painted in a few years but was smooth enough, and he bunched the tee at his belly where he bent over the side.

Parker propped himself on his elbows and spread his legs as far as he could with his pants around his ankles. He glanced over his shoulder and found Adam with his own jeans and briefs down, his meaty cock hard and leaking in his grasp. But he seemed frozen, staring at Parker with parted lips.

"Do you want a written invitation or something?" Parker pushed his hips back.

Adam spread his palms over Parker's ass, running them up to his shoulders. Goosebumps spread over Parker's skin as the cool breeze flowed over him along with Adam's fevered touch, and then Adam was kissing down his spine, his mouth hot and wet and open. Parker mumbled, "Yes, yes."

He was so *exposed*, and even though he knew there was no one around, it still felt dangerously daring to be fucking out in the open with the setting sun warming them. In this moment, there were only the two of them in the world.

When Adam sank to his knees and buried his face in Parker's ass, spreading him wide, Parker shuddered and cried out. Then Adam's tongue was pushing inside him, and it was the greatest thing he'd ever felt. He'd never been rimmed before, and the way Adam ate him out was feral and almost unbearably intense.

Adam worked him open with his mouth, and Parker could only moan and flop down, his arms already giving out. He pressed his cheek to the table, and he might get splinters, but he didn't fucking care because his ass was alive with pleasure.

And they'd survived. Nothing else mattered.

He protested when Adam's mouth left him, but he could hear Adam rummaging in their pack, and soon his slick finger pushed into Parker's hole. Maybe he'd used the little tube of salve Parker had lifted from the ranger station, but it didn't really matter because he was working some kind of magic, easing his finger in farther and farther, and then squeezing a second one in too. Then a third. It burned, but Parker wanted more.

Parker had fingered himself plenty of times, but he'd only had a dick in his ass twice. He hadn't come either time, since Greg Mason was an epic douche and hadn't lasted more than two minutes—and had been out the door as soon as he'd tossed the condom.

He thought of Adam's thick, uncut cock, and Parker's mouth watered. "Please. Fuck me, Adam."

He didn't give a shit about condoms since they were both tested, and Adam didn't even get sick, and the world was a disaster area, so *fuck it*. He was alive now, and he wanted this. He held his breath as Adam pushed inside, the stretch flaring into searing pain.

"Breathe," Adam murmured, stroking Parker's hair with one hand, the other tight on his hip.

Parker forced his lungs to expand, closing his eyes as he concentrated on *in and out, in and out.*

Trembling, Adam inched inside. "Good," he gritted out. He was clearly holding back as much as he could.

When he was all the way in and Parker could feel his balls against him, Parker moved his hips experimentally and squeezed his butt muscles.

Groaning, Adam tightened his fingers in Parker's hair. "Fuck. You're so tight."

"Do I feel good?" He craned his neck to see Adam's face.

"Perfect." Adam's eyes gleamed, and his lips were slack. "I need… God, Parker."

"Do it. Fuck me." The burning was fading, and Parker pushed back. "I want it. Want you."

He didn't have to ask twice, and Adam began thrusting, shallowly at first. Then he was going deeper with long, hard strokes. He still gripped Parker's hair, and Parker loved it, the feeling of being held down, of being filled so completely. His dick had gone a little soft from the earlier pain, but now it was straining.

"It feels so good. Want you to fuck me forever."

Adam was panting, his hips slapping against Parker's ass. On one of the strokes he rubbed against Parker's prostate, and Parker cried out, making nonsensical noises that weren't really words. There were sparks behind his eyes, actual bursts of color as Adam pounded him, and he was flushed and sweaty all over.

The mix of pleasure and pain had tipped firmly to the side of mind-blowing joy, and Parker heaved himself up on one elbow so he could jerk his cock. It only took three strokes before the tingling in his balls pin-wheeled through his body and he shot, his whole body shaking with the release.

All he could do was collapse back down as Adam continued thrusting with low moans. Parker's mouth was dry, and he licked his lips as he looked back. "I wanna feel you come inside me. I want you to fill me up with everything you've got, and—"

Eyes blazing before he threw his head back, Adam came in long spurts. His hips stuttered with his release, and it was hot and deep inside Parker. It felt like something they were meant to do— like his ass was made for Adam's cum, and Adam was marking him the way animals did.

His breath hot and chest heaving, Adam bent over him, his dry lips gentle on the back of Parker's neck as he ran his fingers through Parker's sweat-damp hair. As the stars twinkled into view, they stayed slumped together with Adam still twitching inside him.

"Parker," Adam breathed, and it sounded so tender. Parker reached for Adam's hand, and they clasped their fingers together.

When Adam finally pulled out, Parker could feel the wetness dripping down his inner thighs. It should have been gross, but instead, he found himself wondering how long they had to wait until they did it again. He shivered as Adam smoothed his fingers over his swollen hole, swirling the sticky mess around.

Adam cleaned him up with some kind of cloth—probably one of their T-shirts from the backpack—and pressed little kisses to Parker's ass cheeks.

"Was it too rough?" His breath whispered across Parker's skin, and he rubbed his hands up and down Parker's legs.

Boneless, all Parker could say was the truth. "It was everything."

Chapter Twelve

THEY WERE IN the heart of the Nevada Badlands when they passed a sign for Highway Fifty, proclaiming it: *The loneliest road in America.* Parker muttered, "Let's hope so."

It lived up to its billing until a vehicle appeared on the horizon of the two-lane blacktop.

Parker squinted at the new addition to the landscape. The sun blazed overhead, and he was thankful they'd picked up sunglasses at an abandoned gas station. He called back to Adam. "People."

"Yeah."

They'd settled into a routine of taking turns driving, with Adam always driving in the dark so they could keep the headlight out. It was slower going than with a car since riding a motorcycle took more energy and focus, especially for Parker.

They slept as little as they could and tried to make good time. Still, they'd hit mountains soon, and there was no telling how long it would take to make it across the country with all the potential threats in their path.

"Should we try to avoid them? Go off the road? Obviously they've seen us, but they can't follow far. Looks like they're in a minivan."

"I guess we can't avoid people forever," Adam answered.

"Guess not. I hope this goes better than last time."

"Would be hard for it to go worse."

Parker groaned. "And now you jinxed it. Knock on wood!"

Adam reached up and rapped his knuckles on Parker's skull.

"Ha, ha. You're hilarious."

He eased off on their speed as the minivan neared. It appeared to be slowing too, and halted about twenty feet away. Parker rolled to a stop but kept the engine running. Through the minivan windshield, he could see an older man and woman. They all watched each other uneasily, until Parker raised his hand and called out, "Hi."

The couple exchanged a glance, and then the man in the passenger seat opened his door and stepped out. He wore a Tilley hat and a windbreaker over slacks, and Parker was struck by a memory of his grandpa heading out for a weekend sail. Grandpa had died years ago, but in that moment, Parker missed him intensely.

The man waved. "Hello there."

Adam remained silent and tense behind him, so Parker cleared his throat. "I'd ask how it's going, but I don't suppose it's going much better for you than it is for us."

A smile tugged at the man's lips. "I don't suppose so, son. Look, we don't mean you any harm, and we don't have anything of value. We'd like to talk if you're amenable to that."

He sounded like his grandpa too. Parker glanced back at Adam, who nodded. Parker turned off the engine, and the minivan rattled down as well. He climbed off, Adam following closely on his heels, and neared the man with his hand extended.

The man shook his hand warmly. "I'm Charlie." He led the way back and opened the side door of the minivan. "That's my wife Annette behind the wheel, our grandchildren Nora and Hannah, and in the back are Rebecca and her two boys, Logan and Dylan."

Annette's silver hair was cropped to her chin, and her smile was tentative. The kids ranged in age from about eight to twelve, and Rebecca looked around thirty. Parker waved at the group. "Hey. I'm Parker. This is Adam." He nudged Adam, who raised his hand in greeting. "We came from the Bay area. Where are you from?"

"Just outside Vegas," Charlie answered. "The kids had dentist appointments. Their parents work in the city at the casinos, so Annette and I said we'd take them." He shook his head and spoke softly. "We waited as long as we could, but it was spreading like wildfire. The whole city was just…"

Parker thought of visiting the Vegas Strip with his family when he was a kid. Going up the fake Eiffel Tower and watching the fountains outside the Bellagio, eating his weight in shrimp cocktail at the buffet and slopping seafood sauce all down his shirt. "I'm sorry."

"We left a note for them. Just in case." Charlie motioned to the back of the minivan. "We met Rebecca and the boys on the way."

"Where are you headed?" Adam asked.

"We have a cabin. Northern California, closer to Oregon. It's isolated, and we thought… Well, we thought it's worth a try."

Parker nodded. "Better than just sitting around, right? We're going to Boston. Cape Cod. My family's there."

Charlie sighed. "I'm not sure that's a good idea. Seems the East Coast was hit awfully hard from what people say. It's all gossip and rumor at this point. We scan the radio band, searching for any signals. Sometimes we hear people talking. No one's saying anything good."

Parker tried to smile. "I know. We're just hoping… Well, I have to try. The Cape might be okay."

"Maybe," Charlie said.

In the awkward silence, one of the girls piped up. "I'm huuungry."

"Why don't we have a picnic? Are you boys hungry?" Annette asked.

"We never say no to food. Right, Adam?" Parker nudged him again, and Adam nodded.

They helped spread out a blanket on the shoulder of the road and sat with the kids while the other adults perched in the open minivan. Annette passed out sandwiches—actual fresh sandwiches!—and Parker groaned as he bit into it. "Oh my god, this is the best tuna salad ever. Where did you get this bread?"

"Rebecca made it yesterday in a house we stayed in. She's quite the baker," Charlie replied.

Rebecca waved her hand. "Bread's easy as long as you have yeast."

"It's amazing," Adam added before taking another big bite.

As they ate, Parker focused on enjoying every morsel. His grandma had always said to cherish the little things in life, which was easy for her to say since she'd been stinking rich. But now more than ever, Parker wanted to enjoy the little things—like tuna salad on fresh, soft bread.

"What if your family's not there?" one of the boys asked. "What if it's all zombies out there?"

"*Logan*," Rebecca said sharply.

"What?" Logan's cheeks flushed. "It's not like they don't know that's what could happen. I'm just wondering what they'll do then."

Parker tried to think of something to say but had no answer.

"Then we'll figure something out," Adam said. He sat close to Parker and leaned in with his shoulder.

"I'm sure it will be fine. We'll all be fine. This too shall pass," Annette said. She smiled, but it didn't quite reach her eyes.

One of the girls—Hannah?—asked, "Do you know why this is happening?"

"I wish we did," Parker answered. "Seems like it's some kind of infection. A pandemic, the news called it before… Before the news stopped. The creepers, they're not dead. Not like what we think of as zombies. It seems like they're still alive, but they don't know who they are anymore."

"How do you know that they aren't dead? Or undead, or whatever? Did you get right up close to one?" Rebecca asked.

"Yeah, unfortunately. They seem to be alive. But we're not sure what caused the infection. We've heard it might have been intentional."

"Like a weapon," Charlie said flatly.

"Yeah. But we don't know for sure."

"If it was a biological weapon, I just can't imagine what's in it for them." Annette chewed thoughtfully. "Seems like it would destroy more than just America. Canada, Mexico. Down into South America."

"I suppose anyone who would create something like this might not care about the consequences," Adam noted. "Or maybe that's their goal: annihilation."

They were all silent for a few moments. *Annihilation.* It did seem to be the likely outcome, no matter what the intention. Parker supposed the why and even the how didn't really matter now. What mattered was surviving.

"Do you think it's all over the world?" Logan asked.

"I know it was in London. It could very well be in other places too." Thinking about it was so fucking depressing. Even if Eric was alive, they'd probably never see each other again. Even if one of them got across the ocean, finding each other was a whole new ballgame. Parker's appetite was gone, and he had to blink rapidly to get back in control.

"If it wasn't, I think they'd have come by now. The Europeans. Wouldn't they have come? Their troops? Ships?" Charlie wondered.

Parker realized he hadn't really thought about it after the first couple days. They'd all hoped the army would rescue them, and maybe they still would. Maybe ships and aircraft carriers and submarines would save the day. But until that day came, Parker was operating on the assumption that they were on their own.

"They might have us under quarantine. They might be waiting to see how the infection plays out," Adam said.

"That's a good point. Maybe they're waiting." Annette smiled softly. "Still hope, right?"

Parker returned her smile as best he could. "Always."

"Creepers. That's a good name," Logan said.

"Yeah. We heard it from someone else." Parker wondered how Dave and his companion had fared down south at Big Sur.

"They seem to like the light," Charlie said. "I don't think they see very well, even though their eyes are…well, you've seen them. At night, the light whips them into a frenzy. Who can say why."

"We noticed that too." Adam took a sip from their water bottle. "Now that I think about it, you're right about the daylight. It doesn't have the same effect."

"Creeeeeeepers." Logan tugged on Nora's pigtail. "Don't let the creepers get you tonight."

Rebecca smacked his arm and sighed. "How is that funny?"

With a shrug, Logan said, "Sorry, Mom," and walked into the desert. He started chucking rocks.

Parker was having a hard enough time dealing with it, and he couldn't imagine what it was like for the kids. They sat in awkward silence before Parker cleared his throat. "Thank you so much for lunch. I guess we should get going."

The women insisted on giving Parker and Adam sandwiches for the road, and they didn't refuse. Charlie neatly tore a piece of paper from a notebook. He clicked a ballpoint pen and scribbled.

"I'll give you the address and directions to the cabin in California. Just in case you ever come back west and are looking for some friendly faces."

Parker took the folded paper. "Thank you. It was great meeting you all. Restored my faith in humanity. It was a little shaken."

Charlie clapped him on the shoulder. "You too, son. Good luck to both of you. Oh, can we top up your tank? We loaded up on gas jugs. You've got a bit of an empty stretch coming."

"That would be great," Adam replied. "Thank you so much."

It was Adam's turn to drive, and Parker strapped on the pack over his machete and climbed on Mariah behind him. As they continued east, he glanced back every so often at the disappearing minivan getting smaller and smaller, until it was just him and Adam and the loneliest road in America.

GRABBING AT ADAM'S jacket, his gloves slipping on the leather, Parker jerked his head up.

"Okay?" Adam called.

"Yeah." Parker's heart raced, and he took a deep breath. "No. We need to stop. I'm going to fall asleep and end up as roadkill."

Adam slowed the motorcycle. "There's nothing for at least…twenty miles or so."

"That's okay. We can camp out. I just… Shit, I need to sleep. It's catching up with me."

In the darkness, Adam eased off the road. When he cut the engine, it was silent but for the wind whistling across the barren earth. The temperature drop at night in the desert was extreme, and Parker shivered. "That winter outdoor blanket from the sports store sure is coming in handy." He pulled it from the backpack and unfolded it. "It's weird. That was what? A week ago? I have no idea what day it is. But it feels like it's been a million years."

"It really does." Adam stood with his head tipped back. He whistled softly. "The stars are incredible out here."

Parker gazed up at the thick carpet of constellations, a sea of lights that went on forever. "It's like the sky is closer somehow. You know what I mean?"

Adam nodded. "You want to eat?"

"Uh-uh. I just need to sleep." Parker pulled out his toothbrush and toothpaste, using a few sips of water to rinse as he spat onto the cracked earth. It was a little luxury both he and Adam enjoyed.

While Adam brushed, still keeping his eyes on the stars, Parker found what looked to be the area of ground with the least amount of scrub and rocks. The sand still felt painfully hard as he stretched out, but it would have to do. He sat back up and unstrapped the machete, and then positioned the pack so both he and Adam could use it for a pillow. He held up the blanket so Adam could squeeze under with him.

They moved into each other's arms automatically now. Parker had never felt so physically comfortable with another person. The fumblings at prep school were light years away from the easy way he and Adam fit together. They kissed under the canopy of stars, the waxing moon beaming over the lunar landscape.

Parker sometimes thought he could just be happy kissing Adam forever. The roughness of Adam's growing beard contrasted with the softness of his mouth and tongue and sent Parker's head spinning every single time. He sighed as he broke away to take a breath. "I could kiss you all night."

"Mmm. Won't get much sleep that way." Adam dipped his head and latched onto Parker's throat. He apparently loved to mark Parker's fair skin since he did it every chance he got.

Something scuttled nearby, and Parker froze. "What was that?"

"Nothing," Adam mumbled against his neck.

"Holy shit. Are there scorpions out here? Snakes? Spiders? Something else I can't think of but is equally terrifying and gross?" Parker dug his fingers into Adam's shoulders.

"They'll stay far away from us, don't worry."

"Can you sniff them out?"

Adam's laugh was warm. "Definitely. They'll stay away from the big, bad wolf."

"Seriously? Can they like, sense you?"

With a sigh, Adam lifted his head. "Parker, I'm sure they're all burrowed into their homes for the night." He kissed the tip of Parker's nose. "Go to sleep."

"Okay." Parker resolutely closed his eyes and snuggled closer. His eyes flew open. "Wait, did you actually just refer to yourself as the big, bad wolf? Did that happen?"

Adam said nothing.

"Hello?" Parker reached under Adam's jacket and shirt to tickle his belly. "Admit it. You called yourself the big, bad wolf."

He caught Parker's wrist with a reluctant smile. "Okay, I give. I admit it."

"That would naturally make me Little Red Riding Hood in this scenario. Oh, what big eyes you have!"

"All the better to see you with, my dear."

Even though it was just a joke, hearing the endearment on Adam's tongue made Parker's heart skip a beat. Was he dear to Adam? He thought he was, but were they boyfriends now? Did Adam care as much as Parker cared about him?

He shoved the thoughts back down to deal with another time. "My, what big teeth you have."

Adam flashed a grin and nipped Parker's neck.

"Seriously, did you ever go to the orthodontist? Because your teeth are incredibly straight and white."

"It's all natural."

"Let me see your fangs. I want to check something."

Adam's smile faded. "You don't want to see those. Come on, we should sleep."

"No. Show me." Parker frowned. "Why are you so tense all of a sudden? I've seen them before."

"Not like this. Only when I had to." Adam tried to roll over. "Time to sleep."

"Uh-uh." Parker splayed his hand on Adam's chest. Of course Adam was far stronger, but he stopped moving. "It's nothing to be ashamed of. I want to see."

Adam still wouldn't meet his gaze, but after a few moments, his eyes glowed, hair spread down over his forehead, and his beard grew far thicker. Two of his teeth seamlessly elongated into fangs. Parker teased the new hair with his fingertips. It was thick and surprisingly soft, just like the rest of Adam's hair. Then he ran his index finger over each fang. Adam was completely still and didn't even seem to be breathing as Parker explored.

When Parker leaned in and kissed him gently, tracing each fang with his tongue, Adam shuddered and gripped his shoulders. Parker reached down between them and felt Adam's thickening cock through denim. He pulled back from the kiss and bit the side of Adam's neck. His exhaustion had evaporated, and desire pooled low in his belly.

With a growl, Adam rolled on top of him. Almost as quickly as the transformation had occurred, his werewolf attributes receded, and he plunged his tongue into Parker's mouth. They rutted together frantically, and Parker spread his legs and locked his thighs around Adam's hips. He didn't care if he messed up his jeans. He needed to come. Needed Adam.

Adam pushed himself up on one powerful arm and tugged at the buttons on their jeans. They both moaned as he took their cocks in his hand, rubbing them together as they thrust their hips in a clumsy rhythm. It didn't take long before their shafts leaked, and Parker's whole body vibrated on the hard earth.

"Jesus, I want you to fuck me again."

Groaning, Adam nodded. "But now… I need…"

"Oh fuck yeah, don't stop. I can't wait now. Need this. Keep going."

With a hard kiss, Adam thrust his hips faster. He panted over Parker, warm bursts across Parker's face.

Meanwhile, Parker couldn't seem to stop talking. "I want you to stretch me open and fill me up again and again. Until it's dripping out of me, and you lick it up and feed it to me, and then you fuck my mouth and I swallow it all and—" Parker gasped as he came in long spurts over Adam's hand.

Adam didn't let up, and Parker's dick was oversensitive, but it was a delicious pain as another wave of pleasure hit him. He whimpered, the glow of release easing his aching body. Adam groaned, the arm holding him up trembling as he climaxed. Breathing hard, he slid onto his hip and buried his face in Parker's neck.

As they came back down, Parker replayed his rambling words in his mind and flushed. Adam raised his head. His brow was furrowed.

"Okay?"

"Yeah, yeah." Parker stared up at the Big Dipper. Or maybe the little one—he was shit at astronomy. "I just said some, you know, raunchy stuff. I don't want you to think I'm weird."

Adam tilted Parker's chin until Parker looked at him. "I don't think you're weird."

"You don't?" Parker smiled tentatively.

"I *know* you're weird." He kissed him lightly.

"Shut up!" Laughing, Parker smacked his shoulder. "You know what I mean."

With a gleam in his eyes, Adam lifted his right hand. He kept his gaze locked on Parker's as he slowly licked his sticky fingers clean one by one.

Parker's breath hitched. "You're going to make me hard again."

Sweeping his tongue languorously against Parker's, Adam kissed him. Parker could taste both of them, and *he loved it.*

Adam leaned their foreheads together. "Whatever you think might be too kinky or weird?" He traced the shell of Parker's ear with his tongue and whispered, "I guarantee I want it too."

Another spike of adrenaline made Parker's heart skip. "Good

to know."

For a few minutes, they rested, tangled together, and Parker watched the stars. "I don't think I can sleep after all. Got my second wind. What about you?"

"Let's keep going." Adam smiled slyly. "Find a bed."

Parker grinned. "Shit, what are we waiting for?"

STRETCHING HIS ARMS and legs, Parker let out a long, silent yawn. The motel sheets may not have been the highest thread count, but they felt positively luxurious against his bare skin. It had taken until dawn, but they'd found a bed, goddamn it. He opened his eyes and blinked at the clock radio's glowing numbers.

7:47 P.M.

Miracle of miracles, the deserted roadside motel on the out-skirts of a small town had power. Well, it did after they'd turned on the Desert Retreat's emergency generator. Even though he hadn't been sure of the exact time, Parker hadn't been able to resist setting the clock earlier. It was a little slice of normalcy that made him happy. A search of the radio bands had come up empty.

Adam slept naked beside him in the dark room, tangled in the cheap sheets and flopped on his stomach, his arm over Parker's waist. For all their grand plans of fucking each other's brains out, they'd showered in the mildewy little bathroom, devoured a pile of half-melted chocolate bars from the empty office, and pulled down the blackout blinds before crashing.

It was the first time either of them had slept properly in days, but especially Adam, who Parker knew stayed on guard far more than he did. But apparently, werewolves needed their sleep too, and this crash for Adam was overdue.

He knew it was indulgent to stay in the room for a whole day, but burning themselves out wouldn't do them any favors. He'd wake Adam soon, and they could get back on the road. Although he wasn't leaving this little oasis until they'd fucked every which way to Sunday—and Wednesday and Friday too.

He watched Adam in the faint glow of the clock. He was still dead to the world, snoring softly in a way that was ridiculously adorable and made Parker grin stupidly. He loved how easy and *right* it felt to sleep with Adam and look at his body. He resisted the urge to turn on the light and lick every mole and freckle he could find.

He eased out of bed, tiptoeing on the threadbare carpet. He pulled on his underwear and jeans before shoving his bare feet into his sneakers. His eyes had adjusted, and he could pick his way around the vague shapes of the room. He rubbed his arms.

The air conditioning probably sucked up way too much power, but the day had been scorching, and they hadn't been able to resist. It hummed and rattled loudly, and the sound was so reassuringly ordinary that Parker decided to keep it on for a bit longer.

The ice bucket sat on the cheap desk. Grinning, he grabbed the plastic container. They'd found a fridge full of warm soda in the office, but now it should be cold, and by now the ice machine should have filled. Oh yes, there would be ice. Parker wondered if there was any beer around, although an ice-cold cola would pretty much taste like liquid crack at this point.

With his flashlight in hand, he tiptoed past the bike, which they'd brought inside for safekeeping.

"Where are you going?" Adam mumbled. "What's that noise?" He groaned.

"It's the A/C. Keep sleeping."

"No—got to get up. Turn on the light. That'll help. Damn, this bed is comfortable."

Parker flicked on the overhead light, holding up his hand to block the harsh glare. "I'll be right back." He unbolted the door and twisted the handle.

"Wait!" Adam shot up.

But Parker was already staring at the writhing sea of creepers in the parking lot. Blinking, he realized the motel's flashing neon sign had come on in the twilight, a three-story beacon to the hundreds of chattering creepers that jerked around its base as darkness set in.

WELCOME! POOL TV VACANCY

"Parker!"

There was no time to answer, because nearby creepers on their pilgrimage to the neon sign detoured straight for him and their bright room, moving faster than he could.

Chapter Thirteen

PARKER SCRAMBLED BACK and tried to slam the door, but it was no use. The creepers shoved into the room, five or six of them reaching for him with rigid fingers and open, bloody mouths. Panic stole his breath. He lunged for his machete.

With a roar that rattled the windowpane, Adam put himself between Parker and the invading creepers. He was still naked, and hair spread over his thick shoulders and thighs. He was already slashing with his claws, laying waste to the nearest infected, tearing into their throats as he shoved them toward the door.

More poured in.

Parker frantically hacked at the arm of an old woman who didn't scream, but instead chattered with a new ferocity, lunging for him.

Fuck, fuck! No!

He stumbled back, tripping over something on the carpet. She followed, her teeth smashing together as she descended on him. He slashed at her neck, but then her head was torn free, Adam turning away from the door to rescue him.

Before Parker could blink, they were on Adam.

Jumping to his feet, Parker whacked at one as its teeth sank into Adam's neck, another taking a glistening chunk of Adam's shoulder.

"No!" Parker screamed and raised his blade again and again, hacking into them in a bloody frenzy until he and Adam were able to drive the rest back out the door.

Adam dug in his heels and pushed back against the shuddering piece of wood as Parker flipped off the damn light.

"Adam?" His voice was little more than a croak. In the sudden darkness, he could only see Adam's golden eyes glowing. "Oh god. They didn't… You're okay. You're okay!" Parker's mind spun. He gasped, a thick band squeezing around his chest and constricting his lungs. "You're okay!"

He has to be. Oh fuck. They bit him.

Adam still held the door. His voice was little more than a growl. "Get the pack. Get on the bike."

"You're okay, right?" Parker's chest was unbearably tight.

Please. Please, God.

He didn't answer.

"No." Parker shook his head violently. "Do you feel different? It might not work on you. You're a werewolf. You'll be okay!"

"Too many. If I'm infected, you'll never make it. I'll kill you."

"But—"

"*I'll kill you.* You only have a minute." Every word was bitten out around his fangs.

"But—"

He roared, "Pick up the pack and get on the fucking bike! *Now!*"

With trembling hands in the dark, Parker slung the pack over his bare back and straddled the motorcycle, the machete still clutched in his right hand. He started the engine, and Mariah hummed to life beneath him. "Get on, Adam."

"I'll distract them. Don't look back. Go."

"Not without you!" Parker's heart pounded so hard he thought it might explode.

"You're going to stay alive, Parker." Adam flicked on the light. For a moment, he smiled, so much tenderness and sorrow in his golden eyes. "If I'm still me, I'll find you."

With a mighty shove, Adam toppled the door backward and

off its hinges, splintering the frame as the nearby creepers went flying. The parking lot was thick with them, and Adam was a blur as he sliced and ripped. Parker raced through the open space, weaving into the crowd and hacking at the infected in his way.

But fuck, fuck, fuck—there were still too many. Something tugged hard on the pack, and he slashed back desperately, gunning the engine as others came from both sides, closing in. Then Adam was there in a burst of thunder, and Parker was free, Mariah zooming through a gap in the crowd.

He skirted the edge of the parking lot in seconds, and then he was back on the blacktop of the highway, escaping into the night and the cold, empty desert. Creepers filled the road in the direction of the town, so he headed the way they'd come.

He forced himself not to look back.

Some miles down the road, Parker stopped. He had no idea how far he'd gone, and he staggered off the bike, cracking his knees on the asphalt as his legs gave out and he vomited the remnants of the chocolate. He trembled violently, his teeth chattering so loudly that for a moment he thought maybe he was infected after all.

Parker crawled away from the mess and struggled to get the pack off. It took forever for his hands to cooperate and unzip it. He pulled on a T-shirt and zipped up his hoodie and jacket. Sitting back on his heels, he wrapped his arms around himself.

He couldn't stop shaking.

He clenched his eyes shut.

Please, God. Please let me wake up. I need to wake up. This isn't happening. It's not real.

He whimpered when he opened his eyes.

The moon was almost full, illuminating the stretch of the highway in both directions, the faint dotted yellow line disappearing into the distance. The wind swept across the dry land, and he thought of last night, huddling with Adam under the stars, safe and alive.

He would give anything to go back there. In a heartbeat, everything had changed.

They'd let themselves relax. They'd figured out in the desert, there wouldn't be any creepers. How the fuck the infection had gotten to the town, Parker didn't know. But it didn't matter. It had. And they'd bitten Adam.

"If I'm still me, I'll find you."

He had to be okay. He'd come. The infection wouldn't get him. It couldn't. Shuddering, Parker squeezed his eyes shut again. He thought of Adam, who had annoyed him so much when they met. Adam, who had saved him again and again. Adam, who was so brave and beautiful and generous and patient, and who he'd just woken up beside.

Adam, who'd kissed him like he couldn't get enough.

Alone on the asphalt under the rising moon, endless miles from home, Parker gave in and sobbed.

"I HAVE TO do something."

His voice was hoarse—his throat unbearably dry and scratchy. Parker shivered and fought down a fresh wave of tears.

Get it together. Get up!

But he didn't. He sat on the road, his legs folded beneath him and cramped. He wasn't sure how much time had passed. He was a snotty mess, and his head pounded. He couldn't seem to move as he stared into the shadows of the desert. He could have been on the surface of the moon. He wanted to curl up and disappear.

He'd never been so wholly and utterly alone in his life.

With a grunt, Parker staggered to his feet. "Okay. Stop feeling sorry for yourself. Adam's fine. He's going to be here any minute. He's coming."

But when Parker squinted into the distance, there was only the empty highway and the night.

He breathed in and out the way Adam would, counting to ten. "Water. Drink some water."

He rummaged in the pack and was relieved that the bottle was still half full. He gulped and coughed and forced himself to slow down and save some for later just in case. Swiping impatiently at his wet eyes, he took stock.

He still had the machete, but no holster for it. After a few moments of debate, he carefully packed the weapon in the backpack, leaving enough room at the top for the handle to stick out. It would have to do, and hopefully he wouldn't slice up the few belongings he still had.

After straddling Mariah, he sat and closed his eyes for another moment. "Okay. I'm going back, and Adam will meet me halfway. He's fine. He's not dead. He's not one of them." He turned the key.

One step at a time.

Given how straight and flat the road was beneath the stars and moon, he didn't need the headlight. Mariah thrummed under him, and Parker took a deep breath. He'd find Adam. He accelerated. As he drove back the way he'd come, the road still his, he tried not to think of what he'd do if Adam wasn't okay. Because Adam was okay. Adam had to be. Then a thought hit him.

Shit. Gas.

Without the lights on, Parker couldn't see the indicator, so he rolled to a stop. Peering into the distance, he could barely see what might be the halo of light of the motel's sign, but what could have just been a particularly bright star on the horizon. He had to take the chance. He flicked on the lights and checked the gauge before turning them off again. Half a tank. Should be enough to get them to a safe gas station.

Because Adam was still alive. Yes. Adam was just fine.

A flicker of movement caught Parker's eye. His breath stuck in his throat, and he squinted down the road, turning off the bike to listen. There was only the whistle of the wind across the flat land. His heart pounded in his ears, but then he realized it was getting louder.

Thump, thump, thump, thump.

Adrenaline ricocheted through him. There was definitely someone—or something—coming his way. He yanked out the machete and held it in a trembling hand. It had to be Adam. It couldn't be the infected. Right?

Thump, thump, thump, thump.

"Parker!"

His name was a whisper on the wind, still far away. But then a figure came into focus, running so fast that it was only a few seconds before he could make out Adam's familiar silhouette, right down to the leather jacket and jeans, his boots pounding the road.

Parker leapt off the bike. His feet were moving. He dropped the machete with a distant clatter, running now. If he was losing his mind, he was going with it, because Adam was getting closer and closer with each heartbeat, and his eyes were glowing golden, and they weren't bugging out, because *he was still him.*

With a half laugh and sob, Parker threw himself into Adam's arms. Adam lifted him off his feet, and Parker wanted to whoop for joy. He breathed him in and ran his hands over Adam's back and shoulders.

"Are you real? Are you here?"

"I'm here." Adam's voice was muffled where he buried his face in Parker's neck. When he lifted his head, he put Parker back down and ran his hands over him. "Are you hurt?"

"No. Not really." He clutched him. "God, don't ever… Just don't." He swallowed hard. "I was so afraid you were gone."

"So was I." Adam gently brushed away the fresh tears from

Parker's cheeks. "I don't know why I wasn't infected. I must be immune."

"Because you're a big, bad wolf."

Adam laughed, and it was the most beautiful sound Parker had ever heard. They pressed their foreheads together, and Parker breathed him in, all leather and earth and *Adam*.

"That must be why—it doesn't affect you since you're a werewolf. But you were gone for so long."

"I had to heal, and I had to be sure I wouldn't change. It might have just been delayed. We saw with Carey it happens in minutes with humans." He leaned back and gripped Parker's shoulders. "You have to promise me that you'll take Mariah and go if I have a delayed reaction. Promise."

"You won't. I know you won't."

"We don't know anything. The thought that I could hurt you—*kill you*—it's… Just promise me."

"Okay. I promise." He wrapped his arms around Adam's waist, keeping him close. He didn't think he would be able to stop touching him for hours. "What happened after I left?"

"I killed a lot of them. Figured I could take out as many as I could before I changed. I turned off the generator. The others started drifting back toward the town once the light was gone. It seems like unless you're close to them, they get easily distracted and don't really have a memory." He pulled something from his pocket. "Thought you might want this."

It was the machete holster, all wadded up. "Thanks." Parker bit his lip, tears threatening again.

Get. It. Together.

"When I opened the door and they saw me…" He shuddered. "It was so fast. They seemed to come faster, didn't they?"

Adam nodded. "I think they're getting hungrier. It makes sense. The more the infection spreads…"

"The fewer of us there are to eat." What a cheery fucking

thought. "It's only going to get harder."

"Yes. But we'll make it. I'll be more vigilant. It's my fault. I let myself relax in that bed. With the A/C on I didn't hear them. I should have smelled them. I'm sorry. I'll be better."

"Don't be sorry! We're doing our best. You've done so much. You were exhausted. You still saved me."

Adam ran his thumb over Parker's lips. "I was afraid I wouldn't find you."

"I'm so glad you're here. You…I…" Parker couldn't find the words and kissed him instead.

For a glorious moment, their lips pressed together. It was only a simple kiss, but as they clung to each other, it was everything Parker had prayed for.

Then Adam yanked away.

Parker blinked, reaching for him. "What?"

But Adam staggered back out of reach. "What if I'm immune, but I'm carrying the virus?"

The bottom of Parker's stomach dropped. "I don't…" He shook his head. "Do you think that's possible? No. I'm sure it's fine." Parker reached for him again, but Adam dodged.

"We don't know that."

"Well, we don't really know anything."

"Exactly. We can't take the chance. We know it isn't transmitted through the air, or at least we don't think so."

"Right. With Carey, it was a bite. So you won't bite me— problem solved."

"What if it's like a sexually transmitted disease?"

"Then we'll find condoms." Parker reached out again, but Adam stayed away from his grasp.

"We can't risk it. We can't risk anything. I could pass it to you through saliva. Any bodily fluid."

"But…" Parker dropped his hand.

"We should get moving." Not looking at him, Adam headed

toward Mariah.

Parker knew Adam was right, but that didn't soothe the ache growing in his chest.

Chapter Fourteen

P ARKER REACHED OUT with his gloved hand, but there was
only hard ground beside him. He'd barely woken, and already
the day was off to a shitty start.

When he opened his eyes, he could see the splash of orange
through the trees as the sun rose. Adam stood nearby with his
back turned.

They'd camped, sleeping on pine needles, well off the road
where the trees grew so thickly they had to walk the bike and duck
branches. Parker stretched his stiff muscles. Jesus Christ, it was
freezing, and he was wearing pretty much all the clothes he had in
bulky layers. The Rockies in October were not his idea of primo
camping season.

It had been extremely slow going in Colorado as they took the
long way over the mountains. Tunnels on the interstate were too
much of a risk in case they became trapped with the infected, so
they zigzagged their way onward. They spent a lot of time
scrounging for gas, which was a constant worry.

With a little groan, Parker pushed himself to his feet. After a
moment of debate, he cautiously approached Adam. He knew
Adam could hear him coming, and maybe… But the second he
reached out, Adam wrenched away from him.

Parker bit back the disappointment and hurt, and tried to
keep his voice light. "Hey. Sleep okay?"

"Yeah. You?" Adam didn't look at him as he crouched down
to rummage in the pack and unfold their map.

"Sure."

It had been two weeks since that night in Nevada. While they'd always huddled together before, now Adam slept with his back to Parker, just an edge of the thermal blanket over him. Sometimes Parker would inch closer, but it was as if Adam had a proximity alarm. He always kept a space between them.

Parker cleared his throat. "So, how much farther until we're down the mountains?"

"Could be a few more days. Once we're in the Midwest, we should be able to make better time."

"Cool. How are you feeling?"

Adam kept his eyes on the map. "Fine."

"Good. Still no virus, I see."

With a sigh, Adam refolded the map. "Parker, we talked about this."

"I know, but seriously, you're overreacting. You're paranoid."

"What if I'm not? It isn't worth it."

"But it's been weeks. Even if you were carrying it, wouldn't it be dead by now?"

"Typhoid Mary carried the disease for decades. There are HIV carriers who are asymptomatic for years."

Super.

"Okay, so maybe we can't fuck, but…"

Can't you at least look at me?

He'd felt closer to Adam than he ever had to another person, yet now this chasm had cracked open between them. They hadn't kissed. Had barely touched—even a brush of fingers was rare now.

"But what?" Adam's nostrils flared. "If you got infected, you'd be gone in minutes." He shoved the map into the pack. "Let's get moving."

They packed up in silence and wheeled Mariah to the road. Parker climbed on and wrapped his arms around Adam. This was the only time he was allowed now, and he'd take what he could get.

"THE PINES." PARKER read the sign at the foot of the driveway. The sign was expertly crafted from wood and beveled glass, and from the back of the bike, he leaned closer and ran his fingers over the smooth, wet grain. "This could be nice."

They'd followed a paved lane off the main road early one gray morning as a steady rain turned to sleet. They'd driven through part of the night since the temperature had dipped even more, and it was too cold to sleep outside.

They were almost on the other side of the Rockies now and hadn't seen any infected—or anyone else—in days. The possibility of a comfortable place to rest was hard to pass up, especially as the roads got messy. "It sounds like it has beds. Maybe a shower if there's enough water pressure left. God, I need a shower."

Adam was staring intently down the driveway, where manicured trees loomed. "There are people here."

"Shit. I guess we should go. I was really looking forward to not stinking for a few hours at least." Sleet dripped off his hood into Parker's eyes, and he swiped at it, shivering. Adam was soaked, but it didn't seem to bother him as much.

"There's someone coming." Adam vibrated with tension.

"What? How did they know we're here?" Parker swiveled his head and caught sight of the camera mounted high on a tree. The camera moved, sweeping the area. "Whoa. Security system. How do they still have power? I guess we should talk to them? They might have information."

"I guess." Adam was rigid, gripping the handlebars.

The hum of an engine reached Parker's ears, and he grabbed the pistol out of the pack and clicked off the safety. He hoped he'd never have to shoot anyone who wasn't infected. They waited on the bike, Mariah's engine still running.

When the black SUV came around the curve in the driveway,

Parker glimpsed *The Pines* written on the side in dark green. The vehicle came to a stop, and two men in matching forest green raincoats and jeans climbed out. The passenger, a young man in his twenties, carried a shotgun, but pointed it at the ground.

The middle-aged driver closed the SUV door and raised a hand to tip his cowboy hat. "Howdy."

Adam nodded. "Morning."

"Where are you coming from? East or west?"

"West," Adam answered.

"How are things looking out there?"

Parker spoke up. "Not great." He gave them a brief rundown on what they'd seen on their journey. "But we made it through. Uh, obviously."

The younger man said, "Glad you did. Some of our people are from Denver. They barely made it out."

"You're headed east?" The driver nodded toward the horizon.

"We are," Parker answered. "Have you heard anything from out there?"

"We have a couple who came to us last week from the coast. From what I understand, things are looking pretty grim."

Although it wasn't unexpected, it was still a blow. He'd tried not to think too much about his parents since it only upset him, and when he did, his chest tightened like there was a python around him.

Are they alive? Is Eric? Are Jessica and Jason? Even if they are, will I ever see them again?

Adam squeezed his knee gently, and Parker managed to suck in a breath. Yeah, this was why he tried not to think about it.

The driver went on. "You're welcome to stay here. We've got lots of space, and the way we see it, there's strength in numbers. We've heard stories of people turning on each other. That'll be the end of us for certain, even if this sickness isn't. So, we've got rules here."

"You can get cleaned up and have a good meal. It's a nice resort. But no pressure," the passenger added.

Adam and Parker shared a glance.

"We'll let you discuss it while we turn the vehicle around. You can follow us back if you like. If not, we wish you safe travels." The driver tipped his hat again.

"I think they seem okay?" Parker whispered.

Adam nodded. "He's telling the truth."

"How do you know?"

"I can hear his heartbeat. It's steady. When people lie, they give off all kinds of signals. Their hearts skip around, sometimes just a little, but enough. He seems honest."

"Whoa, you've got a werewolf lie detector? That's awesome. Also, you should have mentioned that, jackass."

For a wonderful moment, Adam smiled. "You're a terrible liar anyway."

The SUV headed back down the driveway slowly. Parker said, "We should check it out, yeah? Hot food would be pretty amazing right about now."

Adam nodded. "If it doesn't feel right, we'll leave."

They followed the SUV down the long, winding driveway, and Parker flicked the safety back on his pistol. The drive was paved, and the asphalt was pristine. As they rounded a corner, a tall wooden fence came into sight.

It had to be twenty feet high, made of logs that blended into the natural surroundings. A huge metal gate was half open across the driveway. A young woman in a guard's booth smiled and waved as they drove in. With an electronic whirr, the gate slid closed behind them. The SUV stopped, and the driver unrolled his window.

"Christy, we've got two visitors. Sorry boys—didn't get your names. I'm Steve, and this is Jake."

The girl popped out of the booth, her blonde curls swaying as she pulled up the hood on her green uniform coat. "Welcome!"

"Thanks. I'm Parker, and this is Adam." He indicated the fence with this thumb. "Are you sure this place isn't a prison? What's with the security?"

"Anti-paparazzi," Christy answered. "This was supposed to be the hot new escape for the rich and famous, where they could come and commune with nature and have total privacy. We were getting it ready for the grand opening. It was supposed to be next week, but obviously that's not happening." Her smile was forced. "Oh well. At least we're alive, right?"

Parker smiled back. "Yeah. Thanks for letting us in."

"Of course! It's not safe out there. I can hardly believe the things people have told me. I was lucky to be up here."

"When's your shift over?" Steve asked.

"Not until noon. I'll see you all later." With another wave, Christy returned to her stool in the booth, shutting the door firmly.

They drove on, and when they came around another bend, Parker gasped. "Holy shit."

The hotel was massive—a gorgeous three-story wood and glass building that stretched across the center of a large clearing. There were mountaintops every way Parker looked, and it felt as if they were nestled right in the heart of the Rockies. Even in the sleet, the view was impressive. They pulled into a lot off to the side. He and Adam both hesitated to leave Mariah.

"I guess she'll be okay out here, right?" Parker asked.

Adam didn't seem convinced but nodded.

Jake motioned for them to follow the flagstone path to the hotel. "Come on, we'll get you settled."

In the grand lobby with a cathedral ceiling, skylights, and exposed brick and wooden beams, a group of people greeted them. They ranged in age from children to seniors. A woman of about fifty with charcoal hair knotted into a sleek bun and angular, black-framed glasses stepped forward. She wore a crisp blouse and pressed trousers.

"I'm Angela Yamaguchi, the general manager of the Pines." She smiled tightly. "At least I was. My duties have changed somewhat, but I'm still in charge of keeping everything running smoothly here."

Parker raised his hand and waved to the group before unzipping his soaking coat. "Hey, everyone. I'm Parker." He waited for Adam to introduce himself, but when he glanced over, Adam was staring at someone in the welcoming committee. "Uh, this is Adam." He nudged Adam with his elbow, and Adam nodded a hello.

"Wonderful to meet you both." Angela smiled. "We'll make all the introductions later, since I'm sure you'd both like to rest and clean up. We have hundreds of rooms, so you can each have your own, or you can share a suite. Whatever you'd like."

"We'll share a room," Parker said. Anyone who didn't like it could bite him. (Well, not literally.)

Angela nodded to a man near her, who was about thirty, Hispanic, and incredibly hot. "Perfect. Ramon? Do you want to go tell Chef we'll have two more for breakfast?" To Parker, she added, "We can have it sent up to your room if you'd like."

"Of course." With a smile, Ramon disappeared down a hallway off the lobby.

"Right this way." Angela motioned them toward the grand staircase in the middle of the lobby, her heels clicking on the slate. "All of our guest rooms are on the second and third floors, offering maximum privacy and mountain views." She paused at the top of the stairs. "Sorry. It's hard to snap out of hotel mode. It's been more than a year of preparation for opening." She smiled ruefully. "Sometimes I find it a challenge to accept these new circumstances we're living in. But I'm sure they're only temporary."

God, Parker wished he could believe that, but any semblance of his old life seemed impossibly out of reach. He forced a smile. "Let's hope so." Adam said nothing, and Parker wasn't sure he was even listening.

Angela pointed down to the hallway where Ramon had disappeared. "The kitchen and dining room are at the end of that corridor. We eat dinner in the staff lounge in the basement since the main dining hall doesn't have any window coverings, and we've been told the infected are attracted to light."

"Yes, they definitely are," Parker confirmed.

"As an eco-focused facility, we fortunately have some solar power and our own greenhouse. Part of the appeal of the Pines was that we were going to offer locally grown organic food all year long. We weren't fully stocked for opening yet, but Chef is doing the best he can with what we have in the freezers and greenhouse. Everyone is welcome to eat breakfast and lunch in the dining room, or to take a plate to their room anytime. Our only rule is that food isn't wasted and that we clean up after ourselves."

Parker glanced at Adam, who really seemed to be spacing. Worry clenched his gut. Adam definitely needed to catch up on his sleep. Parker turned his attention back to Angela. "We'll follow the rules, no worries. How many people are staying here?"

"With you two, we have seventy-three. Forty were staff. The rest are a mix of family and friends who escaped Denver and were smart enough to come here, and travelers like yourselves." She pointed to the other side of the foyer. "There's a full gym, indoor pool, and ballroom in the west wing. For now, we still have electricity. We have a very powerful generator to back up the solar power, but we're hoping we won't have to overuse it. With winter coming, it's a concern."

"Have you had any creepers up here?" He didn't add *yet*, although it was only a matter of time.

She blinked. "Creepers? That's quite a...descriptive word. So far, we haven't encountered any. We do have a strict lights-out policy. Currently it's six p.m., and all blinds must be closed, and lights in rooms with windows extinguished. That includes all guest rooms. Even with the wooden Venetian blinds, which were specially designed for absolute privacy, from the outside light does escape around the edges. Every room is equipped with flashlights that use electromagnetic induction. We have a stock of emergency candles, but obviously they can be a dangerous fire hazard, and we prefer to keep them out of the guest rooms. Anyway, you just need to shake the flashlights to activate them. These flashlights are for inside use only, and never around an uncovered window. We can't be too careful."

Parker nodded. "Right. Sounds logical. If you have power, can you go on the internet? Have you found out anything about what caused all this?"

She sighed. "*We* have power, but our ISP apparently doesn't, so we can't get online. Phone lines are also dead, and we don't have cable or a television satellite since part of the mandate for the resort was that it was a retreat from the world. Staff were going to have satellite TV access, but it hadn't been installed yet. Amazing how dependent we've become on technology, isn't it? We do have a transmitting radio that was intended for emergencies. We have shifts manning it so the bands are being monitored twenty-four hours a day. There's scattered information from all over. It seems to be mostly rumors, unfortunately. We're working on extending our range."

"Do you have notes on what you're hearing?" Parker asked.

"Of course. Logs are detailed and filed daily. I'll be happy to show them to you. And once you're settled, if we could sit down and get some notes on your experiences it would be greatly appreciated."

"Sure. Do you know what the worldwide situation is?"

She sighed heavily. "I'm afraid it's not positive from what

we've heard. There are rumors a group claimed responsibility. The Zechariahs, they call themselves. God sent them to cleanse the Earth—you know, all that end times nonsense. But as I said, it hasn't been confirmed."

Angela continued walking, leading them down a hallway decorated with enormous framed watercolors of the mountains. Parker's mind spun.

The Zechariahs. Wonderful. Nutso zealots with biotechnology were just what the world needed.

Angela put on a wide smile, firmly changing the topic. "And lest you think you have some long, boring evenings ahead, we've been having movie nights in the staff lounge, which is in the basement, as I mentioned. Everyone is welcome to attend. We have quite a Blu-ray collection."

Boring evenings sounded goddamn amazing, actually. "A movie would be pretty awesome, right?" Parker nudged Adam.

"Uh-huh." Adam smiled wanly. "Thank you. We appreciate your hospitality."

"As I'm sure Steve told you, we believe there's strength in numbers. We want to build our community here so we can face whatever challenges the future brings together. The Pines was founded on the ideal of sustainability and teamwork." She grimaced. "Sorry for the corporate speak. I mean, let's be honest. This place was designed to be a hideaway for the filthy rich. But I wanted to run it on teamwork and striving for a common goal. That goal used to be providing our guests the best and most discreet service. Now it's survival."

"I'm not sure how long we'll stay, but count us in for the team while we're here," Parker said.

Angela smiled and adjusted her glasses. "Excellent."

She led them down the second-floor hallway of the east wing. "For now, you're free to use all the electricity and water you want, within reason, of course. Normal amounts. I have a suite on the third floor that I'm sure you'll enjoy." She opened the door to a stairwell midway down the hall. "We've locked the elevators since we don't want to risk anyone getting stuck if there's a power issue."

On the third floor, they followed Angela to the end of the hall. She pulled a key card from her pocket and slid it into the door. The light went green.

"What happens to the doors if there's no power?"

"They won't lock, except for the safety chains inside the rooms. We're hoping it won't be an issue." She opened the door. "Here you are. Someone will bring your breakfast tray shortly. Don't expect any more pampering, but we like to give our new friends a warm welcome. Please come down later for lunch, or you can sleep and join us for dinner. You're free to do whatever you like, really. Everyone is expected to clean their own rooms, and our only other guideline is that we treat everyone here at the Pines with respect and remember the golden rule. I'm assuming you learned it as children."

"Absolutely. Do unto others, etc. That sounds great. Right, Adam?"

Adam nodded. "Thank you, Angela."

"Oh, do you have a phone charger?" Parker asked.

"Yes. You can drop by my office later and pick one up. Although none of us have had any service in weeks."

"I know. I just want to see if it still works. It got wet."

"Well, I hope you'll be with us for some time." She smiled warmly and turned to go. "Oh, there's one more rule: no weapons. We're keeping everything locked safely in my office. We have a full security system and four guard outposts, including the front gate. If there's an event, we'll have plenty of time to arm ourselves. With children in the hotel, we don't feel comfortable with anyone having weapons in their room. Of course, when or if you leave, they'll be returned to you immediately."

"Right. I guess that makes sense." Parker glanced at Adam, who nodded. Parker unstrapped the machete and passed it along with the gun to Angela, who held them as if they might bite.

"Thank you, gentlemen. I hope I'll see you later today."

They closed the door behind her, and Parker kept his voice low. "How about her? She seems nice, but what's your lie detector saying?"

"She's on the level."

"Okay, good." Parker hung up his sodden jacket and whistled. "Check out this view." The windows were floor to ceiling, affording a perfect snapshot of the surrounding snow-capped peaks, miles of pine forest, and brilliant orange and red autumn colors. "And this room is sweet. King bed and a sitting area."

"Mmm."

Adam wasn't even looking, instead apparently preferring to stare at his shoes.

Parker flicked on the bathroom light and turned on the tap in the nearest sink in the double marble counter. He scrubbed at his hands with a bar of creamy soap. "Dude, there is the biggest shower I've ever seen in my life in here, plus a separate hot tub built for two."

"Didn't you grow up with stuff like this? I thought your family was rich." Adam was still not looking at him.

"There's rich, and then there's this." Parker shifted self-consciously. "We spent most of our vacations on our sailboat. Which I admit was pretty big and expensive. But I can still appreciate a nice room. Especially considering our accommodations lately. And it's not like my dorm room at Westley was fancy. I wasn't *that* spoiled. I'm not saying I wasn't privileged, but..." He stopped before he sounded any more ridiculously defensive.

"I didn't mean anything by it," Adam said and turned to the window.

"Fine."

Then why'd you say it?

Parker unlaced his sneakers and kicked them off. "You know, if you want your own room, you should've said something."

Adam turned, his brow furrowed. "Why would I want my own room?"

Seriously?

"You just seem kind of… Whatever, it's fine. You're okay staying in here with me?"

Adam looked at him like he was crazy. "Of course, Parker."

A soft rap on the door stopped Parker from biting out anything else, which was probably a good thing. He opened the door to find a girl and boy of about ten and maybe twelve. The redheaded boy held a tray carrying covered plates, while the brunette girl's tray had a pitcher of orange juice and two icy glasses.

The girl smiled widely. "Hi. I'm Evie, and this is my brother Jaden. I hope you're hungry."

Parker grinned back. "Hey, it's my two new best friends. Is that bacon I smell? Come on in."

Giggling, the kids carefully placed the trays on a small dining table by the wall of windows. "Are you going to come downstairs later?" Jaden asked. "We're going to play soccer in the ballroom at eleven."

"We're a little tired, but we'll try to make it. Thanks for breakfast. Tall, dark, and brooding over there is Adam, and I'm Parker."

"It's fun having new people," Jaden said. "We're going to watch *Avengers* tonight, so you should definitely come for that."

"Music to my ears! Believe me when I tell you I wouldn't miss it." Parker raised his hand and gave both kids a high five. "See you then."

"Oh, and we're supposed to tell you to bring down your laundry later, and you can use the machines."

"I've never uttered these words in my life, but laundry would be heaven. Will do."

The kids waved to Adam, and Parker closed the door behind them. "Clean clothes. I bet they even have fabric softener. And a movie! That'll be fun. Nice to do something normal for once, right?"

"Mmm. Uh-huh." Adam took off his leather jacket and hung it on the back of a chair.

Parker bit back a surge of irritation and tried to keep his tone light. "What's up with you? This is all pretty cool, isn't it?"

Can't we even enjoy a bit of comfort now?

Adam didn't meet his gaze. "Sorry. I'm tired. Going to get cleaned up. You go ahead and eat."

"Are you sure? It'll get cold."

"Yeah. Don't wait for me." Adam disappeared into the bathroom and closed the door.

Parker listened to the shower come on.

He's tired and stressed. It's fine. We'll be fine.

The bacon was perfectly cooked—just crispy enough, but still tender—and the scrambled eggs and buttered toast melted in his mouth. Parker scarfed down the first hot meal he'd had in weeks and tried to enjoy the view.

Instead, he obsessed about Adam, dissecting every word and glance, wondering what he'd done wrong.

Chapter Fifteen

"*THIS IS YOUR last reminder. Lights out in two minutes, please. Dinner will be served shortly in the staff lounge, followed by a movie. Remember to turn off all flashlights by uncovered windows.*"

When Angela's announcement was over, Parker pressed the button for the blinds, horizontal wooden slats that descended with a whisper from the very tops of the high windows. When they were in place and closed, they blocked out the last rays of sunset. He switched on his flashlight, sweeping the beam over the room. "We'll have to take one of these when we go."

"Hmm." Adam was stretched out on the bed, fully dressed aside from his boots and jacket, his ankles crossed as he stared at the ceiling. He'd shaved off his beard, leaving only artful stubble.

It was delightfully vain that he'd made the effort to get his facial hair back to the way it had been at Stanford. Parker wanted to tease him about it but bit his tongue. Parker had shaved the scrubby bits of facial hair he'd grown, and it felt nice to have his face perfectly smooth again.

Adam frowned and shielded his eyes with his hand. "That's bright."

"Shit, sorry." He sat at the table and aimed the beam at the floor. "It's kind of weird, right? This place? I mean, it's nice— more than nice. But after what we've seen out there, it's like... It's weird. Rules and movie nights. I guess it's not bad. But you know what I mean?"

"Yeah." After a long moment, Adam added, "It's surreal. I

think I'd just gotten used to the way things are out there, and this feels like...playing house."

"Exactly! Although the bacon was amazing, I have to say. Come on, let's see what's for dinner. Might as well get all the hot food we can. We're going to leave tomorrow, right? Or the next day at the latest? We'll be nice and rested."

"Mmm."

"So, ready for dinner? And *Avengers*?"

"You go on."

Disappointment flared. "You don't want to come?"

"I'll catch up with you. I need some fresh air."

"Oh. Sure."

"I don't want you to miss the start of the movie. You've been looking forward to it. Go ahead."

"Okay."

Adam was clearly distracted and distant, but Parker didn't want to be clingy. Maybe Adam just wanted some time to himself. It wasn't unreasonable. Parker shouldn't get upset about it. "I guess you can see without a flashlight. But they're in the drawer in the desk just in case." He opened the door. "Later. Try to make it in time for when Bruce Hulks out and fights Black Widow. It's the best part."

"I will."

Flashlight bobbing, Parker made his way down the stairwell to the basement. It was the first time he'd been voluntarily separated from Adam in weeks, which was a strange feeling. Part of him wanted to march back upstairs and get Adam to talk.

No. Give him some space.

Downstairs, Parker could hear the hum of voices and smell something that made his stomach growl.

Don't get used to it.

"No, but I can make the most of it," he muttered to himself.

The basement corridor was lit with long fluorescent bulbs that seemed unnaturally bright. The door to the staff lounge was open near the stairwell, and Parker poked his head in hesitantly. Dozens of pairs of eyes turned to him, and he shifted from foot to foot and raised his hand. "Hey."

"Parker!" Evie shouted. She pushed back her chair from one of the many small tables that reminded Parker of a food court. The room sprawled out beyond the eating area to include video games, ping pong, and game tables, and a distant den with couches and a big-screen TV. After squeezing by some other tables, Evie grabbed his hand. "Come meet everyone!"

She took him table to table, reciting names and relationships that Parker would never remember, even if he and Adam weren't leaving tomorrow. Parker shook hands and smiled endlessly before Evie took him through a swinging door to the kitchen. A stout chef of about forty stood by a counter filled with serving dishes.

"A newcomer. Welcome to the Pines," he said. "I'm Mario Moretti."

"Parker Osborne. Great to meet you." Parker offered his hand.

The man gave a curt shake of his head. "I never shake hands. Even before all this nonsense. Don't want to pass on any illnesses to my diners. You wouldn't believe how easy it is for the common cold to wreak havoc."

Parker shoved his hand in his pocket. "Right. That makes sense." He inhaled deeply. "This smells amazing."

With a flourish, Mario removed the lids from the platters. "Pan-seared venison steaks with wild mushroom risotto and grilled zucchini."

"Wow. Evie, what are you guys going to have? Because I'm pretty sure I can eat alllll of this myself."

She giggled. "Save room for popcorn."

"Oh my god, seriously?" His mouth watered at the thought.

"Yes, my popcorn is very good," Mario said with a satisfied smile. "Now, one piece of venison, or two?"

When Parker's plate was loaded up with steaming food, he took a seat at a table with Angela and a thin older man who was oddly wearing a lab coat. Gray flecked his black hair, and dark circles shadowed under his eyes. Parker wanted to shovel the food into his mouth but forced himself to shake hands and be polite. "Parker Osborne."

The man took his hand with a firm grip. "Doctor Andrew Yamaguchi."

"Oh, are you two related?" Parker waved his fork between Angela and the doctor before scooping up a mouthful of risotto. He moaned softly. "God, that's good."

Angela smiled. "Only the best here at the Pines. And yes, Andrew's my big brother. He's a researcher with the University of Denver at the Rocky Mountain Center for Conservation Genetics and Systematics. He and his assistant were able to escape with a good amount of their equipment and supplies."

Andrew laughed hollowly. "To think I was worried about saving my research on the Canada Lynx and continuing the project. Now it's the preservation of humanity we must concern ourselves with." His lips quirked in a half smile. "The lynx are on their own."

Parker sliced into the tender venison. "Zombies put everything into perspective, that's for sure."

"Zombies?" Andrew's voice rose sharply, drawing looks and a sudden hush from the room. "The subjects I've seen were still alive but consumed by an unknown virus spread into the bloodstream through a bite. Have you encountered any infected without vital signs?"

"Um…" Parker glanced around and felt his cheeks flush. "No. It was just… I didn't mean it literally."

Angela put her hand on her brother's arm. "It was a figure of speech."

Andrew loosened his iron grip on his fork and placed it down neatly on his plate beside an uneaten strip of zucchini. "Of course. My apologies, Parker. It's that I've been conducting my research on the principle that the affected are still alive, and if that's not the case, it would change everything."

"I understand. You're doing research? Here? I was wondering about the lab coat."

"Sometimes I think he sleeps in it," Angela noted wryly.

Andrew chuckled. "Yes. It's not a—what's the term? A fashion statement. We've set up a lab on the other side of the basement. I can at least put my knowledge to use. We haven't been able to contact anyone at the CDC or any other regulatory bodies. Communication is a huge challenge right now. I'd love to reach my colleagues in Europe, but it's proving difficult. I feel my research could be vital."

"Wow. What is it you do, exactly? Not that I'll understand any of it, I don't expect."

And what do you know about werewolf physiology?

His tired eyes lit up, and he gestured with his hands. "I use molecular genetic tools to address conservation issues. I analyze DNA and study population dynamics and viability, gene flow, and genetic diversity. So now I'm applying my knowledge to the biggest conservation issue we've ever faced. I completed a fellowship in epidemiology, and I'm using those principles to—"

"Movie will be starting in ten minutes," a man announced loudly. "Can we see a show of hands so we can bring over enough chairs?"

Parker dutifully raised his hand.

Andrew wiped his mouth with a thick paper napkin and folded it neatly. "I should get back to work."

"Why don't you relax? I'm sure Neil has everything under control in the lab." A furrow appeared between Angela's sculpted brows. "You need a break, Drew."

Let the man do his work! Sleep, schmeep.

Parker wisely kept his mouth closed for once.

"I'm fine. I came to dinner, didn't I? I'll see you later." Dr. Yamaguchi smiled tightly and gave Parker a nod before leaving.

Parker cut another piece of meat. "So, you guys have a whole lab down here? That's amazing."

"It's strictly off limits." She practically barked it.

Parker blinked. "Of course. I wasn't—I didn't mean…"

Her face relaxed into a placid smile. "My apologies. As you can imagine the research is very delicate, and the equipment could be dangerous in the wrong hands. With children here, we have to emphasize that no one is to visit the lab at any time. But you're an adult, and you understand why."

It was strange to be referred to as an *adult* by a person his mom and dad's age. He'd sure as hell still felt like a kid when he'd gone to college, but that Parker was gone now. He fleetingly thought of Jessica and Jason and shoved away the sorrow.

"Definitely. I won't go near it."

Angela's smile was still in place. "Thank you. I need to check in with the guard houses. Enjoy the movie, Parker. Is Adam not hungry?"

"He'll be here soon, I'm sure. The food's incredible. Thanks again for your hospitality."

"It's our pleasure to have you. I hope you'll be able to stay for some time."

"I'm not sure. We need to get to the East Coast. My family…"

"Yes. I understand. I was lucky Andrew was able to make it here. Our parents passed away some years ago and neither of us married. Both married to our jobs, I suppose." She rose gracefully and picked up her plate. "There are bins for dishes and cutlery by the sink in the kitchen. Be sure to scrape your plate. I'll see you in the morning, Parker."

Once he was finished piling his plate on top of the neat pile in the kitchen, he made his way to the couch area and squeezed in with Evie and Jaden on the thick carpet in front of the TV. Mario set up cold cans of soda on a long table against the wall and filled small paper bags with buttery popcorn. The TV was at least seventy-five inches, and a surround-sound system was built into the walls.

As the Blu-ray started and someone dimmed the lights, Parker crossed his legs and popped the top on a cola with a grin. Time to shut out reality, at least for two and a half hours.

ADAM DIDN'T MAKE it in time for the Hulk and Black Widow fighting. Or the battle of New York. He didn't even make it for the awesome shawarma scene at the very end of the credits.

As the group dispersed, Parker hung out in the lounge after the movie and debated the relative merits of Captain America versus Iron Man with Evie and Jaden. "Look, Iron Man's great. We all love him. But the Captain is underrated. Chris Evans is also really hot."

Evie giggled. "He totally is. Did you see *What's Your Number?*"

"Did *you?*" He flailed his hands. "He was almost naked in that movie! Do your parents know about this?"

Evie's smile vanished, and Jaden spoke up. "It's just our dad right now," he said quietly, nodding to the pensive man sitting in the corner staring off into space.

Parker couldn't remember their dad's name, which made him feel even shittier. "Oh. I'm really sorry about your mom."

Jaden gave Evie's shoulders a squeeze. "It's okay. She's going to come here as soon as she can. We know she will. We left directions. Our uncle Paul works here."

"Oh, cool. Yeah, I'm sure she'll be here soon." Parker tried to sound like he believed it.

Evie gazed at him intently. "What's it like out there? We didn't really see much. Our dad made us keep our heads down in the car."

"It's…" Parker tried to think of anything he could say that wouldn't be a lie. Looking into their serious little faces, he couldn't. "It's scary. Like the kind of movie you're probably not allowed to watch yet."

"You were scared coming here?" Evie asked.

"Oh yeah. Really scared."

"Why didn't you find a place to hide until it gets better?" Jaden asked.

Because I'm afraid it's never getting better.

"I thought about that. But I really want to find my parents if I can, or else I'll always wonder. It's weird—you kind of get used to it. Surprisingly fast. It's like… You have to. You don't have a choice. You have to suck it up and keep going. After a while, the way life used to be feels like a really long time ago."

Evie seemed to ponder this. Then she asked, "Where's your boyfriend? He's cool."

"He was tired."

Also, he's not my boyfriend. Is he? We were fucking, but now we're barely talking, and it's stupid and weird and awkward, and I hate it.

He kept his voice even. "Yeah, he's cool."

"That's an awesome motorcycle," Jaden said. "Think he'll take me for a ride in the parking lot?"

"How do you know it's not mine?"

Evie shot him a look. "Seriously? He's totally the motorcycle type. You're cool, though."

Parker pretended to be wounded. "You think I'm Steve Rogers pre-transformation, don't you?"

"Nah. You're at least as good as Bucky."

"Hey, Bucky ends up pretty badass. I'll take it."

"I guess I'll be Nick Fury. I'm the only Black guy here, after all."

They all turned to the slim young man standing by the snack table. He had a white lab coat slung over his arm, and his worn blue T-shirt bore a Transformers symbol. His hair was shorn closely to his head.

Evie brightened. "Hi, Neil! You missed the movie again."

Neil picked up one of the few bags of popcorn left and ate a handful. "That's okay, hon. I'll catch it next time."

Parker stood and extended his hand. "I'm Parker. You're Dr. Yamaguchi's assistant?"

"Sorry, I'm buttery." Neil wiped his hand on his lab coat and shook Parker's. "And yes, that's me. I'm working on my PhD. Well, I was, at least. Now I'm working on saving the human race, apparently."

"No pressure, huh?"

"Nah, none at all."

"How's it going in there?" Parker asked.

"Okay, I guess. Do you have a science background?"

"Not even a little bit. I'm going to be a lawyer. I mean, I was. Maybe I still am?" He was aware of the kids listening, watching him and Neil carefully. He wondered how much their father had told them, and guessed it wasn't a lot. "But I'm sure everything's going to be okay."

Neil glanced at them and smiled. "Definitely. So, a lawyer? Why'd you choose that path?"

"I..." Parker tried to think of an answer that wasn't *because I wanted to make my dad proud* or *because that's what I was supposed to do*. "I'd always wanted to be one. Since I was a kid."

It was the truth, although now he really wasn't sure why. Would he have really been happy representing big businesses like his father and examining contracts all day? Would the world ever need lawyers again? Would society ever be the same? He supposed they'd find out eventually. But either way, Parker was struck with the conviction that he'd never be a lawyer.

Neil picked up another bag of popcorn and tucked it under his arm. "I'm going to see if I can scare up any leftovers. Nice to meet you, Parker. You two rascals be good, okay?"

"Okay," Jaden and Evie replied in unison.

"Kids. Time for bed." Their father stopped by the couch with a weary smile as Neil disappeared into the kitchen.

"Parker, what should we watch tomorrow night?" Jaden asked. "How about *Spider-Man?*"

"Andrew Garfield, Tobey Maguire, or Tom Holland?"

"Definitely Andrew Garfield," Jaden answered.

"That's because he has a crush on Emma Stone," Evie stage whispered.

"Hey, who doesn't?" Parker said. "She's awesome."

"So, you'll watch with us tomorrow?" Jaden asked.

"Wouldn't miss it." Shit. He was getting swept up in the fantasy of the Pines; he had to focus. "We might have to move on, though. We'll have to see."

The kids' father frowned. "Move on? To where?"

"We're heading to Cape Cod. My family's there. My mom left me a message when everything went down. We have a house in Chatham, and it might be okay there."

Has to be.

"I wouldn't count on it." The man glanced at his children and cleared his throat. "Get your flashlights. And you're both flossing as well as brushing because you had popcorn. No arguments."

The kids grumbled and followed their father out of the lounge. Parker pocketed a can of cola for Adam. It was barely cold anymore, but there was probably an ice machine by their room. He wondered if Adam was asleep. There seemed to be so much they needed to talk about, and as much as Parker wanted things to be right again, he was dreading it too.

What if he's sick of me?

On the main floor, he snapped off his flashlight and made his way to the guest dining hall, keeping one hand on the wall to guide him in the murk. The ambient star and moonlight streaming in the grand windows of the dining hall soon showed him the way. He'd go talk to Adam…in a bit.

Parker skirted around tables to the wall of glass and leaned his forehead against the cool, smooth surface. The temperature had dropped, and he wrapped his arms around his waist. Angela had mentioned they weren't heating all the rooms to capacity since it seemed such a waste.

A flicker of movement caught his attention, and he was immediately on edge, reaching for the machete that wasn't there. He squinted as two men came into sight. His gut clenched.

Adam in his familiar leather jacket, and…what was that guy's name? Ramon?

They stopped on a pathway and were talking intently. Parker wished he could read lips, even though they were too far away and the moonlight wasn't enough to combat the shadows over their faces.

Then Ramon placed his hand on Adam's arm.

What. The. Fuck?

Parker clenched his fingers into fists as jealousy burned through him. He knew it was ridiculous because Adam wouldn't cheat on him. Firstly, because Adam wouldn't do that, and secondly because of the whole Typhoid Mary thing. Still, he wanted to punch Ramon in his stupidly square jaw for having the nerve to touch Parker's man.

Instead, he stalked upstairs and attempted with great effort to retain a shred of dignity. The soda can sloshed in his hoodie pocket, and he resisted the urge to throw it across the room when he returned to the suite. He searched for the damn ice bucket, because maybe he'd drink the soda himself.

There. That'll teach him.

No ice bucket.

He took a glass in the bathroom and shook his flashlight violently. When the light came on, he searched the hallway for the ice machine or a sign pointing to one.

No ice machine.

As Parker stomped back toward his suite, his flashlight shone over a pair of flip-flops and manicured toes. He squawked, the glass flying from his grip and landing with a solid *thud* on the plush carpet.

"What are you doing out here?" Angela asked. She wore a thick terrycloth robe with *The Pines* embroidered delicately on the breast in forest green.

"Looking for the ice machine. Also having a heart attack, for the record." He bent over and retrieved the glass, which remarkably hadn't broken. "Did I miss the machine?"

"It's in the kitchen. At the Pines, guests call down for ice and we bring it up."

It was unnerving when she spoke about the hotel services in the present tense. "Ah. Sorry, didn't realize. I guess Adam can just have warm soda."

"See you for breakfast, Parker."

"Good night."

He hurried back to the room and held the flashlight in his mouth so he could see to slide home the key card. Inside, he left the soda and glass on the table. The flashlight beam waved over a shiny black rectangle on the polished wood surface, and Parker's heart skipped. He'd almost forgotten.

With shaky hands, he turned on his phone.

Probably shorted out in the pool weeks ago anyway.

But a few moments later, the white apple appeared. Parker held his breath as he waited for his lock screen. As the startlingly blue waters of Cape Cod appeared, impending tears burned behind his eyes. There were no notifications, but he thumbed in his code anyway.

The phone company would have to be operating and have power for his voicemail or texts to work. He'd known there wouldn't be anything waiting, but the disappointment still sent a shudder through him, his throat tightening painfully.

Do not cry. Don't do it.

The screen flickered, likely some aftereffect of the dunking, but the phone still seemed to work well enough.

It was comforting just to see his icons again and to flick through his photos. He stared at the last pictures he had of Jason and Jessica—the three of them laughing with mouths open, taking silly selfies with their tongues out on the deck of his parents' boat. It had been just before college started and they went their separate ways. Had that only been months ago?

Parker turned off the phone.

This wasn't doing him any good. He was tempted to have another shower, but instead, he brushed his teeth and stripped down to his boxers before climbing onto the left side of the king-sized bed. He wondered what side Adam usually liked to sleep on. They'd often curled up with Parker on the left, and it had become a habit.

Now it was just Parker alone in the huge bed. "I should sleep in the middle to spite him."

His chest burned as he imagined Adam with Ramon in the moonlight, their heads close. What would he be talking about with Ramon? Parker knew there was no answer until he spoke to Adam himself, but that didn't stop the question from swirling through his mind endlessly.

THE DELICATE GREEN glow on the sleek digital clock showed after midnight when Parker blearily opened his eyes. He wasn't sure what time he'd fallen asleep. He reached out and found the mattress cold—but an instinct told him there was someone else in the room, breathing heavily. His heart skipped a beat as he peered into the inky darkness beyond the bed.

"It's me," Adam said quietly. He sounded like he was maybe sitting in one of the chairs close to the covered windows. Maybe he was doing that meditation thing.

Parker wanted to ask a million questions, but instead, he just reached out his hand. "Come to bed?"

"Soon."

He rolled over and closed his eyes, curling into a ball. The feather duvet was wonderfully warm, but he still shivered. He was almost asleep again when he felt Adam caress his hair. The touch was barely a whisper, but it was there.

Chapter Sixteen

"H OLY SHIT."

"What?" Adam called out through the open bathroom door, his voice tight.

Parker blinked and rubbed his eyes as the wooden blinds ascended, folding up into a slot in the ceiling. Nope. Still there. "Snow." He was only wearing his boxers, and he shivered even though it was warm inside.

Then Adam was beside him, shaving cream on half his face. He'd already been dressed in jeans and a maroon Henley when Parker woke, and Parker wasn't even sure Adam had slept at all.

Adam stared. "Snow."

And lots of it. It blanketed the ground with at least a foot already, and fat flakes continued to come down. The world had gone entirely white, the mountain peaks hazy in the distance.

Parker said, "I guess we should wait until it stops coming down before we leave."

"We have to wait until it melts."

His heart thumped. "What if that's not until spring? I know it's only October, but we're in the mountains. For all we know this is the start of winter. No, I'm sure we can go when—"

"The roads won't be plowed, let alone salted."

"Fuck." Parker thumped his forehead against the glass. "Fuck, fuck, fuck."

"It's okay. I'm sure it'll melt soon. It's still early for winter. Even up here. We'll figure it out." Adam stared down at the snow-covered lawn.

Parker followed his gaze, and a lead ball dropped in his stomach. There was Ramon, having a snowball fight. The kids appeared to be shrieking with laughter, but the window was completely soundproofed. Stupid Ramon with his square jaw and broad shoulders dove behind a half-built snow fort, one of the kids tackling him as Adam watched closely.

Be mature. Don't flip out. You're an adult now, remember?

So, Adam apparently had an interest in Ramon. It was natural, right? After all, he and Parker had been thrown together by circumstance.

It's not like he had any other options. I was the only guy available. Now I have competition.

Parker wasn't sure if he should punch something or curl up and go back to sleep. He cleared his throat. "I guess we'll see what it's like tomorrow."

Adam's gaze was still on Ramon. "Yeah. Sounds good."

"And then I was thinking we could murder one of the kids and eat them for lunch. That tender meat should grill up really well. It'll go great with leftover risotto."

"Hmm. Sure."

"Oh for fuck's sake!" Parker exploded, stalking away. "Why don't you go share a room with your new pal?"

His brow furrowed, Adam turned from the window. "What?"

"Ramon's obviously hot. You barely even look at me, but you're sure keen on eye-fucking him. I get it. Message received."

"Parker, you're being ridiculous." Adam shook his head wearily.

"I am not! You won't even touch me, and I'm... I'm..." He wanted to scream his frustration.

"Look, I know you're horny, but—"

"Horny? *Horny?* Are you kidding me right now?"

Adam held up his hands. "Are you telling me you're not

horny?"

"Of course I am! But that's not the fucking point! But fine, sure. I'm horny. I guess I'll just jerk off, and that'll solve everything." He stormed into the bathroom and grabbed a tube of K-Y from the basket holding every kind of lotion and whatnot a guest could want.

When he came back out, Adam was facing the window again, which made Parker's blood boil even hotter as he stripped off his boxers and kicked them across the room.

"Look, I—" Adam froze as he turned, his breath seeming to catch in his throat.

Gaze locked with Adam's, Parker stretched out on the bed atop the duvet. Spreading his legs wide, he bent his knees, his feet flat.

"Parker." Adam scraped the word out, his voice hoarse.

He flipped the lid on the tube and squeezed a cool dollop into his palm before smoothing it over his cock with long strokes. As blood rushed to his groin, he teased his nipples with his other fingers, pinching and caressing.

He'd never exposed himself like this to someone who was only watching, and *Jesus Christ* it made him so hard. His heart pounded, and arousal hummed through him, roiling with his anger. He barely blinked, his eyes locked with Adam's as Adam stared with lips parted, his chest rising and falling rapidly.

Parker reached for the lube and squeezed more onto his left-hand fingers. As he stroked his dick again with his right hand, he spread his legs even wider and lifted his hips so he could reach down and finger himself. First, he teased the rim of his hole, skating around it.

"*Parker.*" Adam barely gritted the word out.

Moaning shamelessly, Parker pushed into his ass roughly, tightening around his finger.

Eyes flickering, Adam *growled* and stalked to the bed, pushing up the sleeves of his Henley. He knelt between Parker's legs on the huge bed and shoved Parker's hands away, replacing them with his own. Parker gasped as Adam started fingering him in a staccato rhythm, first one, then two digits seeming to find the right spot like magnets on metal.

"*Yes*," Parker groaned.

He was spread out wantonly, laid utterly bare. His whole body thrummed, and he was practically whimpering. Using more lube, Adam shoved in a third finger, stretching Parker mercilessly.

"You like that?"

He moaned. "You know I do."

"You love it." Adam's eyes flashed. "Want more?"

Parker nodded frantically. "Wish it was your cock."

It burned like hell as Adam worked in a fourth finger, and Parker pulled his knees to his chest, gasping. "Don't stop."

He was begging for release by the time he came with four fingers deep in his ass and Adam's other hand around his dick, stroking him through his climax. He shot over his belly and chest and barely had time to take a breath before Adam was lapping it up, his fingers still jammed inside Parker.

Adam's breath was hot on Parker's stomach as he licked almost frantically, sweeping his tongue to capture every drop. He rested his head on Parker's belly and pressed little kisses there as Parker let his legs flop open. When Adam slid his fingers out, Parker felt unbearably empty again.

He gripped Adam's shoulder. "Don't run away." He swallowed thickly. "Don't leave me. Please."

They were both breathing hard, and Adam flattened out, his head on Parker's belly and his feet hanging off the end of the bed. "Parker..."

"It's about more than sex. You know that, don't you? It's about the way you make me feel when you touch me. When you look at me like I matter. When I make you laugh. When I wake up in the middle of the night, and I know I'm okay because I'm in your arms. When we have a stupid fight, but then it doesn't matter because you kiss me like you could do it all day." He sucked in a breath. "Adam, I'm dying to kiss you again," he whispered.

Adam gripped Parker's sides, his face rubbing against Parker's stomach. "You think I'm not?"

"I have no idea what you're thinking. You don't look at me. You're right here, but you're hiding. I feel alone."

Adam pressed kisses to Parker's skin. "I'm sorry. I'm sorry," he murmured.

"Do you still want me?" It was barely a whisper.

Pushing himself up, Adam sat back on his heels and met Parker's gaze. "Always."

"Then if I can't touch you, let me see you. Stop hiding."

With a shaky breath, Adam shoved down his jeans enough to pull out his dick. He was already leaking and flushed a deep red, and he jerked himself, panting softly, his eyes on Parker's. It felt achingly intimate in the hush of the room, and the rest of the world disappeared. It was just the two of them again, in the moment together as Adam pleasured himself, vulnerable and open.

When he came over his hand, tipping his head back with a little cry, he was *beautiful.*

Parker blinked back tears, and before Adam could close off again, he sat up and tugged him back down into his arms, pulling Adam's head to his chest and wrapping his legs around him. "Thank you," he murmured, petting Adam's thick hair.

"Parker, I want you so much. I can't. I'm afraid I won't be able to stop. That if I let myself touch and be close to you, I'll lose control. I wanted to throw your legs over your shoulders and bury myself inside you, but I can't. We can't. Not if it means risking you."

Parker groaned. "Okay, first off? That's a hell of a visual. Second, we really need to figure this infection thing out because I need that to happen. Like, yesterday."

With a real smile brightening his face, Adam pushed himself up and rested on his elbow on his side, his other palm warm and solid on Parker's chest. "You still make me laugh. Even about this."

"It's my superpower, I guess. Hey, maybe we can ask Angela's scientist brother more about how the infection works. He's actually already set up a lab in the basement and everything, and he knows about epidemiology." He traced his fingertip down Adam's nose and over his mouth. "Or his assistant, Neil. He seems cool. I could ask him a few questions. Try to be casual."

"Ramon might be able to help too."

The tension returned to Parker's body like the flare of a headlight on a dark road. "How the hell would *Ramon* be able to help?" He enunciated the man's name as if it were a strain of particularly virulent diarrhea.

With a sigh, Adam rubbed his face. "Parker, it's not what you think."

"Then what is it? Because I saw you two outside having a private little moment, and—"

"He's a werewolf."

"Plus, I—" Parker blinked. "Wait. What?"

Adam raised his eyebrows. "He's. A. Werewolf."

Parker opened his mouth and closed it. "Are you shitting me?"

"Yes, Parker. I'm shitting you. That's precisely what I'm doing."

He sat up and stared down at Adam incredulously. "Why didn't you tell me?"

Adam sat up too. "I was going to. Today. I just needed to process. It was a lot to take in." He took a deep breath, and Parker waited for him to say more. "I've never met anyone like me before.

I guess I wanted to talk to him first and make sure I was right. Make sure he seems okay and not dangerous. I didn't know what to think."

"Are you sure he's a werewolf? How do you know?"

"I could sense it right away. There's a scent. A feeling. I can't explain it. But he knew it too."

"And you talked to him, so he confirmed it? Is he the only one here?"

Adam nodded. "He's got a sister in Florida and parents in San Diego. He came here to run the outdoor programs. Rock climbing and that kind of stuff. He got a text from his sister when the infection happened, saying she was going to make her way here."

"Did you tell him you were bitten by a creeper? That you guys seem to be immune?"

"Not yet. But maybe he can help. He knows a lot more about being a wolf than I do."

"That's cool, right? Hey, does he know how to turn into an actual wolf?"

"Apparently." Adam shrugged, but the lines of his mouth gave away his nerves. "He said he can show me, but not until the right time. Whatever that means. I guess he's leery. Understandably—he doesn't even know me."

"Right. Well, obviously you can get to know him. At least a little." A horrible thought dawned on Parker, and he suddenly felt like puking.

"Parker?" Adam frowned.

"It just occurred to me that you and Ramon wouldn't have to worry about infecting each other. So you could… If you wanted."

Adam raised an eyebrow. "We could what? Have sex? Hmm. You know, that's a great idea. I'm going to go do that. Not sure if he's gay, but I bet I can talk him 'round. Can you grab me a bagel at breakfast? I'll be hungry afterward."

The pillow made an enjoyable *thwacking* sound as Parker

smacked Adam with it. "Okay, okay." He huffed out a laugh. "But the guy's hot, and you got stuck with me, and you have this mystical bond with him."

Adam brushed back Parker's mussed hair. He smiled. "We got stuck with each other, remember? Parker, you're the only one I want."

"Even if—"

"Even if *everything*. Okay?" He watched Parker seriously. "You're the one I want."

That was sure nice to hear. "Okay." Parker leaned back on his elbows. "It must be weird, meeting him. But nice? Especially if he can tell you things."

"Yeah. I have a lot of questions, and he said he's happy to help."

"I bet he is. Just tone down the eye-fucking, okay? Or whatever that whole intense staring thing is."

Adam laughed, and he seemed so much lighter. "Deal." In a graceful movement, he rolled off the bed to his feet. He stripped off his jeans and underwear and padded into the bathroom, where the tap ran. "What do you want to do today? Just you and me."

Parker stretched his limbs and yawned. "How about a nap?"

"How about I go down and get us breakfast to go?"

"Mmm, breakfast in bed? Yes please. In the meantime, I'll lounge here. Naked. Thinking of you."

"I'll see if they have any grapes I can peel you."

"I like the way you think." Parker grinned to himself as Adam redressed and left. He closed his eyes and splayed out on the soft sheets, feeling better than he had since everything went to hell at the Desert Retreat Motel.

He heard the door close sometime later but didn't open his eyes. He listened to the clink of plates and silverware and inhaled the delicious aroma of—"Is that sausage? And something sweet. Pancakes? No—French toast. Am I warm?"

"Mmm-hmm."

Parker opened his eyes to find Adam filming him with a thin, square silver camera. "What are you doing?" He laughed but didn't move to hide his nakedness. "Where'd you get that?"

"Angela. She has a box of them, so I took a few. Extra batteries too. It's Samsung's new HD camera. Smaller than a smartphone with a terabyte of storage, and the battery lasts a year. It hadn't even come out yet. She got samples to give to the rich and famous."

Adam was positively glowing, and Parker loved every second of it. "What was your thesis going to be? A documentary about what?"

"Found families. The bonds people can create without blood ties." He turned off the camera and laughed sheepishly. "I know. Don't exactly have to be Freud to dissect that one. Come on. It'll get cold."

Parker wanted to say something profound or insightful or comforting. Instead, he said, "We can eat at the table. I don't want to get syrup on the sheets. I prefer to get them sticky with other substances." He rolled out of bed and pulled on his boxers and a tee before sitting down across from Adam at the table by the windows. "Had you done much research yet? For your movie?"

"A little. Mostly on confessional techniques—talking head camera angles and that kind of thing. It's not that interesting."

"Tell me."

Adam did, and Parker poured maple syrup over the stack of food on his plate and listened, letting himself be utterly content as the snow fell.

Chapter Seventeen

"**P**ARKER!" EVIE APPROACHED the table in the main dining hall, wearing a too-big parka and earmuffs. "Are you coming with us? There's a good hill behind the west parking lot. The snow's starting to melt. I'd ask Neil too, but I know he'll say no."

Neil shrugged. "Sorry, little lady. Duty calls. I've already been gone twenty minutes."

"Dr. Yamaguchi's working you to the bone, huh?" Parker asked.

"Nah. I want to do it. For all we know it'll be useless, but we have to try."

Parker gave Evie a smile. "I'm not much for tobogganing, but have fun." A complete lie—holy cats, he *loved* tobogganing, but he needed to get Neil alone. "Snow's melting, huh?" It had been two days since the blizzard, and as luxurious as the Pines was, he was getting antsy.

"Yep," Evie replied. "Ramon says we'd better get while the getting's good." As if on cue, the man himself appeared and headed toward them.

Don't be a dick. It's not Ramon's fault he has a bond with Adam.

With effort, Parker smiled. "Hey. I hear you guys are hitting the slopes."

"We are indeed. You're welcome to join us." Ramon wore a red ski jacket and a headband that should've made him look ridiculous but was rather dashing in a sporty way. "Adam's coming along."

"Oh, cool."

By which I mean, not cool at all, because I'm still irrationally jealous even though I know you can help him.

"I'm good. Have fun!" Parker focused on sounding enthusiastic. He waved to Evie as she skipped off with Ramon.

"What's the deal with that?" Neil asked.

Parker pushed around a tortellini with his fork. "With what?"

Neil snorted. "That was convincing."

"Okay, okay. That guy just bugs me. I have no good reason."

"Fair enough. Plenty of people bug me."

"So, you were saying, about the virus? You don't think it's possible for someone to carry it and be asymptomatic?" Parker had been trying to get Neil alone for two days, and this was the first time he'd even seen him. He'd tried to casually approach the lab after sneaking out during a movie the night before, but Angela had spotted him and briskly herded him away.

"Doubtful." Neil swallowed a bite of garlic bread. "This thing is a beast. You should see the way it takes over the cells. It's a steamroller."

"How do you know? Do you have live virus in the lab? Like, samples?"

Neil focused on his plate and took another mouthful. "Yeah. We've got samples."

"Huh. I thought the creepers hadn't been up this way? How did you get cells or blood or whatever from them?"

"Dunno. Not my department. Man, Chef is amazing, huh? Wait until you taste his chocolate cake. He calls the chocolate in it some fancy French word—ganache. But it's basically cake. So good."

Parker smiled. "Look forward to it."

Neil was clearly lying—Parker didn't need to hear his heart-beat to figure that much out. But it wasn't as if he was rolling in choices for friendly scientists. He cleared his throat.

"Hey, could you take someone's blood and test it for the infection? Like to see if they're a carrier?"

Neil swallowed his bite of pasta. "Sure. It wouldn't take long. Are you worried about yourself?"

"No, it's Adam. He got scratched a few weeks ago. It was nothing, but he's been really paranoid ever since that he's Typhoid Mary or something. He's afraid he could pass it to me if we even kiss. And honestly, I really need to get laid. It's stressful enough nowadays without blue balls." It was partly the truth.

Neil laughed. "I hear you, man. I hear you. No prob. I'll swing by your room before lights out and take a sample. I only need a drop." He leaned in. "Just don't mention it to anyone. Especially not Dr. Yamaguchi. He's getting really intense. He's practically sleeping in the lab, and every time I leave, he gives me a guilt trip. I mean, we're way out of our league here. But he's convinced we can crack this thing."

"Hey, maybe you're underestimating yourself. Thanks for helping me out. It would be great to put our minds at ease."

Neil chugged the rest of his glass of water. "Sure. I've gotta get back."

Parker was just finishing his lunch when Ramon appeared at the table, his red jacket unzipped and headband looped around his wrist. Parker swallowed. "Um, hey. I thought you were tobogganing?"

"One of the kids landed hard. Just a bump on the head, but I brought him back." Ramon pulled out the chair across from Parker and plopped down.

Awesome.

"Sorry to hear that."

Ramon smiled easily, his very white teeth also very straight and his lips plump. "No worries. Better safe than sorry. Anyway, I just wanted to say hi. We haven't really had a chance to get to know each other."

"Right. Yeah." Parker tried to think of something to say. He gestured to the dining hall. "This place is amazing, huh? Would have been a great resort."

"And now it's a great home for all of us."

"Yeah. I hope the creepers don't come up the mountain and you guys can stay safe."

"You can stay safe too. You're already part of the community. Evie and Jaden were waxing poetic."

Parker chuckled. "They're sweet kids. But we have to get going now that the snow's melting. Probably tomorrow."

"Why?" Ramon raised his hands. "Sorry if I'm being too nosy. I guess I just don't understand why you'd take the risk out there. Especially since Adam wants to stay."

Um, excuse me?

"I need to find my family. Or try at least."

"Man, I totally understand. I'm worried sick about my folks and my friends. But getting myself killed out there won't help them." He lowered his voice and leaned in. "Parker, I can count on one hand the number of weres I've run into in my whole life. Adam told me his family died when he was a kid. Most of his life he's been without a pack. You can't imagine what that's like. The pain and loneliness—it's visceral. It is for humans too, but for us, it's even worse. I got my sister and cousins jobs here so we could be together. They were supposed to start this week, and I have faith they'll make it in the end. There's strength in numbers. In community. In a *pack*. Adam can be part of that. So can you."

Looking at Ramon's earnest, open face, Parker had to admit the man made good points. "It's something to think about. I hear what you're saying."

Ramon leaned back and smiled ruefully. "Sorry. I don't mean to pressure you. I understand being torn, believe me. Not knowing is the worst, isn't it?"

"It really is. It's like..." He hesitated, but Ramon was looking at him so understandingly. "I feel like I'd always wonder. I'd always hate myself for not trying hard enough."

"I get it, man. It's still hard to believe this is even happening. It's like, a month ago I was planning resort activities. This was my dream job, and now..." His nostrils flared. "I hate thinking about it. That all this could have been caused by religious freaks."

"The Zechariahs, or something? Angela mentioned that."

"To destroy so many innocent lives. I can't wrap my head around it. To take something written in the Bible and twist it into *this*?" He hitched his shoulders. "It's mindboggling."

"Yeah. I wasn't a regular at Sunday school, but I seem to remember a lot of talk about loving thy neighbor and not throwing stones."

Ramon smiled humorlessly. "I looked up the passage someone on the radio in Oklahoma mentioned. Zechariah fourteen-twelve: 'And this shall be the plague wherewith the Lord will smite all the people that have fought against Jerusalem. Their flesh shall consume away while they stand upon their feet, and their eyes shall consume away in their holes, and their tongue shall consume away in their mouth.' Cheery stuff, huh? I kept reading it over and over like I'd find some answer there. Some reason."

Nausea rolled through Parker. "If that's what they were aiming for, I have to say they've done a bang-up job."

Ramon briefly squeezed Parker's forearm. "Don't go out there again without really weighing the pros and cons. Okay?" He stood and zipped his ski jacket. "I'd better get back and make sure no one's breaking their necks. See you soon." He hesitated. "You and Adam seem to care about each other a lot. I shouldn't stick my nose in, but like I said, there aren't many of us around, you know? I'd really like more time to get to know him better. Know you both better." He lifted a hand and hurried out.

Mind whirling, Parker watched him go. Adam talked to Ramon about him? Did Adam want to stay at the Pines? He thought they were on the same page about leaving when the snow melted. Was he being selfish for wanting to go? He thought of what Adam had said about found families. Maybe Adam really did want to stay.

Parker gazed around. There were certainly worse places to live. What if his parents weren't there? What if he was risking their lives for nothing?

His mom's voice echoed in his mind. *We love you.* Parker's stomach churned, and when one of the chef's assistants offered dessert, he shook his head.

HE FOUND ADAM at the top of the makeshift toboggan run with a sled at his feet. "Hey. I ran into the kids and they said you were still out here." Parker took in the view of treetops and distant peaks. The sun beamed out from the scattering clouds. "I can see why."

"It's peaceful."

Parker had second-guessed himself the whole walk in his borrowed, too-big boots, and now he faltered.

Maybe I shouldn't say anything. I'm going to ruin everything. No. I'm being mature. We can discuss this like grown-ups.

"Are you... If you want to be alone, I can go." He jerked his thumb over his shoulder, already hoping for a temporary reprieve.

Super grown-up, Parker.

"Why would I want you to go?" Adam frowned. "Your heartbeat's all over the place. Are you sick?" He reached for Parker's forehead.

"No!" Parker batted his hand away. He took a deep breath and blew it out. "Do you want to stay here? I wouldn't blame you. It's a good place with good people, and it's safe and insanely comfortable. And you'd be able to bond or whatever with Ramon."

Adam stared for a long moment, his face blank. "What are you talking about?"

"Ramon understands you in a way I can't. I know that must mean a lot to you, after all these years without your family. Without another…" He waved his hand and thought of the word Ramon had used. "Without another *were*. I don't blame you, and I don't want to pressure you."

"Pressure me about what?" Adam's brow creased.

"I don't want you to come with me because you think you have to. Because you're being honorable or something. If you want to stay here and have a…pack or whatever, I don't want to stand in the way."

"A pack?"

"Ramon said it's really important."

"Is that what you want?" Adam asked carefully. "I thought after the other day, we were on the same page again."

"We are." Parker reached for Adam's hand. They were both wearing gloves, and the leather squeaked together. "I want you to be happy. I want you to have a choice. This place could be so great for you. For me too. I don't know what to do."

"You know what the best decision I ever made was?"

Holding his breath, Parker shook his head.

"Giving an entitled freshman who didn't try hard enough a C-minus."

Parker's head was suddenly light, and he gripped Adam's hand.

"There are a million what-ifs and maybes in our lives. What if the pandemic had never happened? Maybe you would have dropped the class like you'd promised, and I'd have never seen you again. Maybe I'd have gone back to my studio apartment after I ran into you on campus and spent another night alone watching reality TV and eating takeout. Maybe I'd have gone on filming other people's lives. Gone on watching life happen through a lens. But I didn't because I gave you a shitty grade, and because I was lucky enough to run into you. Because we needed each other. Maybe if the world had stayed the same, I wouldn't know you. But I can't imagine my life without you now."

All Parker could do was suck in a breath before he threw himself at Adam and hugged him tightly, desperate to kiss him but knowing he couldn't, not until Neil did his tests. "I can't either, Adam."

Adam wrapped his arms around Parker and buried his face in his neck. "Whatever we do, it's together."

"Okay. Yeah. Good." He breathed deeply and relaxed against Adam. "I love you." It took a heartbeat for Parker to realize what he'd said, and he pulled back and met Adam's gaze, his mouth going dry. "I didn't mean—you don't have to—is that crazy?" He forced his lungs to expand. "Maybe it is, but it's how I feel."

Taking Parker's face in his hands, Adam rubbed their noses together. "What isn't crazy now? We don't know what will happen tomorrow. Falling in love with you is the one amazing thing that's come out of this mess. The one thing that makes it all worth it."

His heart thumped. "Really?"

"Duh."

Parker laughed, feeling like he could float up right over the peaks of the Rockies. "I guess you're my boyfriend, huh?"

"Boyfriend. Partner. Significant other. Whatever you want to call it."

"So, we're making a conscious coupling here. Officially."

Adam laughed, his warm breath skating over Parker's cold cheeks. "Yes, Gwyneth." He leaned their foreheads together. "Whatever we do, we do it together."

He loves me. I love him. We could be dead tomorrow, so why the hell shouldn't we love each other?

After a minute of nuzzling, Parker leaned back. "I don't want to die on some insane quest, but I think it would drive me nuts, always wondering about my parents. But then I think maybe I'm crazy to want to leave this place. We've got everything we could want, and not a creeper in sight."

"But?"

"Is it me, or does it feel like the calm before the storm? Right now, there's still electricity and heat and gourmet food. Movie nights and salsa classes in the Vista Lounge. Seriously, they were salsaing this afternoon. Everyone is really nice, and they talk about building a community, and it all sounds great."

"But it's going to hell fast as soon as the creepers get through that gate."

"Exactly! They're all trying so hard to be normal. Like this is a retreat and we're guests here at the hotel. But winter's coming. What if they run out of food? What if a hundred new people show up at the gates and want in? I feel like shit's going to go down sooner or later. This is a fantasy. It can't last."

Adam nodded. "I think we should go. No matter what might happen here, you have to try to find your family. I know I would."

Parker exhaled. "God, I want to kiss you right now."

"The feeling is extremely mutual."

"But I think I have good news on that front. Neil's going to take a sample of your blood so he can check it for infection."

Adam was silent for a moment. "You think we can trust him?"

"Yes? Do you think he'll see anything…werewolfy in there?"

"I don't think so. In high school biology we had to do blood tests, and mine looked normal. I think my white blood cell count was high? That was about it. Regardless, I can't imagine Neil would have a clue about werewolves."

"You'll do it? It's your choice, obviously. It just seems like too good an opportunity to pass up. I don't think we're going to run into many more epidemiologists."

Adam's lips quirked. "Seems unlikely. Yeah, let's do it. If I'm being paranoid for nothing, I want to know." He rubbed his gloved thumb over Parker's lower lip. "I want to kiss you for days."

Parker repeated Adam's words. "The feeling is entirely mutual." He pressed his lips to Adam's cheek. "I guess we should get back," he murmured.

"Wanna take a ride first?" Adam nodded at the sled.

Parker grinned. "Hell yes."

They squeezed onto the wooden rectangle, Parker wedged between Adam's legs. With a big push, they zoomed down the steep hillside, Parker's laughter echoing through the pines. At the bottom, they tumbled into a heap in the soggy snow.

Parker groaned. "Ugh, wet jeans are the worst."

"We'll just have to get you out of them. Maybe we should take a shower." Adam waggled his eyebrows. "I hear it's big enough for two."

"What are we waiting for?" Parker sprang to his feet. "Oh, right. We need to walk back up this hill. Wanna carry me?"

Adam wrapped the sled's rope around his wrist. "Hop on."

"Seriously? Man, having a super-strong boyfriend/partner/SO has its perks."

Parker took a running leap at his back, and Adam hooked his arms under Parker's knees.

"If I tell you to mush, will you toss me back down when we get to the top?"

Adam's shoulders shook. "Definitely."

"I'll just be thinking it then."

Adam motored up the hill with a speed and grace Parker could only dream of, and he looped his arms around Adam's neck, holding on tight.

PARKER'S HEART SKIPPED a beat as he spotted Neil walk into the dining hall the next morning.

Across the table, Adam chewed his western omelet and frowned. "What?" he asked around a mouthful.

"Neil!" Parker called out and waved. To Adam, he muttered, "Maybe he has the test results."

It was still early, the sun rising in a brilliant blue sky over a patchwork of orange and red leaves and evergreen pines. The dining hall's wall of glass truly offered an impressive view. Parker could see why people had gotten comfortable here. But only patches of snow remained, and he and Adam needed to go before the weather worsened again.

Only a dozen other people were scattered across the hall, talking quietly amongst themselves. Neil pulled out a chair beside Parker and Adam at their four-person table. He was wearing a ratty He-Man tee that looked like it had been in his wardrobe for years.

"Do you want the good news, or the bad news?" Neil asked without preamble.

Adam and Parker shared a glance, and Parker's palms went clammy.

"Bad," Adam replied.

"Nah, I'm just messing with you. It's all good news. You don't have a trace of the virus in your bloodstream. Your antibodies are off the charts. I've actually never seen white blood cells like yours before. What's your genetic background?"

Parker exhaled the breath he was holding. "You're positive? He's okay?"

"Yep. Free and clear. So, Adam, where were your parents from?" Neil pulled a notepad and pen from his pocket.

"Uh, they were both from Minnesota. My grandparents came from Germany and England. Nothing exciting, I'm afraid." Adam met Parker's gaze intensely.

He knew he was grinning like an idiot, but Parker didn't care. "Neil, can we talk later? We've got to do something. I forgot about…this thing. That we need to do. Now."

Neil looked up from the notes he was scratching. "Sure. Just a few more questions. Adam, what's your typical diet?"

While Adam answered Neil's seemingly endless questions, Parker jiggled his foot and played with the zipper on his hoodie, relief, excitement, and hard-core lust zinging through him. Finally, Neil capped his pen.

"Thanks so much. I might have some more questions later. You guys will be around, right?"

"Uh-huh," Parker answered, already pushing back his chair. "Thanks again, Neil." He clapped him on the shoulder as he passed by.

He and Adam waited until they were in the stairwell to run. Of course, Adam beat him to the third floor by a mile and was already naked when Parker stumbled through the door to their room. The sun streamed in the windows, showing every bit of Adam's lean flesh, powerful muscles, and the dark hair dusted over his body.

"Jesus, you're gorgeous." Parker tossed the key card over his shoulder before yanking off his hoodie and T-shirt and sending his sneakers flying. He struggled with his fly, then couldn't wait another moment to kiss Adam, closing the distance between them and lunging for his mouth.

They both groaned as their tongues met. Parker wasn't sure how long they stood there, just kissing and rubbing against each other. Adam tasted so good, and Parker wanted to lick every inch of him. When he broke the kiss, Adam chased after him with his mouth, but Parker dropped to his knees on the thick carpet.

"You want me?" Parker teased.

Adam growled low in his throat. His eyes flashed bright, and Parker swallowed the head of Adam's thick cock, teasing the foreskin with the point of his tongue. Then he began sucking in earnest.

As he watched through his lashes, Adam's eyes flared golden, and his claws and fangs extended, hair spreading more thickly over his body. He throbbed in Parker's mouth.

"Parker!" Adam gasped. "Fuck, I'm sorry. We shouldn't. Not like this." He pulled his cock free. "Give me a minute."

"*No*." Parker clutched Adam's hairy thighs. "I want to see you like this. It's who you are." Desire ran thick in his veins, and he rubbed himself through his jeans. "I don't ever want you to hide from me. Fuck me like this."

In one movement, Adam picked up Parker from his knees and tossed him onto the bed. Heart pounding, Parker shimmied out of his jeans and underwear and reached for the lube where he'd left it on the side table.

Kneeling between Parker's spread legs, Adam watched with glowing eyes as Parker opened himself with his fingers. Adam's hairy chest rose and fell quickly, and he stroked himself with a loose fist, his claws barely skimming over his shaft. In his werewolf form, his cock seemed to swell even thicker, and Parker's throat went dry with a mix of fear and hunger.

He slathered the lube over Adam's dick and lifted his legs. Heart hammering his ribs, he bent his knees to his shoulders and opened himself. Adam was growling now, and he lifted up Parker's ass and leaned over him as he rammed inside.

It burned painfully, but Parker cried out and arched his back. "Yes! Like that." He could feel Adam's claws on his skin, but they didn't cut him.

It was rough, and the bed thumped against the wall as Adam pounded into him. All Parker could do was hang on, his ankles up around his ears as Adam bent him in half with punishing strokes. Parker felt like he was being shattered into a million pieces, but filled in every little corner as well, consumed completely as Adam fucked him with low grunts and snarls through his fangs.

Maybe it should have felt wrong, but Parker's cock thrummed, his balls heavy and tingling as he was stretched and filled. The extra hair on Adam's body rubbed against Parker's sac and ass, and he ran his hands over the pelt on Adam's chest and shoulders. "You're so hot. I'm gonna come so hard." He licked Adam's neck and the sheen of salty sweat there. "Love you," he mumbled.

With a gasp, Adam's rhythm stuttered. When he spoke over his fangs, it was deep and strained. "Even like this?"

"Every part of you." Parker squeezed around Adam's huge cock opening his ass. The pain and pleasure blurred, and he moaned. "I'd fuck you if you were an actual wolf on four legs. I'd get on my hands and knees and let you lick me open. Let you mount me and plow me with your huge cock. Feel your fur against my skin, and your claws digging into my shoulders, and—"

Adam came with an actual howl, his head thrown back and fangs gleaming as he filled Parker's ass, splashing hot and wet. He trembled with pulse after pulse until it was leaking out of Parker's hole.

Before Parker could formulate a thought, Adam pulled out and dropped Parker's legs to the mattress. On his knees, he rose up to straddle Parker's hips and guide Parker's cock into him as he sank down in a swift motion.

"Fuck!" Parker bucked up into Adam's tight ass. The heat and pressure were incredible, and even though there was no lube, Adam didn't seem to feel any pain as he rode Parker hard, leaning his palms on Parker's chest. His claws grazed Parker's skin just enough to send shivers through him.

As Parker clutched Adam's hairy thighs, he was moaning and shouting and being far too loud, but all he could care about was the sensation of being *inside* Adam—of having everything between them stripped away for good.

He cried out Adam's name as the orgasm rocked through him.

He spurted into him, and Adam squeezed and coaxed, getting every drop Parker had. As they panted, Parker watched Adam come back to himself, the transformation something he didn't think he'd ever tire of seeing.

They were both wet and sticky, but they stretched out and kissed, rolling together. Adam whispered into Parker's skin that he loved him, over and over until they did it all again.

Chapter Eighteen

"LEAVING?" ANGELA GAPED for a long moment before a thoughtful and calm expression slid into place and she rose from her desk. "I'm sorry to hear that, Parker. May I ask why? Are you and Adam not comfortable here at the Pines? If there's anything I can do to help, please tell me." She motioned to one of the two guest chairs in front of her wide wooden desk.

"No, no. It's great here." Parker didn't want to be rude, so he sat. Angela's large office was impeccably appointed with silver accents and polished furniture, similar to being in the middle of a Restoration Hardware, right down to the chenille throw over a low sofa. Through the window, the sun dipped toward the tree line.

She folded her hands on the desk. "Because if there's anything you need, just ask. We want to make sure everyone feels at home here."

"It's not that. This place is amazing, and you've all been so welcoming. But I really need to get to the Cape and find my family."

"Parker..." Her face softened and her tone was soothing. "We've heard horror stories out of Boston. A new group arrived yesterday. They barely made it out alive. While I understand your desire to find your family, I beg you to reconsider. You're safe here. We're safe together. As a group, we can build up our defenses."

"And you're doing a great job, you are. But my parents were

going to the Cape, and there's a chance they survived. I have to try. I just—I have to."

Angela sighed. "I do understand. Truly. I'll have Chef prepare some supplies for you. When do you leave?"

"Early tomorrow morning. We figure we'll have one last night in luxury, and I want to be sure to say goodbye to Evie and Jaden, and Neil."

"Neil? I didn't realize you'd become friendly."

"Yeah, he's a great guy. I'm sure he and your brother are doing excellent work."

She smiled, but it seemed strained. "Andrew always wanted to expand his research. Make an impact. Now it seems he has his chance." She stood and extended her hand. "It's been a pleasure, Parker. You and Adam are always welcome back. I wish you safe travels."

"Thank you." Parker clasped her hand. "Oh, can I get my weapons back?"

"Of course. I'll take them out of the vault before bed tonight." She smiled widely. "It's prime rib for dinner, so I hope you're hungry. Frozen, but Chef works wonders."

"That he does. I look forward to it." Parker returned her smile and left the office with a wave.

On his way back to the room, he admired the arching ceiling of the lobby and the intricate craftsmanship of the carved wooden railings on the grand staircase. The Pines really was beautiful. Maybe it would be able to keep going, hidden away in the mountains, self-sufficient and protected from the chaos out there.

"Parker!"

The few people in the foyer turned to watch Adam stride to the stairs and take them two at a time.

"What's wrong?" Parker stopped halfway up.

"We have to leave. Now."

He blinked. "Huh? Why?"

"I have a bad feeling." Adam was already hurrying back down, tugging Parker with him.

"About what? I haven't said goodbye to the kids yet, and I have to get my weapons from Angela. We don't have any of our stuff."

"We'll get more weapons somewhere. We can't wait."

Parker wanted to dig in his heels and insist Adam tell him what happened, since something clearly had, but he trusted Adam's judgment. In the fading daylight outside, Parker squinted at Adam's jacket. "Are those scratches on your sleeve?" Anger flared in his chest. "Did Ramon do that?"

As they reached the parking lot, Adam nodded and pulled the motorcycle keys from his pocket. "I shouldn't have trusted him."

Something whistled strangely through the air, and Adam grunted and skidded to a stop. He pulled his hand away from his neck.

There was a red-tipped dart between his fingers.

They stared at each other in horror, the moment seeming to stretch out infinitesimally. At the same time, it happened too fast, and Adam crashed to the ground before Parker even blinked.

"Adam!" He stumbled to his knees and shook him roughly.

Footsteps pounded on the pavement—Ramon running toward them with a rifle in his hands. Something sharp on the ground dug into Parker's shin, and his fingers closed over Mariah's keys. He shoved them in his pocket as Ramon raced up with Dr. Yamaguchi on his heels.

"What the fuck?" Parker exploded to his feet and shoved Ramon's chest.

With one hand, Ramon swatted him down. Parker landed on his ass. "We don't want to hurt you," Ramon said. "Calm down and listen."

Adam was frighteningly still beside him, his lips slack. Parker put his fingers to Adam's neck and breathed a sigh when he felt a pulse beating there steadily. "What did you shoot him with?"

"He'll be fine." Ramon still gripped the rifle.

"What was it? And what the hell is going on? Answer me!"

"We have to get him downstairs," Dr. Yamaguchi hissed. "Hurry."

As if he was picking up a bag of potatoes, Ramon easily slung Adam over his shoulder in a fireman's lift. "We'll explain in the lab. Everything's going to be fine." He turned on his heel with the doctor scurrying ahead to open a side door.

Parker had no choice but to follow.

The smell of dinner wafted through the basement, but they didn't go into the main hallway, instead winding through a labyrinth of access corridors. When they entered what had to be the lab, Parker blinked at the bright fluorescent lights overhead.

Storage shelves were pushed aside along one wall of the twenty-foot square room, piled with jars and bottles and scientific equipment. Vials and slides lined the shelves of an industrial-sized fridge with glass doors, and soundproofing batting covered the walls.

Neil sat in front of a microscope at a long table that looked as if it belonged in a dining room, with his notes fanned out on the surface. He blinked owlishly. "What's happening?"

Ramon dumped Adam onto a low cot in the corner near a closet. "Everything's fine."

"Everything is not fucking fine!" Parker yelled. "You just drugged Adam with god knows what."

"It's grizzly tranq," Ramon answered. "He'll be good as new."

Neil knocked over his stool as he shot to his feet. "It'll kill him! Are you insane? Doctor, what's going on?"

"He's a werewolf," Yamaguchi replied. "It will wear off soon enough. Now draw more of his blood. We need tissue samples as well."

Neil stared at Adam, then the doctor, and then Parker.

"Werewolf?"

"He's immune to the virus," Ramon explained. "So that means he's the key to creating a vaccine." He turned to Parker. "I'm sorry. We couldn't let you leave without learning more."

"You're sorry?" Parker clenched his hands into fists. "For starters, *fuck you*. Secondly, you're a werewolf too, so they can run their tests on you!"

"And they will! But I haven't been bitten by an infected person. I'm not sure if I'm immune or not." The rifle slipped off Ramon's shoulder, and he straightened it. "We're like any species. There are variations. There aren't many werewolves left, and we can't afford to let one go. I tried to talk to Adam, but he bolted. Dr. Yamaguchi isn't going to hurt him. As soon as he takes some samples and runs some tests, you're both free to go."

"That's really big of you." Parker ran his hands roughly through his hair.

Fuck, fuck, fuck.

Neil shook his head in wonder. "Werewolves. This is a thing? Werewolves are a thing?"

"Yes!" Parker snapped. "And now one of them has been kidnapped to be used as a lab rat."

Neil raised his hands defensively. "I had no idea about any of this. I really didn't, Parker." His face lit up. "But if he's immune to the virus, we really might be able to create a vaccine!"

Parker eyed Ramon. While he certainly couldn't deny the obviously desperate need for a vaccine, something felt off. He wished Adam would wake up and do his lie detector thing. He wished Adam would wake up, period. He crossed to the cot and knelt, taking Adam's lifeless hand in his. "I won't let you hurt him."

"We have no desire to hurt him," Yamaguchi insisted. He picked up a hypodermic needle from a tray of instruments. "Time to get started."

Parker jumped up and spread his arms. "You're not going near him. No way."

Yamaguchi gave Ramon a sharp look, and Ramon yanked Parker out of the way so hard Parker thought his shoulder might dislocate.

"Whoa." Neil held out his hands again. "There's no need for violence. We all want the same thing here, right? We're on the same side. We're friends."

Ramon smiled. "Of course. I'm sorry, Parker. Come on, why don't we go get some dinner and let these gentlemen get to work?"

"I'm not leaving him." Parker's nostrils flared as he tried to contain his fury. "No fucking way."

"This is a laboratory. You can't be in here," Yamaguchi said as he rolled up Adam's sleeve and tapped for a vein.

"Get away from him!" Parker lunged, but Ramon held him back easily. "Jesus fucking Christ! This is a *storage room in a basement*. This isn't a lab! Do you even know what you're doing?"

"I don't see anyone else working day and night to find a way to stop the infection," Ramon said as he tightened his grip on Parker's shoulders. "We do the best we can with what we have. Come on. The sooner they can get the samples, the sooner you and Adam can leave."

"What's going on?"

They all turned to find Angela in the doorway holding a set of keys. She glanced over her shoulder and quickly closed the door. "Andrew? Ramon?" She tried to look around them, pushing up her black glasses on her nose. "What happened to Adam?"

"Good ol' Ramon here tranqed him so your brother can do experiments on him. You didn't know about this? Come on, you've got the place covered in soundproofing. Where the hell did you even get it?"

She opened her mouth and closed it, blinking repeatedly. "Andrew, what are these experiments Parker is talking about? My god, you can't do anything against Adam's will."

"Ramon will explain," Andrew said dismissively. "Neil, hand me those slides. We have to get started. I'll inform you when our work is complete."

Angela's gaze skittered to the closed door in the far corner, and Parker's mouth went dry. "What's in there?" he croaked.

He had a very bad feeling he knew the answer.

"Time for dinner." Ramon tugged on Parker's sore shoulder.

Parker dug in his heels but slid on the dull tiles. "I'm not leaving him!"

Ramon's eyes flared yellow, but his tone was conciliatory. "I know this is hard. We'll just go down the hall and have something to eat. We can talk it through. Angela, after you."

She hesitated but opened the door. "All right, but I'm expecting a hell of an explanation, and fast." Her heels clicked down the hallway.

Before Parker knew it, he was in the hall with Ramon's fingers digging into the flesh of his arm. The door locked behind them, Adam out of his reach.

"I CARRIED A watermelon," Jennifer Grey told Patrick Swayze.

"They're going to fall in love now," Parker muttered. "Spoiler alert." He didn't even know why he was talking. It made him feel like he was doing something, he supposed.

Across the small table, Ramon ignored him. Parker, Ramon, and Angela were the only ones left in the dining area, sitting together at a table in the corner. At the other end of the staff area beyond the games tables, the blue light of the huge TV flickered, and a song that made Parker think immediately of his mother blared from the speakers.

Dozens of residents and staff crowded the couches and chairs, watching with rapt expressions. Evie and Jaden had wanted Parker to watch, but he'd managed to beg off.

Once dinner finished and the movie started, he'd paced back and forth, knowing Ramon would easily catch him if he made a break for the hallway. He'd tried anyway, but Ramon had shoved him into a chair so quickly he hadn't even had time to squeak, and no one else had noticed.

Angela shook her head. "I can't believe this is happening. Werewolves. And you were born this way?"

Ramon sighed. "Yes. How many times do I have to explain it?"

"There's a learning curve for most of us, asshole," Parker snapped. He bounced a knee up and down and tapped his fingers on the table, ready to burst out of his skin. "Give her a break. Anyway, it's been an hour, and I'm done waiting. I want to see Adam. Now."

"He'll be out cold for a while yet. There's no point."

Parker gritted his teeth. "Maybe not to you, but I need to see him. I'm staying with him tonight. He's always looked out for me, and now it's my turn."

He wished he had the pistol or his machete, but they were presumably still in Angela's vault. He'd never wanted to use the weapons on another person so badly. When he looked up, Ramon was watching him with hard eyes. With Ramon's speed and strength, Parker knew it was pointless to even try an attack. He had to be smart about this.

"Maybe you should get a good night's sleep," Angela suggested weakly.

"I can't sleep knowing Adam is being experimented on."

"I don't blame you. But Andrew won't hurt him. I know he won't," Angela insisted. "Are you sure you don't want to eat?"

Parker was about to reply that no, he'd somehow lost his god-damned appetite, but he stopped. "Maybe. At least I'll be doing something. Can I go get leftovers?"

Ramon was opening his mouth, but Angela glared at him and replied, "Of course. Help yourself to anything, Parker."

"You can't get to the lab from the kitchen, so don't bother trying," Ramon said softly.

Parker nodded, doing his best to keep his heart rate steady as he skirted tables and made his way to the kitchen. He thought of how Adam breathed to calm himself, and Parker counted his inhalations and exhalations so they matched.

One, two, three, four. One, two, three, four.

The kitchen was empty, with only a small overhead light remaining on in the corner. Parker went to the fridge and rummaged around in it loudly, still breathing as steadily as he could as his gaze darted around the room.

Come on, come on. There has to be—

The carving knife Chef had used on the prime rib stuck out of a wooden block. Whoever had done the dishes hadn't slid it all the way back into its holder, and the thick part of the blade gleamed.

In a heartbeat, Parker snatched it and tugged up the leg of his jeans. He tucked the smooth handle into the side of his thick sock, then pulled up the wool over the blade. The sock reached the top of his shin and had a tight elastic.

Praying it would hold—and that he wouldn't have to use it—Parker quickly unwrapped some leftovers from the fridge and slapped them on a plate. Back in the dining room, he forced himself to take a few bites, acutely aware of the cool blade against the side of his calf.

After a few minutes, he spoke as calmly as he could. His throat was raw. "I want to go back in there and check on Adam."

Ramon shook his head. "Dr. Yamaguchi will get us when it's time."

Angela stood and straightened her pencil skirt. "Adam and Parker aren't yours to command, Ramon." Her voice was steely.

"We don't keep prisoners at the Pines. Andrew can do his tests, and then they're free to go. And Parker is free to stay close to Adam in the meantime. I'm in charge, and don't you forget it. Parker, go ahead. I want to speak to Ramon for a minute."

The silence stretched out, sixties music from the movie the only sound. Then Ramon smiled. "Whatever you say."

Parker quickly left them behind before Ramon could change his mind. He needed to get Adam the hell out of there. The door to the lab was locked, and he rattled the handle impatiently, knowing they'd hear that inside.

When Neil opened the door, he glanced anxiously over his shoulder. "I think you should wait outside. We're just—"

Pushing past Neil, Parker rushed to the cot. "What are you—stop!"

Yamaguchi stood over a pale, unconscious, and half-naked Adam with a jar in one hand and a bloody knife in the other. "He heals so quickly. It's absolutely remarkable. The practical implications are numerous, and—"

Parker grabbed him by his lab coat and shoved him to the floor. The jar went flying, smashing on the tile in a mess of blood, glass, and chunks of Adam's flesh. There were already three other jars on the nearby table, labeled *Arm*, *Leg*, and *Back*.

Parker's stomach roiled. "You're cutting him up? Jesus Christ!"

"But he heals so easily!" Yamaguchi pushed himself up on his hand. "Like there was never a wound at all."

"He still feels pain, you psycho!"

Yamaguchi scoffed. "He's under sedation. When animals are tested in labs—"

"He's not an *animal*!" Parker trembled with rage. He snatched a jagged piece of glass from the floor. He didn't want to pull out the carving knife just yet—Ramon could disarm him easily when he returned. "You've got your pound of flesh. If you try to cut him again, I'll cut you."

"Okay, everyone needs to calm down." Neil still stood by the now-closed door. "Dr. Yamaguchi, I think Parker's right. Surely we have more than enough samples now?"

Yamaguchi grunted and heaved himself off the floor. He returned to his microscope and opened one of the jars without comment.

Adam was shirtless, his Henley and leather jacket discarded on the floor. His jeans were pulled down to his knees, and blood stained his skin where the wounds had healed on his body. Blood had dripped onto the top of his briefs from the last cut on his belly, stark red on the white cotton. Parker tried to bite back his fury.

Just play along. Get Adam out.

"Neil, can you help me?"

With Neil's assistance hefting Adam's dead weight, Parker was just finishing redressing Adam and zipping up his leather jacket when Ramon and Angela entered the lab. Angela gaped at the bloody mess on the floor.

"Good Lord, what's this?" she demanded. "Andrew, this has gone far enough. These are our *guests*."

"For God's sake," Yamaguchi spat. "Take your head out of the sand! This is a new world. You've heard what people are saying on their ham radios. The chaos is global and only getting worse. Governments and infrastructures have crumbled already. The virus is spreading incalculably every day. Every hour! This is Armageddon—the old rules don't apply. We need to do whatever it takes. Don't you understand how important this work is?"

Angela's face creased. "Of course, but you don't have to hurt anyone to do it!"

"Um, I think he's waking up," Neil said. He backed away, his eyes on the cot.

Parker turned away from the rest of them and squeezed Adam's hand. "It's me. It's okay. You're okay."

Adam blinked blearily, and Parker sighed in relief to see those golden hazel eyes again. Adam tried to speak, but could only groan softly.

"I know." Parker brushed Adam's hair back from his forehead. "I know."

"He shouldn't be waking up yet." Ramon frowned.

As Adam struggled to rouse himself, his eyes began focusing, and he turned his head to take in their surroundings.

Parker kept his tone soothing and calm with great effort. "We're in the lab in the basement. Dr. Yamaguchi just needed some of your blood. We're leaving soon. You need to cooperate. Okay?" He tried to tell Adam everything he couldn't say with his eyes.

I won't let them hurt you again. Don't fight or I think they might chain you up. Play along.

"You understand?"

Adam nodded, only a small movement, but it was enough. Parker hoped to God Adam did understand. He kissed him gently. "It'll be okay."

Someone made a sound of unmistakable disgust.

When Parker turned his head, he found Ramon grimacing down at them. Anger whipped through him and the words flew out. "Oh, fuck you."

Pain exploded in Parker's jaw as he sprawled onto the tile. The blow had come so fast he hadn't even seen Ramon raise his hand. He tasted blood and touched his jaw tentatively. It didn't feel broken, at least. On the cot, Adam growled, his eyes glowing, claws and fangs extending. But he was clearly still too weak from the tranquilizer to move.

"Ramon! What is the matter with you?" Angela stared, aghast.

"Seriously, this is not cool," Neil added. "I'm not comfortable with this. Any of this."

Yamaguchi said nothing, hunched over his microscope as if

they weren't even there.

Adam growled again, and Parker took his hand, mindful of the claws. "I'm fine." He spat blood on the floor and wiped his mouth. "I'm fine," he repeated.

Slowly, Adam transformed back and closed his eyes. His chest rose and fell rapidly.

"Wow," Neil breathed. "I've never… I can't believe I just saw that."

Parker focused on Adam, caressing his hair and touching him lightly. He ignored Ramon, who still loomed nearby.

"He shouldn't be polluting himself with you," Ramon gritted out.

Parker kept his gaze on Adam. "Okay, you're homophobic. Got it. Thanks."

"I don't care about that. It's *you*. He should be with his own kind."

"Apologies—you're just racist." He shot Ramon a snarky smile. "My bad."

Ramon's nostrils flared. "This is about *survival*. Our numbers were already dwindling, dying out because of breeding with humans." His tone softened. "You're a kid. You don't understand. We need to stick together. Adam needs to be with his kind. My family will make their way here, and we'll build a new pack. We'll find other survivors, and we won't have to hide who we are ever again. Adam will be a leader. He'll help us create a new generation."

"A new generation? What, like he's a werewolf stud horse? Fuck that."

"We need a new bloodline. I couldn't believe it when he showed up here. Don't you see? It was meant to be."

"Ramon." Angela's tone was icy. "You can't force him to stay. That's not how we do things."

Ramon faced her. "Maybe it's time for a change in management. Sometimes you have to put the good of the many above the good of the few. Adam needs to think about the future of our kind." He motioned to Yamaguchi. "And if this quack can actually create a vaccine that will protect humans from this infection, isn't that worth it?"

"Worth what, exactly?" Angela raised her eyebrows. "You've got Adam's blood. You've got his tissue. What more do you need?"

Yamaguchi spoke up. "Ramon, I need your samples to compare."

"Of course." He rolled up his sleeve. "I put my money where my mouth is. We could be able to save you all. We'll have the power. We'll build a new society."

"Then we need to infect the subject and take more samples," Yamaguchi added.

"Infect? Infect Adam?" Parker shot to his feet. "How are you going to do that?" He followed their gazes to the mystery door. "I fucking knew it. You have creepers in there, don't you?" He shook his head. "With soundproofing up in there too so we can't hear them, I bet."

Neil shivered. "That sound they make is the worst."

"What if you're wrong? What if it was a fluke that Adam didn't get infected when he was bitten? I won't let you do this. No way." Parker squared his shoulders, his fingers itching to reach for the handle of the carving knife. *Not yet.* "No fucking way."

"We're not taking a vote. This is for the good of everyone." Ramon held out his arm to Yamaguchi, who stuck in a needle and removed a vial of blood. "You should all wait outside. I'll take him in."

"Remember, let them bite him, and then get out." Yamaguchi pulled a set of keys from his pocket. "Without the facilities to cultivate the virus properly outside a host body, we need them alive."

"Andrew, I don't think this is a good idea," Angela said sharply. "I've sent the residents to their rooms and told them there's a plumbing leak down here. Let's all take a breath and go sit down and talk about this. We need to agree on a plan."

Parker glanced at Adam, who struggled to sit, shaking with the effort. Parker cleared his throat. He needed to stall. "This is a bad fucking idea. What if Adam does get infected? Then you'll have creepers with werewolf strength and speed, and trust me when I tell you that won't end well. We all want a cure or a vaccine, but this is out of control."

"I agree," Neil said. "I think cooler heads should prevail. We're all tired and stressed, and—"

Before any of them could react, Ramon had hauled Adam to the interior door, holding him up by the back of his jacket. "I'm doing what needs to be done." He grabbed the keys from Yamaguchi.

As the door swung open, a cacophony of chattering reverberated through the enclosed room, sending a chill down Parker's spine. Inside the other room, a padlocked storage cage held a female and male creeper, their eyes bulging as they screeched and rattled their container.

Oh, Jesus. This is it! Do it!

Parker reached down for the knife, snatching it out of his sock as he lunged for Ramon's back. At the same time, Adam kicked out Ramon's feet, sending him crashing to the tiles.

With a high-pitched scream, the creepers ripped the door off the cage and launched themselves forward, sinking their teeth into Ramon as the room exploded into chaos.

Chapter Nineteen

As Ramon roared and transformed into his werewolf form, Parker grabbed for Adam and caught his hand. Adam stumbled, struggling to stay on his feet. He slammed to the floor when the female creeper clutched his boot and gnawed at the rubber sole.

Parker slashed his blade into the creeper's face, hitting bone with a sickening jolt. She still twitched and clawed, and Adam connected his heel to her nose and sent her spinning back into the cage, where Ramon ripped into the other creeper with a feral growl.

Parker hauled Adam up, supporting as much weight as he could. They staggered past Yamaguchi, pressed against the wall, frozen in gaping horror. Neil blocked the door, his skinny arms spread.

"Wait! We have to contain—"

"Move!"

"Let them go!" Angela commanded, backing away from where Ramon grappled with the creepers, tearing the head clean off the female, the carving knife still embedded in her eye socket. "We won't let the infection spread." She winced as the creeper made a last screech. "I don't think they'll be the problem. I'll try to stop him from coming after you."

"Thank you!" Parker shouted back as they escaped and Neil slammed the door behind them. In the sudden silence, they lurched down the corridor, careening into the stairwell door.

Parker shoved at it and started on the stairs, his shoulder scream-ing as he tried to get a better grip on Adam.

"Leave me," Adam mumbled, stumbling.

"Oh my god, shut the fuck up and run!" Parker jammed his shoulder under Adam's arm and heaved him up the stairs, reeling under Adam's weight, fear powering every step.

In the lobby, Christy with the blonde curls and bright smile looked up from behind the polished reception desk. "Hey, guys. Were you downstairs? There's a leak or something." Her smile vanished. "Oh my gosh, are you okay?"

Zigzagging to the front door, Parker didn't pause.

"What happened?" she yelled after them.

They teetered into the frosty night air, and Parker dug in his pocket for Mariah's keys. The parking lot seemed a million goddamn miles away. His muscles burned, but he gripped Adam and didn't stop moving. "Come on, come on."

"He's coming. It's me he wants," Adam gritted out.

With a grunt, Parker ran faster across the pavement.

Almost there, almost there, almost there...

He skidded to a stop and dragged Adam onto the motorcycle. "Shut up and get your ass on the bike." He jammed in the key and revved the engine as Adam wrapped his arms around his waist, swaying dangerously. From the corner of Parker's eye, he saw a flash of movement, but he gunned it and didn't look back. "Hang on!"

The winding driveway hadn't felt this long when they'd ar-rived, and Parker's heart thumped with each second that passed, sweat prickling his neck and adrenaline thrumming through him. He needed the headlight to see, but Ramon would be able to spot them in the dark anyway, so it didn't matter.

The light flashed over the closed gate as they barreled around the final curve, and a man stepped from the guard booth. It was Jake, the young guy from the morning they'd arrived.

Parker weighed their chances of simply smashing through the gate, but it was too solidly constructed, so he braked. "Open the gate!"

"What's going on?" Jake raised his hand to shield his eyes from the headlight's glare.

There's a psycho asshole werewolf chasing us. "He's sick," Parker blurted out. "Look at him!"

Jake jolted back, his eyes wide. "What do you mean? Like, infected?"

"Yes!" Parker lied. "He's infected, so open the damn gate!" He couldn't hear another vehicle, but then he realized the pounding in his ears wasn't only his pulse, but Ramon closing the distance between them on foot.

Possibly paws.

Tripping over his feet, Jake spun and reached into the booth to slam the button. As the gate slowly slid open, Jake pointed the way they'd come. "What's that?"

Parker spared a glance at the blur of motion speeding their way before zooming through the opening in the gate, leaving Jake in the dust. "How fast can he go?" he shouted.

Adam's voice was hoarse. "Fast. But he'll slow down. Can't...keep up." Adam wavered and then righted himself.

Gripping the handlebars, Parker strained to keep balanced as they left the resort's private drive and shot onto the two-lane road down the mountain. While most of the October snow had melted, the road was slushy and slick. He prayed it wasn't icy. "Is he still coming?"

"Yes."

Fuck, fuck, fuck.

"Concentrate," he muttered, following the curving yellow line and staying in the middle of the road so he could take the turns wide. Even so, they veered frighteningly close to the guardrail, and Parker's chest tightened painfully. The wind whipped through his hair, and his arms shook as he took another turn, leaning into the road and praying they wouldn't skid out.

A roar in the night made the hair on his neck stand up. After the next curve, he dared a glance back at a feral Ramon in the moonlight, snarling through huge fangs, eyes burning as he hunted them down, running after them so low to the ground he was almost on all fours.

Adam growled in response, but he was clearly weak, and Parker knew their only chance was Mariah outrunning Ramon. He hunched over the handlebars, head down as he increased the throttle and flew around the next bend. Another roar rattled his eardrums, but he didn't look back.

Blocking out everything but the yellow line and the void beyond, Parker whipped around each curve until Adam spoke again.

"I can't hear him." He leaned heavily against Parker's back, but his voice was stronger.

"I'm not stopping until we're off this fucking mountain." He eased up and flicked off the lights. "Whoa." He turned them back on. "We'd better hope the creepers haven't made it up this far, because I can't see shit. But I'll take my chances with them at the moment. Keep your ears open. Can you stay awake?"

"Yeah. Keep going."

Adam hugged Parker's waist tighter, and even though Parker was the one in control, he felt a surge of warmth and comfort.

We're going to be okay. We're together.

He reached back and squeezed Adam's knee before turning his concentration back to the road.

BY THE TIME the sky began to brighten in the east, they were in the foothills with Denver sprawling in the distance. They'd lost their map, along with their pack and weapons, but Parker managed to find his way around the city, out of reach of the grasping infected that overran the area.

They were still on the outskirts of Denver, weaving through the lonely cars clogging the roads when one of the bike's lights flashed. Parker's stomach dropped. "Shit. We need gas." He glanced around. "And soon."

A yellow sign beckoned them a mile down the road, and Parker pulled into the seemingly deserted gas station. He left the engine running. "We have any company?"

Adam closed his eyes. After a moment he shook his head.

Parker turned off Mariah, groaning as he stood and stretched his stiff muscles. He reached out a steadying hand as Adam swung his leg over the bike. "Careful."

"I'm fine." He swayed on his feet.

"Uh-huh." Parker wrapped his arm around Adam's shoulder and helped him down to the pavement to sit against the side of an abandoned and blood-spattered Toyota parked at one of the pumps. Parker crouched in front of him and nodded to the road. "You keep watch."

"Okay, but I'm fine."

"Dude, you got shot up with enough tranquilizer to take a *grizzly* out of commission for a day. And that's not even the craziest thing that happened last night. You're white as a sheet and you can barely stand, so sit there and shut it."

Adam's lips twitched. "Have I ever mentioned that you're bossy?"

"Oh, you love it. You can't fool me." He moved toward the pumps.

Adam caught Parker's hand. He was paler than Parker had ever seen him, and blood stained his cheek. "I do, you know."

Parker squeezed his fingers and managed a smile despite the golf ball of a lump in his throat. "I know." As Adam took a shuddering breath, his lip trembled, and he blinked back tears.

Parker dropped to his knees. "Hey, hey. It's okay." He took Adam's pale face in his hands and kissed him gently.

"When I woke up, I was so afraid. Powerless. Then I heard your voice." He smiled tremulously. "I knew you wouldn't back down. I knew you'd save me."

"Figured it was my turn." Parker tried to smile. He wanted to fold Adam into his arms and keep him safe forever. "I'm sorry I couldn't—" He exhaled sharply. "They cut you. It healed, but I couldn't stop them. I tried, but…"

"You saved me, Parker. You could have left me behind."

"No fucking way." He took Adam's hand in his and entwined their fingers. "Never."

Nodding, Adam sniffed loudly and wiped his eyes. "Sorry. I don't know why I'm being so emotional."

"I think we're both due a breakdown or two. Or three or four."

Laughing, Adam nodded. "I guess that's true." His watery smile faded as he grazed Parker's swollen jaw with his fingertips. "Does it hurt?"

Parker honestly hadn't thought about it. He ached all over. "Yeah, but it's okay."

"I'll never let anyone hurt you again." Adam stared intensely. "Ever."

Parker's breath stuttered as his heart swelled. "I know."

"It's been a long time since I didn't want to hide. Since I wasn't ashamed of who I am. I don't know what I'd do without you."

"Me either. Without you, I mean. In case that wasn't clear. I'm rambling. I do that sometimes."

Adam kissed him tenderly, and Parker melted into him before forcing himself to stand and focus on the task at hand.

Obviously, there was no power and the pumps were dead, but he rummaged in the garage and found a piece of clear plastic tubing he could use to siphon. A battered Broncos backpack sat near the workbench, and he grabbed that too, along with a red gas can. He hurried back outside and knelt by the Toyota's gas tank. "This is going to be super fun, huh?"

"I can do it."

"You've done it every other time. My turn."

"Be careful not to swallow any of it."

"Thank you. That's very helpful. Any other pro tips?"

Adam rolled his eyes. "I'm just saying. Have you ever done this before?"

"No, I have never sucked gas through a tube. But I'd better get used to it." He stuck the tube into the tank, hoping the Toyota owner had managed to fill up before getting his or her face eaten. He gripped the plastic and took a deep breath. "Here goes nothing."

"Say hi to the folks at home."

"What?" Parker looked over to find Adam filming with the small recorder Angela had given him. "How do you still have that?"

"It was zipped in my coat pocket with an extra battery."

"Well, here goes nothing, Mr. Scorsese. Although he didn't make any documentaries, I don't think. Mr. Moore? I can't think of another famous documentarian."

"This is exactly why you needed to pursue film studies."

Parker laughed. "Touché."

"Now suck."

He raised an eyebrow. "Ah, I see. This is some kinky shit going on, huh?" He licked the rim of the tube. "You like this?"

Adam's shoulders shook. "Work it, baby."

After the incredible stress of the previous night, it felt so good to actually laugh and breathe. Parker grinned. "Okay, ready or not, here I go."

In the end, siphoning gas was just as much fun as it sounded, and Parker narrowly avoided a mouthful of the stuff, managing to pull away just in time as it splashed out of the tube. He quickly filled the gas can and transferred the fuel to Mariah's tank, repeating the process until she was full.

After tying the gas can to one of the straps on the Broncos pack, he sat next to Adam with a sigh, their shoulders and thighs pressed together. He leaned back against the Toyota and stared up at the gray clouds before glancing at Adam.

"Why are you still filming me?"

Adam kept the tiny camera steady. "Because you're beautiful."

"Oh. Um, thank you." Parker ducked his head, a blush heating his cheeks. "Okay, save your battery."

When the camera was safely tucked away in Adam's jacket, they sat with their heads together and hands clasped, and he wished they could just find a place to curl up. He sighed. "We should keep moving. Put as many miles between us and Ramon as possible. Just in case."

Adam nodded. "Just in case."

"I hope they'll be all right up there."

"Me too."

"What if Dr. Yamaguchi will be able to create a vaccine? At least all the bullshit would have been worth it."

"I hope so. Maybe one day we'll find out. Maybe Ramon's right, and in the new world, werewolves won't have to hide who they are." Adam shook his head. "Maybes and what ifs. Who knows what'll happen."

Parker knew there was no answer, but he asked anyway. "After we get to the Cape, whether my family's there or not, what are we going to do?"

Adam squeezed his hand. "We'll figure it out."

It was all they could do, and Parker found it was enough somehow.

Chapter Twenty

BOSTON BURNED.

The acrid smoke hung low over the city in the dusk like an early morning fog rolling off the Atlantic. Orange flames licked tall buildings on the horizon. The suburban streets teemed with creepers, the chattering a constant din even at a distance.

Parker imagined the brownstone in Cambridge, and his old room with the Red Sox posters he'd put up when he was thirteen so he could ogle the players and their tight pants while pretending to care about baseball.

"It's all gone." His voice sounded strange to his own ears. He sat behind Adam on Mariah, hidden in the trees, close enough to see the destruction of his home but far enough to stay safe. They were both exhausted and hungry, their clothes grimy. The filthy Broncos pack from the gas station in Denver hung from Parker's shoulders, the gas can swaying against his hip.

"I'm sorry."

"I should have ridden the swans again."

Adam rubbed Parker's thigh. "I'm not sure what you mean."

"The swan boats. In the Public Garden? By Boston Common. They have these historic wooden boats, like barges, with benches on them and a swan at the back. You sit on the benches and a guy pedals the boat around the pond. No engine or anything. They can fit, like, twenty people on a boat, so the staff get a good workout. But not anymore, I guess." He blinked back tears. "Sorry. I'm babbling. I didn't think...it was easier when it was places I didn't know."

Adam moved to get off the bike and likely comfort him, but Parker shook his head. "No, don't. I'm fine. I can do this. I'm fine."

Adam settled back down and rested his hand on Parker's thigh again. He turned his head and briefly nuzzled Parker's cheek, the rub of his growing scruff rough but comforting.

For a week they'd encountered desolation and destruction as they made their way across the heartland. The dead and the infected were everywhere with survivors fewer and fewer. Pockets here and there. Convoys heading west, telling them to turn around. Now that Parker saw it for himself, part of him wished they'd listened. He squared his shoulders. "Okay. We need to keep going."

"Are you sure? We can find a place to rest. Wait until tomorrow."

Parker sniffed loudly and swiped at his nose. "No, we're close now. We can make it to Chatham tonight if we keep going. I need to do this." He looked out at the ruin of Boston again. "I thought maybe it would be okay. I know that doesn't make sense. But Boston's survived so much. Somehow, I never pictured it like this. Even after everything. Stupid, huh?"

"No," Adam murmured, with another squeeze of his hand. "Hope is never stupid."

Parker blew out a long breath and wrapped his arms around Adam's waist. "Let's finish this."

With the lights off, Adam steered them through the trees, taking the long way around Boston's sprawl to the coast and away from the creepers who jerked toward the fire illuminating the night sky.

When they drove down the Cape on Highway Six in the early hours, Parker could almost close his eyes and imagine it was Memorial Day or the Fourth of July, the cars packed bumper to bumper on the road.

Almost.

It was nearly November now, and the night was cold, but Parker could still smell the familiar salt in the air. They drove on the wrong side of the road, which had far fewer empty vehicles clogging it. People had indeed tried to escape to the Cape, and now they roamed here with eyes bulging and red-stained mouths.

But Mariah was too fast for the outstretched hands and fingernails grown into their own kind of claws. Adam and Parker wove their way down the Six in a fine, cool mist that threatened to become rain. Parker had traveled this road too many times to count and ticked off the landmarks one by one as he directed Adam off the highway to veer east to Chatham.

It had been mid-August when he was last here, and Jason and Jessica were visiting. They'd walked down Main Street to the restored Orpheum Theater to see *Jaws* on the big screen and spot the local filming locations. Naturally, they'd also stopped at the candy store and made themselves awesomely sick by the end of the movie with Jujubes, chocolate almonds, sour keys, and what seemed like gallons of soda.

The Orpheum's shiny front windows were shattered now. In the pale sliver of moonlight, Parker could read the untouched marquee as they drove by, the black block letters spelling out the name of Tim Burton's last movie.

"Which way?"

Parker blinked and realized Main Street was ending. "Left. No, wait. Right."

Adam paused. "I can hear them that way."

"Can we just look for a second?"

Adam made the turn, and they zigzagged around the abandoned cars dotting Shore Road. They crested the slope up to the lookout over the place where Parker had spent a million summer days, either on a towel with sand stuck to his skin, or sailing through the harbor, or out around the peninsula of Nauset Beach.

Adam braked and they jolted to a stop.

On the right, the Chatham lighthouse stood guard as it had for two hundred years, its Coast Guard station near the base. Of course the beacon was dark now. Parker could imagine what it had been like when it was still running in the early days of the outbreak—creepers choking the station's lawn, circling around the base of the lighthouse, gnawing and clawing at it, writhing and crushing each other in their desperation to get closer, closer, closer.

Some infected wandered the road and lookout, where in summer hundreds of people had once come to picnic and watch the expanse of the Atlantic. He noticed the creepers were getting thinner, and he wondered what would happen when they ran out of people to eat. He supposed they might find out, but not for a while yet.

"I went to the top once. Right up the ladder into the light," Parker whispered. He swallowed hard. "We can go the other way now."

Back down Shore Road, lonely creepers wandered over the lawn of the old Chatham Bars Inn past Adirondack chairs and overturned side tables. The valet parking lot by the sea was empty, and Parker remembered the clambake buffet in July two years ago when his father had insisted on driving his new Aston Martin DB9, even though the walk was barely ten minutes.

But Parker's mother had just laughed the way she always did about his father's new toys. After dinner, they'd put the top down and cruised out to Pleasant Bay, just the four of them for the first time in forever with Eric visiting from London.

Over the next rise, Parker pointed. "Right."

They passed by the summer houses by the shore, standing dark and seemingly empty. Most of their neighbors had closed up after Labor Day, some of them only coming to the Cape once or twice a summer.

When they approached number thirty-four, Parker said, "It's that one. With the green door."

The driveway sat empty, the blinds open on the bay windows that had a matching set on the other side of the house, affording a view all the way to the water and filling the house with light in the day.

"Will you close those damn blinds when you leave?" His father stood in the foyer, briefcase in hand, suitcase rolling behind him. "Anyone can look in. I don't know why we paid a fortune for custom blinds when you never use them."

"This is a house meant for sunshine." Parker's mother pressed a kiss to his father's cheek and swiped at the lipstick mark with her thumb.

Shaking his head, Parker's father couldn't resist a smile. "I don't know where you get these ideas. Don't hang any goddamn crystals while I'm gone." He looked up at Parker on the staircase. "A hundred good schools in Boston, and you insist on California. Have fun with the hippies, kiddo." He turned to go but paused at the threshold. "Call if you need anything. Anytime."

Parker opened his mouth to say thank you, but the door was already closed.

Parker climbed off the bike and somehow got his feet to move. He knew as he reached for the spare key in the hanging planter that the house was empty—that Adam would know if anyone was there; that his parents would have heard the motorcycle and come to the door already.

But as he turned the key and stepped inside, he couldn't tamp down the flicker of hope.

The air was musty, and he could sense the layer of dust that covered everything, even if he couldn't see it in the fading moonlight. He dropped the Broncos pack, and Adam stepped inside behind him and closed the door, hanging back as Parker made his way down the long hallway to the open kitchen.

The antique clock over the fireplace in the living room still ticked the minutes by loudly in the silence, although it tended to run slow, no matter how regularly it was wound.

In the kitchen, an island with a butcher block countertop sat in the middle of the black and white tiled floor. The counter surface was clear but for an upside-down mop bucket on the edge of the island sink, undoubtedly left there by the weekly cleaning woman on her last visit.

No pieces of paper sat on the island—the place where his family had always left their notes to each other for as long as Parker could remember. There were no messages or instructions. No neat script from his mother or messy scrawl from his father. Just the polished wood his mom would never actually dream of using as a cutting board. The notepad hanging by the phone on the wall stared back, blank.

Since that day in September, he hadn't let himself think about them for more than a few moments at a time, pushing the memories and fear away so he could keep going. So he could keep hoping.

Now, standing in the kitchen where he'd eaten ice cream from the carton and wrestled with his brother for the last popsicle, he took a shuddering breath.

"They didn't make it."

He ran his fingers over the smooth countertop and heard Adam's quiet footsteps near. Parker forced another breath into his lungs. "They probably didn't even get out of Boston. I should have called my mom back right away. I should have—" A sob choked him. "I'm never going to see them again. Even if they're alive somewhere, I'll never find them."

That truth hung in the musty air, and as Adam held him close, Parker cried for his family and friends, for ice cream and popsicles, and everything that would never be again.

SUNLIGHT FOUGHT THROUGH the clouds and filled his room, warming Parker's skin as he woke. For a little while, he didn't open his eyes, preferring to remain splayed on Adam's chest, tangled with him on the twin bed.

Adam stroked his hand down Parker's back. "Hey."

"Hey." He blinked at him. "What time is it?"

"Almost noon."

He rubbed the grit from his puffy eyes. For a whole day and night, and now a morning, he'd cried. Parker had retreated to his old bedroom, which didn't have any Red Sox posters since his mother had insisted on tastefully rustic watercolors of Cape Cod scenes for every room. He'd curled up in his bed, and Adam had stayed with him for hours at a time before slipping out to check the perimeter and bring Parker back food he wouldn't eat and water he'd grudgingly sip.

And he'd cried.

But now, it was enough. It had to be.

"So," Parker said.

"So." Adam brushed back Parker's unruly hair. "Do you want to stay here?"

He didn't even have to consider it. "No." It made him queasy to think of staying idle any longer in this empty place where his family had once filled all the corners. They had to keep moving forward. It was the only way.

"What should we do?" Adam asked.

"I don't know. But today, I think we should watch the sunset from the dunes in Provincetown. You'll like that."

Adam pressed their lips together. "Okay."

Parker drew circles on Adam's chest. "Hey, did Ramon tell

you more about transforming all the way? Into an actual wolf?"

"A little. I think he was trying to parcel out information so I'd want to stay and learn more."

"Ugh. That guy was such a dick. Screw him. I'm sure you can figure it out on your own eventually. We can brainstorm and come up with some ideas to try."

"Can we?" Adam caressed Parker's back.

"It'll be a project. A new goal. I like having goals."

"Sounds good." He kissed the top of Parker's head. "Ready?"

"Yeah. I think I am."

After restocking their supplies from the pantry, Parker neatly tore off a piece of paper from the notepad on the wall. A drawing of a cheery lobster smiled at him from the top. He clicked the tip of the pen and wrote six words before placing the note in the center of the island. He weighed it down with a glass from the cupboard. Just in case.

I was here. I love you.

PARKER BROUGHT MARIAH to a stop by the crooked sign on Herring Cove Beach.

No vehicles beyond this point.

They hadn't been able to drive across the dunes without lowering the air pressure in the tires, so they'd stuck to the beach. Parker hopped off. "Guess we should follow the rules, huh? Anyone around?"

Eyes shut, Adam inhaled deeply. "There are some people in the dunes, but not close by. No creepers out here."

Parker tugged off his sneakers and socks. He held out his hand. "Come on."

Every time he'd visited Provincetown, Parker had insisted on coming to the dunes. Art's Dune Tours had a fleet of SUVs with almost-flat tires that had permission to drive over the protected sandy hills, by cranberry bogs and wispy beach grass and clumps of pines and plum trees.

With their bare feet sinking into the cold sand, they walked in the waning afternoon—a crisp breeze setting the grass swaying. They could see tracks in the sand—some animal and some human.

"I always loved coming to P-town." It felt good to talk, and Adam was a good listener. "I remember the first time when I was a kid. I was eight, maybe. All the rainbow flags everywhere, and lesbian and gay couples holding hands. My dad had his arm glued around my mom as we walked down Commercial Street, as if guys were going to drag him into the bushes at any moment and have their wicked way with him. My mom always said if she wanted some affection, P-town was the best place in the world to come."

"I bet you didn't mind all the hot men."

"Not one little bit. Even back then I had a feeling."

"What's that?" Adam pointed to a narrow tower in the distance. "Looks like a turret from a medieval castle or something."

"That's the Pilgrim's Monument in the center of town."

"I thought the pilgrims landed in Plymouth."

"Ah, that's what Plymouth wants you to think. They did end up there obviously, but they stopped here first. They just didn't like it much. We used to joke that it was too gay for them, so they sailed on to somewhere more boring."

Adam chuckled, squinting at a small wooden shack perched on a hill in the dunes that came into sight as they climbed a rise. "How about that?"

"Dune shack. There are a few of them. Ten, maybe? Twenty? I'm not sure. Tiny little things. Some of them are artist retreats, but there are a few still owned by families called the Descendants. Their great-great grandfathers or whoever were squatting on this land before it became a national park. Their families are still allowed to use them, but they can't make any additions to the shacks or bring in electricity. The shacks have to stay the way they were. They can use generators, but that's it. And if their direct line of descendants die off, the shack goes to the artists."

"How long do the artists get them for?"

"Oh, just a week or two. It's run by a non-profit and people apply every summer to get a chance to stay." He knew he should probably be talking about all of this in the past tense but couldn't quite do it.

Adam gazed up at the shack. "What kind of artists?"

"Any kind, I think. Poets, painters." He smiled. "Filmmakers too, I bet. I guess now we could stay as long as we wanted."

"There's someone up there."

Parker stopped and squinted. Then he spotted the shack door opening. A figure emerged—a woman by the looks of it, but he couldn't be sure. For a moment, they watched each other, the woman silhouetted by the cloud-flecked sky. Then she raised her arm high. Parker and Adam waved back solemnly.

They walked on, their fingers entwined.

When they returned to the beach, Parker spread out the little blanket he'd taken from the Cape house and pushed Adam back onto it. They kissed and touched, fingers sneaking under clothing, their moans carried on the wind as they got each other off with mouths and hands. No matter how many times they'd had sex, Parker yearned for the press of Adam's body and the taste of him on his tongue.

The sun seemed impossibly large here at land's end, streaking a pinky red across the fluffy clouds. Parker sat back between Adam's legs, Adam's warm breath tickling his ear. He shivered as the wind picked up. "Winter will be here soon."

"It will." Adam absently caressed Parker's wrist with his fingertips. Then he froze. "There's a boat out there. See the sail?" He pointed to the tiny smudge on the horizon.

"A boat." A surge of excitement—of hope—flowed through Parker. "We could find a boat. My parents' yacht would be at the marina back in Chatham, but there are plenty here."

"Could you sail it? I don't know anything about boats."

Parker sat up and faced him. "Definitely. I used to sail all around the Cape. Sometimes by myself. One summer we went all the way up to Nova Scotia."

"I wonder what it's like up there now."

"There are a couple of islands. Prince Edward and the bigger one." Parker struggled to remember the name. "Newfoundland! It'll be cold though. If we go up there and the infection's taken over, we could get trapped by the ice."

"South, then?"

Parker nodded, excitement growing as a new plan took shape. A new purpose. "South. All those islands in the Caribbean. Maybe some of them are safe. Maybe all of them."

"Only one way to find out."

He took a deep breath. "Are we doing this?"

"Would you rather go back west instead?" Adam asked.

Parker shuddered. "No. We know what's there." He looked out over the water, watching the sun disappear in a symphony of fiery color. "But this way could be a whole other world. We could stock up in town, scrounge up anything that's left. Food and clothes—extremely fashionable clothes, I might add—sailing supplies, maps." He turned back to Adam. "What do you think?"

Adam took Parker's face in his hands and kissed him soundly. "I think we'd better find a boat."

"HERE COMES THE tide."

Parker stood braced at the wheel of a forty-foot sailboat. Its sails were still neatly tied, and it sat on the soggy bottom of the harbor, waiting for the sea to return. It was almost nine o'clock in the morning on a gray day.

Adam poked his head out of the cabin. "You were right. There's room for Mariah."

"Told you. We're not leaving our girl behind. Besides, this boat has the perfect name. It was fate."

Adam chuckled. "I told you that was only a myth." He ducked back down with the last bag of supplies. When he returned, he leaned against the railing next to Parker and unzipped his leather jacket. "How much longer?"

"Not long. We just need to be patient." He winked. "First rule of sailing."

"Guess we'll have to pass the time somehow." Adam edged closer.

Parker could have spent all day kissing Adam in the briny morning air. Finally, he pulled away with a laugh. "If we don't stop now the tide will have come and gone by the time we're finished."

Adam peered out at the water. "Is it high enough?"

"Just about."

"Don't you need to put the sails down?"

"After we clear the harbor. I'll use the engine at first. We shouldn't need it much once we're on our way, though. We can conserve gas."

"This is a pretty big boat. You sure you can handle it?"

"Absolutely. I've got a big, brawny first mate."

"I guess that makes you captain."

"You bet your firm, glorious ass it does. But hey, if you're not up to first mate, there's a cabin boy position available."

Adam grinned. "Sounds tempting."

They were floating freely now, bobbing gently. "Okay. Let's do this." With the push of a button, the engine purred to life.

As they came around the end of Fisherman's Wharf, Adam

turned to see the four enormous black and white photographs of elderly women installed on the ramshackle building there. Two smiled at the camera, while the others were pensive. "Wow," he murmured.

"It's called *They Also Faced the Sea*. They were Portuguese fishermen's wives. My mom sketched it one summer, sitting out on the wharf."

Adam pulled the camera from his pocket. "I want to remember it."

Parker looked back over his shoulder at Provincetown and the Pilgrim's Monument. He wondered where he and Adam would sail, and if they'd ever go home again.

No. Don't think about that. Don't think about them.

He had to let go. It was the only way to survive.

Swallowing thickly, he resolutely faced the bay to find Adam's camera on him now. He blew out a breath, counting his steady exhalation. "Do you want me to say something? Tell the folks at home what we're up to?"

"By all means."

"Well, ladies and gentlemen…" With a flourish, Parker pointed up at a flock of geese, their perfect V formation stretching across the clouds. "We're following these guys south for the winter."

"Is this the stern or the bow?" Adam asked.

Parker whistled slowly. "I see I have a lot to teach my first mate-slash-cabin boy. Yes, the back is the stern, front is the bow, left is port, and right is starboard. That's your first lesson. Good thing we've got nothing but time, because there's a lot more to learn."

Over the camera, Adam met his gaze. "Good thing."

His heart skipped a beat, and Parker found himself smiling. "Come on, you get in it too."

Adam moved around to stand beside him at the wheel, holding his arm out with the camera turned around to capture them both.

"Say something," Parker urged.

"Um...hi."

"*Hi*? That's all you've got?"

Adam shrugged. "What am I supposed to say?"

"I don't know! You're the filmmaker."

"This is exactly why I should stay behind the camera."

Parker shut off the engine as they cleared the harbor. "All right, you can watch me do all the work here."

He gauged the direction of the wind and trimmed the sails to take them around the tip of the Cape and out to open sea, bearing south. When he was finished tying two half-hitches on the mast rail, he stepped back. "That's it. We're ready."

"Now what?" Adam asked.

Parker pointed up, and Adam followed with the camera. The wind caught the sails, and the *Bella Luna* danced across the waves.

About the Author

Keira aims for the perfect mix of character, plot, and heat in her M/M romances. She writes everything from swashbuckling pirates to heartwarming holiday escapism. Her fave tropes are enemies to lovers, age gaps, forced proximity, and passionate virgins. Although she loves delicious angst along the way, Keira guarantees happy endings!

Discover more at:
keiraandrews.com

Made in the USA
Las Vegas, NV
10 August 2024

93608076R00163